Not Just for Kicks

Not Just for Kicks

Lee Reynolds
and
Angela Elwood

Matador
9 De Montfort Mews
Leicester LE1 7FW, UK
Tel: (+44) 116 255 9311 / 9312
Email: books@troubador.co.uk
Web: www.troubador.co.uk/matador

ISBN 978-1905886-593

Cover design: Tony Crosse

Typeset in 11pt Stempel Garamond by Troubador Publishing Ltd, Leicester, UK
Printed in the UK by The Cromwell Press Ltd, Trowbridge, Wilts, UK

Matador is an imprint of Troubador Publishing Ltd

To Maidie Birch

ONE
1966

Suzy ran out of the dressing room and flew down the three flights of stairs to the phone. Bill, the stage doorman sat in his office busy with the crossword. He was used to Suzy, she was one of the few dancers he liked, who normally chatted and shared her chocolate with him, but tonight she had other things on her mind.

She frantically dialled the number.

One ring, two rings…

'Come on you old bag' she barked, 'pick up the phone, the music's starting.'

At last, Beth answered.

'Beth it's me, listen I haven't got long!' And flapping her free hand impatiently, she continued.' The Tiller Girls are auditioning for a TV series on Thursday, so when does your contract finish?'

'The Tiller Girls?' Beth repeated in a daze. 'Er…I'm not…' but before Beth had a chance to finish, Suzy butted in.

'Oh no I've gotta go, the opening number's started, I'll ring you later.'

And that was it. For a moment Beth stood bemused with the phone still attached to her ear, her brain still trying to decipher Suzy's garbled message. As she hung up she allowed herself a wry smile. Was this another of Suzy's hair-brained ideas?

'*The Tiller Girls? What is she going on about?*' Beth thought as she made her way into the kitchen and surveying the carnage of burnt toast, dirty mugs and overflowing ashtray, she remembered

1

the conversation that had taken place that morning. A conversation that took place most mornings, of their shared dreams of stardom, amid copious amounts of alcohol lazing on a Jamaican beach.

They were dreams that hadn't changed since childhood and Beth smiled once again as she lit another cigarette, stretched and closed her eyes recalling that day six years earlier when Suzy came into her life.

It was an unlikely pairing, brought together by their two older brothers, who were friends and deciding that their image in West London could do without a couple of pesky little sisters cramping their style, the perfect plan was hatched. Suzy's brother Rob would introduce her to Jim's nutty sister Beth and the two girls would become friends. The fact they seemed completely incompatible was nicely glossed over, just as long as they left the boys alone.

Back in the kitchen, Beth chuckled as she continued the memories of their first meeting. How Suzy, at eleven years old sat on the edge of Beth's parent's sofa, so skinny and shy, a mop of fair hair and those goofy teeth! Fidgeting with her shorts whilst trying to hide the hole in her sock, she was obviously unhappy at the imposition made on her by Rob. At the front door lay her precious battered roller skates and Beth recalled the obvious nerves on Suzy's face and her own feeling of discomfort with the manufactured meeting.

The two girls exchanged 'hi's', a minimal amount of eye contact and prompted by Joan, Beth's mother, the required small talk about school and family.

'But mum she's so quiet and she looks like a boy in those shorts and scruffy hair' sniggered Beth, escaping to the kitchen to help make the tea. 'Did you see her roller skates? *And* she has a bike! No wonder she hasn't got any boobs doing all that sporty stuff. Can you imagine me on a bike?' She sneered, thrusting out her fast developing chest. 'I think girls should look like girls' and pranced around the room, wailing at the top of her voice 'I'm so pretty, oh so pretty'!

As Joan watched her daughter with her long dark hair, huge brown eyes, and those long gangly legs forever in motion, she wondered how these two were going to get along. They may be the same age, but Beth was certainly very different to the shy tomboy in the other room.

As Joan and Beth reached the living room with the tray of tea they could hear Beth's father Peter telling their young guest his wartime heroics. Suzy, trying to look interested thought how she'd had to endure the same from her dad, except this time it was the Army winning the war, not the Navy!

'Come on we'd better rescue the poor girl and be nice.'

Beth rolled her eyes, sighed but agreed.

Suzy looked up with a grateful smile, as Beth made her way to the sofa and sat beside her. The girls looked at each other and Beth finally took a deep breath.

'So, what do you want to do when you leave school Suzy?' Sniggering to herself she was convinced the only place for this girl was the army!

But wait a minute what was that? 'What did you say Suzy?'

As Suzy repeated her answer, Beth jumped up and stood over her.

'Did you say a *dancer?*' Suzy just nodded frantically as Beth flung herself down again in her usual dramatic way. 'I don't believe it!'

'Oh yeah' replied Suzy rather nervously, unsure of Beth's violent reaction. 'I've always wanted to go on the stage' and added shyly 'actually I'm quite good.'

'But…but' stammered Beth, 'that's what I've wanted to do *all* my life.'

Seizing the moment she turned to her father. 'See dad, it's not a ridiculous idea.' Peter quickly shot a look across to Joan and knew what was going through her mind.

They'd talked about Beth's passion for dancing ever since she could walk and had after all met in the theatre while Peter worked backstage and Joan a dancer at the Prince of Wales. Unfortunately Peter having seen first hand what those dancers got up to was having none of it for Beth. 'Oh God help me, I've got three of them to contend with now.'

Beth impatiently turned back to Suzy. 'Do you have lessons? Please say yes, pleeeese!'

'Well, I've been having lessons since I was eight,' stammered Suzy slightly confused by Beth's overwhelming interest and Peter's growing impatience, who'd now conceded defeat and as any good soldier would, retreated to the bathroom with his newspaper. Two minutes later, Beth dragged Suzy down the hall into her bedroom to find out absolutely *everything* about her newfound friend.

And that was it. Beth joined Suzy at the Maidie Birch school of Dance where their friendship grew from a wonderful understanding of each other's passion for dancing, their insatiable optimism and wicked sense of humour. Their shared dreams of performing and of course becoming famous meant that they sought out each other's company as much as possible.

Back in the kitchen, Beth opened her eyes and laughed at the memory of the shy skinny Suzy and the totally outrageous show-off she now shared a flat with.

Suddenly she remembered the phone call. *'TV series! What the hell was she talking about?'* Lighting another cigarette she paced the floor impatiently. She'd always believed that she and Suzy could communicate telepathically, but Suzy wasn't so sure.

'You're away with the fairies' she would accuse her, but undeterred, Beth gave it a try and puffing on her ciggy took a deep breath and yelled.

'Come on you silly moo, ring me back.' The combination of the weed and screaming psychic commands reduced Beth to the floor in a coughing fit as two minutes later the phone rang. 'There my ESP does work' she spluttered triumphantly.

''Allo mate it's me again.'

'I knew it was you Suz, now just hurry up and tell me your news.'

'Are you all right Beth? You sound a bit croaky.'

'Yes, just proving my powers work on you, so come on give!'

'Ok, Ok, keep your hair on. Right, we've just been told that *The Tiller Girls* are auditioning dancers for The Billy Cotton Band Show. We *have* to go, go on say you will, you know you hate that modelling lark; anyway your boobs are too big! You could fake a pregnancy or a breakdown; you're so good at that.' Suzy didn't give Beth a chance to speak. 'Come on Beth, this is our big chance to work together; it's what we've been waiting for. We'll be discovered! We'll be famous! Today... Shepherds Bush Empire ...Tomorrow... Hollywood!'

A sudden crackling announcement from the overhead tannoy brought Suzy to a sudden halt. 'I've gotta go!' she screeched, 'there's the call for the second half.'

'All right I'll wait up for you; we can talk when you get home.'

'Ok see you tonight kiddo, by the way dig out that silver leotard, you look great in that. On second thoughts I'll wear it, I need all the help I can get, you can wear that old black thing of mine with the holes in it,' laughed Suzy as she slammed the phone down and ran on stage, late again!

Not for the first time that night Beth was left with the phone dangling, head spinning and thoughts racing. *'Oh my God, the Tiller Girls. Is this it? Is this our big break?* This was what they'd been waiting for, dreaming of ever since they could remember and since leaving school some eighteen months earlier their impatience and optimism had almost gotten out of control.

TWO

During those eighteen months Suzy's life had changed dramatically. Having walked out of the school gates for the last time, minus any qualifications, the impatient and ambitious fifteen year old was at last free to pursue her dream, knowing from years off physical abuse and ridicule from her parents that those dreams would only come to fruition through sheer determination, relying on no one but herself.

Sam and Barbara Noden, ruthless with ambition for their two children saw their youngest child Suzy as an embarrassment; for she wasn't particularly bright at school and the disappointment of producing such a plain daughter with seemingly no future, often brought violent outbursts of frustration from her father. Suzy's only solace during that painful childhood was the guilt and remorse that plagued Sam following the regular bouts of temper and allowing her to have the one thing she craved eased his conscience. And so every Saturday eight year old Suzy, tightly gripping her half a crown would run the two miles to the local dance school, where she could forget her torment and take the long dreamed of dance lessons that would change her life forever. As a small child Suzy was confused and terrified of her father's sudden change of moods, but as she got older she became almost grateful for the abuse, realising that she couldn't have one without the other.

And so at fifteen, keen to turn her back on her childhood and the restraints of dreary school life, she walked away from those school gates and heaved a huge sigh of relief.

'Goodbye and good bloody riddance' and tossing her school beret over a garden wall she headed home with just one thing on her mind. She needed to get away, get a place of her own; away from the violence and the constant fear and only then could she even dare to think about her ultimate ambition. She already had savings in the Post Office, from working at the Wimpy Bar after school every evening, but now she could concentrate on getting a full time job, any job, and as soon as possible.

For the following year Suzy worked every waking hour, in shops and restaurants, and no matter how exhausted she felt, or how many blisters she suffered, she would never give up until she had saved enough to be totally independent.

By the time Beth left school the following summer, having had pressure from her parents to gain some form of qualifications, Suzy knew the time was right and keen for Beth to join her in her new adventure, worked on her every chance she had.

'Come on Beth, it'll be fantastic, we can stay out as late as we like and have parties.'

Persuading Beth to move in with her wouldn't be easy. After all she had no reason to move away from her parents, a situation that Suzy understood and envied.

'But Suz, I haven't got a job yet, how am I going to pay rent without any money?'

'Oh don't worry about that, I've got enough for the deposit and two months rent. I can even give up the day job in the shop and concentrate on auditions. Why do you think I've been slogging my guts out, while you've been the snotty sweaty schoolgirl? Anyway it's time you learnt how to make a piece of toast all on your own!' Beth laughed, knowing that compared to poor Suzy she had been totally spoilt, but secretly longed to join her, it all sounded so exciting.

Two weeks after leaving school Beth struck lucky and was employed as an in-house model at Delia Bonet's exclusive fashion boutique in the West End, and so three months later, with Joan and Peter's blessing and Sam and Barbara's obvious relief to be rid of their loser daughter, the naïve seventeen year olds began their new adventure in a scruffy flat overlooking Shepherds Bush Green, but to Suzy and Beth it was a palace.

By the following Christmas Suzy had got a part in the chorus of a local pantomime, while scouring the *Stage* magazine for auditions that would give them their big break. Beth's heart wasn't in modelling and when Suzy had rung about the audition, she was keen to join her.

The week leading up to the audition found the girls unable to concentrate on anything else. The Tiller Girls had only ever been a fantasy on their TV and they spent every opportunity practicing their high kicks. Beth was certain she'd be refused a day off by Delia for the audition, so she invented an agonising tooth abscess needing urgent attention, although she would have preferred something a little more dramatic.

'What if you get it and I don't?' Suzy was panicking.

'Oh shut up! We're both going to stun them and they won't be able to resist us!' Beth, the more confident tried to reassure Suzy. But when the big day arrived, it was Beth locked in the loo, trying to stop herself from throwing up, before they were called into the audition room, where they both smiled and danced for all they were worth. They wanted this job more than anything else in the world.

Three days later, the girls could hardly contain themselves, as the phone call confirmed that their dream was finally coming true and Beth the drama queen got the chance to put on what Suzy described as an Oscar winning performance when she phoned Delia Bonet to be released from her modelling contract. She ignored Suzy's giggles as she croaked that she was *under the doctor* with glandular fever, with warnings that it was highly contagious. Delia had been terse, but keen to keep her reputation and her high class cliental free from threatening germs wished Beth well and hung up.

On the first day of rehearsals Beth and Suzy were sweating with nervous excitement as they walked into the changing room and smiled tentatively at the other dancers who were oblivious to the newcomers as they chatted among themselves. Finding a free corner the two friends silently began to change into their newly acquired rehearsal gear and as Beth, attempting to assume a confident air smoothed the tights over her long slim legs, Suzy nervously fumbled with her shoes, staring at the sea of black fishnets surrounding her. Her heart raced as she remembered that all important phone call confirming they had both been accepted into the most famous dance troupe in the country.

But those days of anticipation were over now, and Suzy's tummy flipped as she realised this was really it, their dream really was coming true. They were professional dancers at last and on Sunday they were going to be on live television! She watched Beth pull on her regulation white blouse and seeing the label still attached to the seam, tugged at it, not wanting the others to see just how naïve and new to the profession they really were.

The door opened and a tall slim attractive woman called them into the rehearsal room. 'This is it' Beth whispered excitedly squeezing Suzy's hand. 'Come on let's show them what we're made of.'

That night they collapsed onto the tube totally exhausted and hardly recognisable as the same two girls who that morning had ran out of their flat looking fresh and confident at the prospect of their exciting new life in show business. The day's rehearsals had proved a lot tougher than either of them had ever imagined, with Beth convinced she'd never walk again, let alone do another kicking routine.

'It's no good, we'll have to move into a ground floor flat' mumbled Suzy as she gripped the banisters and hauled her every aching limb up to the first floor. Staggering through the front door she headed straight for the bathroom, while Beth grabbed two glasses and searched for the bottle opener. Suddenly there was a mighty crash, followed by the less than dulcet tones of Suzy's imaginative swearing. With throbbing leg muscles only allowing a fast shuffle, Beth got to the bathroom to find Suzy on her knees, sleeves rolled up, rescuing the contents of the small wall cabinet from the depths of the toilet. Forgetting the pain she was in Beth leant against the bathroom door for support and burst into hysterical laughter.

'Bloody stupid place to put a cabinet, over a toilet' snapped Suzy, dragging yet another bottle of face cream up from the pan.

'Might improve your skin though, what were you looking for anyway?'

'This!' And with one last plunge she held up a dripping tube of 'Deep Heat'.

As the week progressed Beth and Suzy discovered how glamorous show business could be, with one-hour warm-ups every morning before a gruelling eight-hour day, but they were keen and ready to learn, their confidence and enthusiasm growing as the big day in the studio grew nearer.

There'd been just one thing that had marred their initial excitement at the audition, having been informed they were not only to behave in a ladylike manner and appear neat and tidy at all times, which caused a ripple of nudges and sniggering grunts, but their hair had to be at the regulation length, which basically meant off the shoulders, preferably at ear level. So a quick trim was out and major surgery was necessary.

However, after initial groans and doubts they decided that the long-haired 'Sixties Chicks' were due for a change anyway and avidly explored every likely magazine they could lay their hands on for ideas. Not for them the boring neat and tidy style. Oh no, they weren't interested in approval from their future employer; they wanted absolute adoration! The final decisions were made the night before their appointments. Suzy with her high cheekbones would go for the Mia Farrow look and Beth, confident she would win a Liza Minnelli look alike competition with her new style.

Reluctant to be the first for the chop they tossed a coin, with Beth losing to take the first appointment at 10am and Suzy two hours later.

'You'd better not chicken out on me' Beth warned as they stood outside the Vidal Sassoon salon the following morning. Suzy laughed and reassured her as she shoved Beth through the door, but decided to hang around a while to make sure she didn't change her mind. Ten minutes later, she was satisfied as she spied Beth through the window, sat in the swish leather chair, manically waving her arms at the great man as he graciously nodded, understanding all that was expected of him.

Ninety minutes later Beth left the salon, thrilled with her new-cropped look. With two hours or more to spare she decided to kill time by hitting the shops to complete her makeover and as she sought her reflection at every opportunity between Marble Arch and Oxford Circus her confidence grew.

Some two and a half hours later, all shopped out, she sat by the window of the coffee bar where she and Suzy had planned to meet. She was already on her second coffee and third cigarette. Suzy was late as usual, and impatient to try out the purple Biba eye shadow that would complete her new look, she headed for the loo. Meanwhile, Suzy rushed through the door assuming she was first to arrive and unknowingly claimed the seat by the window. The waitress cleared the dirty cups, brought a clean ashtray and took her order.

Ten minutes later Beth struggled out of the narrow loo door with her shopping bags, cursing that someone else had taken her seat by the window. She sulked into the only other vacant seat and took her mind off her impatience by rummaging through her newly acquired goodies. Meanwhile, Suzy was fidgeting nervously with her non-existent fringe and decided to go to the ladies for reassurance before Beth arrived. Beth glanced up and chuckled at the girl laden with bags struggling to squeeze through the familiar door, but soon lost interest.

Eventually, her confidence renewed, Suzy struggled back through the narrow doorway, when another customer obviously bursting, flung the door open, causing Suzy to lurch forward, dropping all her shopping at the feet of the girl sitting by the door.

'I'm so sorry' she mumbled, embarrassed as she crawled around on all fours trying to pick up all her bags. The other girl chuckled as she bent down to help. 'That's OK'. Suzy's head shot up at the all too familiar voice. 'Beth?' she screamed as she jumped to her feet, dropping her shopping bags yet again. 'Beth! It's me, Suzy!' And she beamed the hugest grin right into Beth's gawping face.

Beth let out a high-pitched scream. 'Oh Suzy! You look fantastic; I didn't recognise you, how long have you been here? Turn around and let me look at you,'

'I've been here ages, sitting over there by the window. But look at you too, you look absolutely gorgeous.' They held each other at arms length in mutual admiration, oblivious of sniggering onlookers.

'Come on *'Mia'* let's go home; I want to see what you've bought.'

'OK *'Liza'* and they linked arms as they made their way to the tube station, singing at the tops of their voices. *'Life is a cabaret my friend, come to the cabaret.'*

THREE

The Sunday of their first TV appearance arrived at last and the tension had increased to fever pitch by the time the girls arrived at the studio for rehearsals before the transmission that night. Pulses raced and the atmosphere became electric when Billy Cotton raised his baton and the band played their opening number for the first time. Suzy, overwhelmed by the whole occasion felt light headed and needed a glass of water and Beth's legs turned to jelly as she stood in line waiting for the cue.

When the rehearsal was over, there were still two hours to go before show time and even the more experienced girls were showing signs of panic in the dressing room as the minutes ticked away, frantically going over steps that had gone wrong in rehearsals and double-checking shoes, gloves and necklaces. Beth and Suzy chain-smoked while putting on their makeup, but Suzy's hands shook so much that Beth tried to help, but nerves were getting the better of her too and it took three attempts to get the eyeliner anywhere near Suzy's eyes!

When the call came for them all to go down onto the studio floor a frisson of panic went round the room as everybody did last minute checks.

'We look amazing!' gasped Beth as they both stood hand in hand in front of the mirror in their black sequined leotards, black fishnets and silver feather headdresses.

'I know I can't believe we're here' giggled Suzy. 'Good luck, or "break a leg" as they say' and gave her friend a quick hug before making their way down onto the studio floor, where the audience were already in their seats. Beth immediately spotted her parents proudly sitting on the edge of their seats in the fourth row and waved frantically. Suzy's heart lurched when for the third time of searching, she was sure her parents weren't there. She was hurt but not surprised, knowing they'd always found her ambitions a huge joke and acute embarrassment. But she'd really thought that tonight would change all that and make them proud of her at last. Beth squeezed her hand. 'They'll be here soon, we've still got ten minutes to go,' she whispered 'come on let's warm up' and led her away from the studio floor and into the wings.

Then at last it was time for the dancers to take their places in the line for the opening routine and the buzz created a heady mix of fear and excitement that neither Beth or Suzy had ever experienced before. With transmission due to begin in little over a minute, a voice from somewhere across the studio bellowed 'Quiet Please' and as a silence gradually settled over the studio and the countdown began, the tension filled air caused many to hold their breaths.

'*Wakey Wakey*'

Half an hour later, as soon as the "off air" lights flashed, the atmosphere changed to immediate relief and spontaneous applause rang around the studio. The two novices, still shaking, allowed themselves indulgent grins as they hugged each other.

'I want to do it again' giggled Suzy, her eyes still dancing.

'So do I, didn't it go quick?' agreed Beth.

It had surely only been a dream! Had they *really* just appeared on live television in front of millions of people? Yes they had and they wanted to do it all over again.

Michael Walsh the producer, made his way from the sound gallery onto the studio floor. 'Well done everybody, a great show,' adding that a congratulatory drink at the bar was in order. Never ones to shy away from such a tempting offer, Beth and Suzy accepted wholeheartedly and raced to the dressing room to change.

Mingling and drinking with the stars seemed a million miles away from 'The White Hart', which was their usual haunt and they were fascinated by the mutual admiration society performing right before their eyes. Gradually, satisfied that their ego's had been suitably massaged, people began to drift off and the two girls having said their goodbyes reluctantly made their way home, still in a state of euphoria. The cold night air filled their lungs, relieving the tension that had gripped their entire bodies for the past week. Linking arms, they excitedly skipped down the road, not remembering when they had felt that happy.

'We done it, we've actually done it...'Wakey Waaaakeeee....Hollywood here welcome!'

FOUR

With just one day off before starting the weeks rehearsals all over again, the last thing the girls needed after celebrating until 3am with a disgusting bottle of cooking sherry that Beth had found in the bottom of the cupboard, was the phone ringing at 10am. Suzy threw herself under the covers and ignored it. Beth tried to, but knew she'd have to answer it. Suzy wasn't human in the mornings and whoever it was would get a mouthful of abuse. Finally Suzy couldn't stand the noise any more and stuck her head out.

'For Gods sake Beth, get that phone before I...'

'All right, all right, blimey you look rough' snapped Beth as she dragged herself from her warm bed and staggered into the living room. Collapsing onto the sofa, she lit her first cigarette of the day and picked up the receiver. It was her mother.

'Beth is that you sweetheart? Sorry I'm ringing so early darling, but I wanted to tell you how much we enjoyed the show last night. We are *so* proud of you both.

Still half asleep, Beth only just managed a mumbled reply.

'Beth you sound awful how's Suzy?'

'Don't ask, she's a dragon in the mornings, can't take the booze like me.'

Joan wasn't impressed, but couldn't be too cross, not today. She invited them both round for a celebratory dinner that evening and Beth readily agreed. With nothing edible in the fridge, the thought of a tasty home feast was too good to miss. She put the phone down, staggered into the bedroom and threw herself onto poor Suzy, who was still unconscious under the blankets. Pulling at the covers, she shook her violently; trying to bring her to some sort of life, but Suzy was having none of it and held on for dear life. But Beth had the advantage and gave the bedclothes a yank pulling them to the floor, with Suzy still desperately clinging on, crashing down on top.

'God Beth, you're so childish. Just sod off and let me die in peace.'

Beth stood back and smiled at the crumpled heap curled up like a baby, attempting to pull her tatty purple T-shirt over her bare cold backside. She couldn't see Suzy's face but was sure she still hadn't attempted to open her eyes.

Suddenly taking pity at the sight of her friend struggling to face the world, she gently laid a blanket over the shivering wreck and quietly crept from the room closing the door behind her. Putting on her face in the bathroom she quietly sang to herself, happy at the memories of the previous day. She wasn't so sure that Suzy's day would be quite so positive, as she was making her usual monthly visit to her parents, who hadn't even be bothered to turn up to watch their daughters TV debut. They'd not left any messages with the stage doorman either, when after the show he handed Suzy back their unused tickets.

Beth had only met Suzy's parents twice in the six years they'd been friends and totally understood her reluctance to face the day ahead. She decided that what Suzy needed was a little pampering and quietly closing the front door behind her headed for the shops.

By 11o'clock Suzy had managed to untangle herself from the heap of bedclothes and collapse into a steaming bath for an hour of total bliss. She relished this quiet time, but eventually knew she couldn't delay it any longer. Anyway the water was freezing and as she stood shivering in front of the mirror, all excitement from the previous night was overshadowed by the day that loomed ahead. As usual, she wondered why she still needed their approval, but she did and today she was determined to get it.

17

Her parents, Sam and Barbara welcomed her with their usual indifference and as Suzy followed her mother into the flat she wondered why she bothered making the visit every month. They lost no time in telling her that they'd preferred to stay at home to watch the show, but the fact that they'd bothered to watch at all was something at least, she supposed. No mention was made of her new hairstyle, so she waited nervously for their reaction to her performance. Sam was the first to speak.

'Well I suppose a TV series is an improvement on that bloody awful pantomime.'

Suzy was incensed. 'How do you know it was bloody awful, you never even bothered coming to see it? And why didn't you come last night? Couldn't you have made the effort, just this once? I'm a member of the *Tiller Girls* now' she wailed, emphasizing the impressive title. 'Why can't you just be proud of me for once?'

Sam wasn't used to being questioned, least of all by his bloody useless daughter and lunging, he smacked her hard across the face, causing her to reel backward, hitting her head against the wall. This was and always had been Sam's way of dealing with what he considered to be a problem.

'It's that bloody tart you live with, she's too cocky for her own good that one.'

Still smarting, Suzy shook her head violently. 'Don't you dare call Beth a tart, she's my best friend and I love her.' Barbara's mouth dropped open; she couldn't believe what she was hearing. 'Oh my God Sam, she's turned into a *lesbian*.'

'Oh mum, I'm not a lezzy; I love her because she doesn't think I'm useless like you.' She was hysterical now, stamping around the shabby living room flinging her arms wildly. 'You don't understand, you never will.' Tears were streaming down her distraught face. 'I thought you'd be pleased for me, but I don't know why I bother!' and ducking to avoid her fathers threatening fist, she ran out of the flat and carried on running as hard as she could, away from a life she'd hated for as long as she could remember.

Beth knew there was something wrong as soon as she got

home that afternoon. Instead of the usual 'Streisand' blaring from the record player, with Suzy attempting not a bad impression, except for those awful top notes, the flat was deathly quiet. Beth dropped her shopping on the hall floor. 'Suz I'm home, where are you, you old bag?'

Opening the bedroom door, Beth's stomach turned at the sight of Suzy curled up on her bed, head resting on her knees, eyes red and swollen, staring blankly into space. She ran over and threw her arms round her. 'Sweetheart whatever is it. What's wrong?'

At the sound of Beth's voice Suzy collapsed into yet more paroxysms of tears. The more Beth tried to console her the more she sobbed. Beth felt helpless. She knew that Suzy's parents caused her anguish and today things were likely to be worse because of their lack of interest in the show, but she hadn't expected her to be this distraught. Eventually, completely drained of any more tears, Suzy calmed down enough to tell Beth all about her awful day. Beth listened sympathetically without comment, quietly went into the living room and rung her mother. She put the phone down and went into the kitchen where Suzy sat at the table furiously puffing away on a cigarette. With a promise of no more tears Beth presented Suzy with a huge bar of her favourite chocolate. 'Thanks Beth' was all Suzy could manage without breaking her promise.

It had been obvious to Joan for some time that Suzy's home life wasn't what it should be. She'd never met Sam and Barbara, but realised there were problems quite early on, noticing Suzy had no self-esteem or confidence. She was very fond of her and found it easy to treat her with as much love and support as she did Beth.

As soon as they arrived Joan noticed Suzy was more subdued than usual and as she hugged them both in turn, she was aware that Suzy hung on a little longer than usual. She decided to leave well alone, today was a celebration and she was determined to keep it that way.

'We're so proud of you both, aren't we love?' smiled Joan giving her husband, the nod. Peter, a compassionate man, walked over to the drinks cabinet and proudly produced a bottle of champagne. 'This is to celebrate my two favourite girls on their first step to fame and fortune, hurry up Joan and get the glasses.'

Beth was grateful for her parents' encouragement. Suzy however, confused by the open affection was unable to stop the tears rolling down her cheeks. Joan and Beth gently put their arms round her, while Peter, slightly embarrassed by all this female emotion suggested he carve the chicken.

The champagne, the meal and the warmth of Beth's family, served to lift Suzy's spirits and the evening turned into a noisy affair with the girls excitedly relaying every minute detail of the previous day. However by 10pm and with heavy eyes they uncharacteristically declared they needed an early night. As they kissed goodbye at the door, Peter ruffled both their hair, complimenting them on their new look.

FIVE

One particular Friday morning, four weeks into the series, it was already 10.30am and Beth and Suzy still hadn't arrived for rehearsal. Ralph Seabrook; top choreographer had been brought in for the series to teach the dance routines, which didn't involve their famous kicking line. On the whole he found the troupe professional, but he had his doubts about Beth and Suzy. It seemed to him that they simply refused to conform to any form of discipline and felt sure that if they continued the way they were, their careers with this well respected troupe would be short lived.

Michael Walsh had been making one of his regular visits with a view for lighting plots and camera angles. Normally a patient man, he paced the floor outside the rehearsal room; these two girls were pushing him to his limit. He stopped abruptly and trying to remain calm, wiped his glasses, put them back on and resumed pacing.

Unable to contain himself any longer he burst through the door and glared at the ten dancers who were sitting around the floor as they waited for rehearsals to start. Silence fell and all eyes followed him as avoiding the sea of legs, he stormed across the room to fix Ralph with a stare. 'They're late again; this is the second time this week.'

Ralph, who had been admiring himself in the full-length mirror jumped up from his chair and tutted. 'Oh Michael *I know*, shall we start without them?'

Ignoring the question Michael spun around to face the dancers, and broke into a reluctant smile, 'I'm sorry ladies,' his voice taking on an all-together softer tone. 'This must be frustrating for you too, so why don't you get yourselves a coffee?'

The girls quickly jumped to their feet and scurried out of the door. It gave them a chance to have a break and gossip about how the shit was going to hit the fan when Beth and Suzy did finally show up.

Suddenly the doors flew open and in burst Beth and Suzy, out of breath, and looking totally dishevelled. They made a beeline for Ralph, throwing their large bags down at his feet. In an effort to avoid the oncoming baggage he stumbled back, fell onto his chair, which wobbled dangerously close to the mirror. In one graceful move he automatically crossed his legs and raised his right hand to adjust his toupee. The two latecomers unaware of anyone else in the room waited for Ralph's undivided attention. Beth nudged Suzy to start.

'Oh Ralph, we're *so* sorry we're late!' She started breathlessly. 'Some dirty old bugger flashed at Beth on the train, and we pulled the emergency cord, and the police came, then we had to make a statement and – Oh Ralph it was awful, we didn't know where to look first!'

Beth shot Suzy a quick look and realizing she was losing her credibility took over. Her big brown eyes now filling up nicely, and lowering her head slightly, she almost purred. 'Ralph, sweetie it was a nightmare.' Ralph wasn't impressed. He took a deep breath, rose from the chair to his full five foot three inches and cranked his neck to look the two girls in the eye, both of whom were four inches taller.

'Well darlings that was *fabulous*! I trust neither of you will need therapy after seeing a penis on the train first thing in the morning? Now get changed, apologize to the rest of the girls, and then take your positions for the number we did yesterday.' *'Was that a smirk on Suzy's face?'* Ralph wondered as he watched the two of them hurry away.

Michael Walsh had quietly taken himself to the back of the room and watched this little performance. *'Flasher on the train, like hell!'* Yet he secretly wanted to applaud the audacity of this troublesome pair, and at the same time knock their heads together. He should have sacked them ages ago, he didn't have to put up with it; he didn't have the *time* to put up with it. The shows were going well, but the pressure from upstairs to keep it under budget was immense. So why did he tolerate such childish behaviour from Beth and Suzy? He'd asked himself that question many times. It wasn't the usual sexual attraction, even though they were both very attractive in different ways, Beth, seductive and flirty, Suzy more open and childlike. Individually they were bright, funny and talented, but then so were thousands of other hopeful dancers and, aware that all the girls were now returning, he knew he had the cream in this very room. No, he couldn't see Beth and Suzy staying part of any troupe for long, but right now they *were* part of *this* troupe and a damn good one it was too, so if they weren't careful... Suddenly he heard Ralph's voice booming across the room. The rehearsal had at last got under way.

'For Gods sake let's try again from the top, and Pam stop flapping those bloody arms around, you look like a fucking fairy!'

Michael grinned to himself as he watched Ralph glaring at the girls, daring them to laugh.

'God I love this business!' He thought as he watched the girls move about quickly getting into their positions while Ralph sat down and lit another cigarette.

The pause gave him an opportunity to leave and storming across the room he bellowed. 'Beth, Suzy, I want to see you in my office as soon as Ralph breaks for lunch' and then he made his exit, slamming the door behind him.

He took the lift to his office, poured himself his usual mid morning scotch, and slumped into his leather chair behind his desk, swivelling round to view the London skyline. He loved his job, the glamour, and the women! Oh yes, the women! Of course he loved the creativity, the buzz, but the real perk was the power to have any women he wanted, at any time. It never ceased to amaze him how women seemed to be turned on by powerful men. How many had he promised to make stars while fumbling under the sheets?

His lifestyle was the envy of many, but to Michael it was no less than he deserved. He shared his five bedroom mock Tudor house in Basildon with Deirdre his wife of twenty-five years. A small attractive woman whose biggest worry was ensuring the swimming pool was cleaned regularly. She enjoyed lunches at the tennis club and was passionate about her rhododendrons that were the envy of her neighbours and fantasising that her Mercedes convertible wasn't the only thing the sexy young mechanic from the local garage would service was common knowledge at the local WI. She'd long ago made it quite clear to Michael that she didn't like show business people, didn't understand them and certainly wasn't interested in his career, but she made no secret of the fact that she relished in the financial security it gave her.

Michael turned back to face the women who shared his life, smiling back at him from the photo on the corner of his desk. What would Deirdre have made of that performance he'd just walked away from? He was certain she wouldn't tolerate Beth and Suzy; in fact as he poured another scotch he chuckled at the thought of them at one of Deirdre's boring cocktail parties!

Maybe it *was* their lively spirits that attracted him. Sure they looked good on camera, and they definitely stood out from the crowd, but on the other hand, perhaps he was kidding himself? Maybe it was purely sexual! Although they were terrible flirts he was willing to bet they were still virgins. They were obviously bright girls, but even with all their cheek, there was still an innocence about them. They usually managed to dispel any tense atmosphere that sometimes arose, even if they had been the initial cause. On top of that, they were good for the show, and with the possible exception of one or two insecure females, everybody liked them. Even Ralph loved them, although he would never admit it. Their timing for humorous outbursts sometimes irritated him, but Michael had to admit he did fancy them both and was well aware that when relaxing in the bar he would often seek out their company. He'd often imagined spending an evening with them, alone away from the studios, in fact more than once he'd fantasized about bedding the two of them, maybe both at the same time. But somehow knew he never would.

For the rest of the morning the two culprits maintained a low profile while they learnt a complicated Charleston routine. When Ralph broke them for lunch, Beth signalled for Suzy to meet in the loo. They had to get their story straight before facing Michael. June, who'd watched them the previous evening flirting with the pop group who'd appeared in the show that night followed them in.

'So, have you been raving it up again?'

'We haven't been to bed, we didn't get home till six this morning,' groaned Suzy, checking her washed out face in the mirror. 'It was worth it though, it was a brilliant night wasn't it Beth?'

'Beth? Oh, she's in love again, look at her.'

June turned to see Beth slumped in an open cubicle, fishnet tights hugging her knees, head propped against the wall and a faraway look on her face.

June sat on the sink and burst out laughing, 'Oh not again, who's this weeks victims then?' And who was it last week? That group over from America,' racking her brain trying to remember their name. 'Didn't the two of you end up doing a runner from their hotel because they wanted a gang bang?'

'The New Christie Minstrels and anyway we're not like that,' snapped Suzy defensively.

'I know you're not, but what do you expect if you go with them to a hotel room - tea and crumpet?' You two are so naïve sometimes.'

'We maybe naïve, but we're still in tact,' grinned Suzy.

Quitting the loo, and leaving a smirking June behind, Beth and Suzy reluctantly dragged themselves into the lift to take them up to Michael's office on the top floor.

'Right, so we stick to our story and don't get carried away' warned Beth as Suzy bravely, if somewhat timidly knocked on the door, and gave her pal a reassuring squeeze.

'Don't worry Beth, he fancies you too much to get rid of you, I'm the one who's in for it.'

'I reckon he wouldn't say no to a threesome,' giggled Beth regaining her confidence. However, the smiles were soon wiped off their faces, when the command to enter boomed from the other side of the solid oak door. Michael seated at his desk, indicated for them to sit down. The silence was deafening, their heartbeats filling the office.

'So, young ladies, how was your night out? I hope it was worth it, because you're in deep trouble' Michaels face remained expressionless.

'We were late because someone flashed at Beth, honest Michael.'

'*Suzy*' He bellowed, his patience running out, 'don't waste my time. I am *not* one of your lust crazed pop stars who you can twist around your little finger. I want the truth and I want it now, or get out and don't come back!'

'*Oh shit, this is serious.*' thought Beth, realising this time he really meant it and once again intervened with the hope of calming things down. She knew Suzy didn't do well with confrontations and could burst into tears at any moment.

'Michael, you know how much this job means to us, and we *love* working for you.' She was thinking fast, and delivering her lines perfectly. If anyone could save the day it was Beth. Even at her tender age, she knew how to use her feminine charms, and so she battled on, dropping her head submissively; then timing it perfectly closed with the most grovelling, insincere apology Suzy had ever heard. Michael allowed her to finish her masterpiece then got up from his chair and slowly walked over to the window. Suzy nudged Beth and quickly mouthed to her '*Brilliant!*'

Meanwhile staring out of the window Michael had to admit she really was very good. 'Thank you Beth,' he turned around and stared her straight in the eye. 'Your story was quite entertaining; however I feel you aren't taking this job very seriously. You know I could replace you both tomorrow; there are thousands of girls who would die to be in your shoes.' He slowly and deliberately made his way round his desk, stopped in front of Suzy and glared.

'I'm beginning to think that would be my best option, what say you?'

'*What say I?*' thought Suzy. '*What say I?*' she screamed inside as she felt the tears slowly starting to roll down her now ashen face. Giving it one last shot, Beth stood up, brushed her hair from her eyes, coughed, and gave a tentative smile to Michael, who was still fixing his steely stare on Suzy. Her voice no more than a whisper, tried again.

'Michael, we really are so very sorry; please give us one more chance. We promise we won't be late again. Dancing is our life; it's all we've ever wanted to do.'

Suzy wiped her eyes with the sleeve of her T-shirt, and seeing Michael's face soften decided to add to the plea.

'We've always had this dream you see, to work together, and now we are, we just get a bit carried away sometimes don't we Beth? But, honestly Michael, we'll work really hard and we won't give Ralph a hard time anymore, will we Beth?'

Having heard enough, but quite enjoying this new humble side to the girls, he raised his hand.

'OK, OK, that's quite enough. But let me make one thing clear young ladies. If you're late one more time, or give Ralph anymore trouble, *or* turn up for rehearsal looking anything like the mess you look today, I promise you I'll make sure the only theatre that either of you work in will be on the end of Cromer Pier! Do you understand?'

'Yes Michael' the girls both mumbled together.

'And we're really really sorry' Suzy couldn't resist adding again.

'Yes I'm sure you are. Now go and get your lunch, and there had better be a change in your attitudes from now on.'

Impatient to escape, the two girls almost bowed in unison to Michael as they gingerly made their way from the now oppressive room. Without speaking, they half ran to the lift and both slammed their hands on the 'down' button. Hearts still pounding they jumped up and down willing the lift doors to open and swallow them up. Once inside and the doors closed, they felt safe. Safe enough for them both to swing round face each other and grin, vowing never to have to go through that again.

Having been given a second chance the girls took no time at all in regaining their confidence and sense of humour. In fact, by the time it took the lift to reach the canteen on the second floor the two girls were back to their normal, cocky selves and had the place in uproar.

The reason for the commotion was of course Beth and Suzy who were holding court, re-enacting their interview with Michael for the girls who'd been waiting impatiently for their return. They couldn't resist exaggerating every move and every word, and the louder their audience laughed, the more they exaggerated.

Back behind his desk, Michael was content with the way he'd handled the situation. In fact, Michael Walsh, major television producer was no different from any other man in that position. He was a sucker for cute blondes and brunettes with big tits!

SIX

Poor Michael this really wasn't his week. Only two days earlier he'd had the confrontation with Beth and Suzy and now, just one day before transmission he had more to contend with. The star for the show that week, Scott Walker, a chart topping pop singer from America, had flown in with his entourage especially for the show, but had arrived at the studio so stoned he had no idea where he was or what he was doing there. However with his manager on one arm and agent on the other, he managed to stagger onto the studio floor for the band call.

'My god, where do they find these creeps?' Michael whispered to his P.A. Marcus, who was trying to keep up with him as he charged from the production box down onto the studio floor to greet Scott. Marcus knew it was pointless answering his boss during times like these, as he wouldn't listen anyway. In fact during the three years they'd worked together, Michael hadn't seemed to be interested in any of his opinions, but as a twenty-one year old university student Marcus was grateful for the fact that Michael always relied on his assistance for the shows. After all he was going to be producing top shows one day and what better way to learn your craft than from the master! Having to keep his patience once more, Michael approached the now staggering singer and suggested he take a break, and as an aside to the anxious manager 'with plenty of black coffee.'

'Hey man stay cool, I'm here for you man.' Scott was enjoying himself and waving his arms in the air, he started singing and gyrating around the studio, only just missing camera four. Michael gently placed his hand on Scott's shoulder, desperate to get this animal out of the studio before he either broke equipment or worse still his bloody neck. He suggested that they break for an early lunch, hoping Scott would use the time to pull himself together. But having spent the majority of his career in a drug abused stupor, Scott still had a vague recollection as to what was required of him, so insisted he take the number from the top, but with the band taking it a little slower and the studio cleared.

'Right we'll go again everybody and all those not included in this number can go for coffee' instructed Michael dubiously, and then continued with apprehension. 'Start the smoke machine.'

'Quiet in the studio' bellowed Marcus importantly.

The musicians played Scott's intro and the smoke wafted in slowly along the studio floor.

Scott was one of Suzy's idols, she had a picture of him on her bedroom wall and had driven Beth mad for a week when she found out they'd be working with him. Ignoring Michael's instructions to clear the studio, they crept back in and sat in the darkness at the back of the stalls. It was a risk, but she couldn't resist the opportunity of watching Scott sing just for her!

'Where the hell is he?' she whispered to Beth, who by now had her hand over her mouth to stop herself from laughing aloud. All they could see was a thick fog swirling around the studio engulfing everybody. The smoke machine was certainly doing its stuff, completely wiping out the whole cast and crew of studio six. The music kept playing and Scott, wherever he was, just kept right on singing. This was too much for the girls who simultaneously lost control and shrieked out loud, rocking in their seats. By now Michael, who'd resumed his position in the production box was yet again on his way down onto the floor to sort out the chaos.

'Turn the bloody smoke machine off and for God's sake open some doors, let's get some air in here.' As best they could people scattered, bumping into cameras and each other. Michael could only feel his way across the floor, eventually finding his guest star still singing, oblivious to the mass confusion surrounding him. As doors were flung open and the smoke began to clear, people were unsure of what to do next. A hush fell across the studio, a hush that was except for the incredible noises coming from the back of the stalls.

'Who the hell is that?' demanded Michael whipping round and shielding his eyes from the glaring lights, tried to peer through the darkness.

'I thought I said to clear the studio!'

As light began to stream in and the smoke all but gone, Michael was still trying to fathom out who was causing the disturbance. By now, exasperated and to the point of needing a scotch, he blinked, he couldn't believe his eyes.

'*Beth, Suzy,* what are you doing in the studio? I asked for everyone to leave.'

Suzy immediately jumped to her feet, feeling relatively safe in the darkness. 'Sorry Michael we only wanted to watch Scott sing, we didn't mean any harm and we didn't touch the smoke machine!'

Scott's ears suddenly pricked up at the sound of a female voice and although his brain wasn't in full swing, his ego was. Another chick to add to his collection was priority, so ignoring Michael he staggered forward, trying to see where the mystery voice came from. Immediately his cigar-puffing sidekicks anticipating trouble stood up, but Scott glared at them and they sat down in unison. 'Hi honey, where are you? Come on up here and join the fun.'

Suzy couldn't believe her ears and tugged at Beth's arm. 'Come on, quick before he passes out or something, we can get his autograph.' Beth more curious than anything, jumped up and they both ran down the aisle coming face to face with the man who'd just given them another great story to tell back in the dressing room. Michael intervened before things got out of hand. He needed to get Scott out of the studio before any more damage was done, including his own reputation. He'd be the laughing

31

stock if this got out. Why did those two bloody girls have to be there?

'Beth, Suzy, go away, I'll deal with you later.'

'Oh! Shame on you Mike' drooled Scott leering at the girls. 'They're the best looking chic's I've seen since I got here!' Michael, embarrassed by the reprimand had no choice but to humour his expensive star and introduced the girls who were in return their most charming. By the threatening look on Michaels face, they sensed they were pushing their luck, leaving them in no doubt as to what he was going to do with them when he'd finally sorted out this fiasco, so excused themselves and headed for the exit, but Scott stopped them in their tracks.

'Girls wait a sec, can I join you for coffee? You did say you were having lunch didn't you Mike?'

Michael's face flushed, he bit his lip and took a deep breath. 'Yes I did and by the way it's Michael.'

Without taking his eyes off the girls Scott threw a dismissive hand in the air, 'sure Mike, well I guess you need time to tidy this place up before we rehearse again, right?'

Without waiting for an answer he made his way up the aisle. 'Shall we go girls?' and linking arms he swept them through the door.

Michael stood for a moment, totally dumbfounded, and then headed straight for the bar.

SEVEN

Christmas was just round the corner and with only two weeks of the series left, Beth and Suzy although sad to be saying goodbye to the other girls were already celebrating. One night in the bar after another successful show, Michael had particular reason to celebrate. The ratings had stayed consistently high and he was having discussions on the possibility of another series. He spotted the girls causing their usual stir across the room, flirting with yet another pop group who were no doubt drugged up to the eyeballs. He called the pair over to join him for a drink and watched them, probably making arrangements to spend yet another night on the town with the over active throbbing groins. Now there's a good name for those arseholes, he chuckled to himself.

'So girls, now that it's nearly all over what are your plans?'

Unlike the rest of the girls who'd been auditioning for other work, Beth and Suzy, far from worrying about next month's rent, had spent most of their time and money on nights out with most of the 'Throbbing Arseholes' that had appeared in the shows over the last six weeks.

'Blimey he must be drunk, he's normally as tight as a fishes arse,' slurred Suzy already on her third Martini, watching Michael fight his way to the bar.

'Perhaps it's our lucky night and he wants his threesome,' smirked Beth.

'Well if that's his game he's on his own.'

'Oh Suz if he could do that he'd be in a circus!'

'Oh my god!' realised Suzy and picturing the whole scenario, they were uncontrollable, delighting in exchanging thoughts of poor Michael in a seedy room somewhere trying to perform the impossible according to a manual.

'So, who's your victim this time?' asked Michael through gritted teeth, as he handed them their drinks, embarrassed and frustrated that he was probably once again the butt of their joke.

'What *do* you mean Michael?' fluttered Beth, 'we were just wondering how many people it takes to make it a party.'

Michael unconvinced and impatient with the secrecy, moved closer until they could feel his breath on their faces. 'Don't come the innocent with me young ladies,' he hissed as they simultaneously bent back to avoid the stench of scotch and cigar. He grabbed their heads with both hands and pulled them in again, ignoring the sudden fear on their faces. 'You two are the biggest fucking prick teasers I've ever met.'

'Michael!' they both shrieked and jumped back spilling their drinks, relieved to be free of his grip. 'Prick teasers! Us?' they screamed at the man with whom they'd taken great delight in prick teasing for the past six weeks. By now the whole bar had come to a standstill. This was better than any fabricated drama being created in the studios. Michael suddenly aware that he was the centre of attention quickly got his head together.

'Excellent girls, that's just the reaction I wanted. Now come to my office tomorrow and we'll run through the rest of the script.' And with that he turned, smiled at his bemused audience and announced 'those two will go far'! And as he strolled from the room mumbled, 'as far away as possible.'

Suzy broke the silence that still hung in the air. 'Bloody hell what on earth was that all about?' Beth stared after him slow and hard, unsure of what to make of it, but reassured Suzy they'd be knocking on his door first thing in the morning to find out.

After Michael left the bar, the girls ordered another round of drinks and discussed their plan of action and at 9.30am the following morning they were knocking on that now familiar office door. Suzy, suffering a massive hangover and finding it hard to focus, regretted that fifth drink.

'God I feel rough, my heads throbbing. Why didn't you stop me finishing that bottle?'

'Because my sweet, watching you perform your headstands in the middle of the bar was classic.'

'Yeah, I must find a new party trick.'

'Still at least you had jeans on, that makes a change.'

The boom from the other side of the door suddenly brought them to attention.

'Come in hurry up, I haven't got all day.'

Once inside Beth confidently stepped forward. 'You wanted to see us Michael and we don't want to be late for rehearsals, so we thought we'd better come in early.' She stood defiant, ushering Suzy to join her. Without inviting them to sit down, he slowly walked round the desk and stood inches from them. He smiled; satisfied that he'd gotten the better of them in the bar. Power was a great asset. He had always known it and now he was abusing the privilege.

'I have to say that you two have been a pain in the arse since the start of the series.' He was enjoying himself and as his eyes flicked from one to the other, they both stared at him unsure of where this was leading. He made his way round to his side of the desk again, took a cigar from the ornate box which Deirdre had brought back from Indonesia for their tenth wedding anniversary, cut the end off and as he lit it, dropped heavily into his leather chair puffing rings into the air and round his victims. Beth suddenly grabbed Suzy's hand reassuring her friend that everything was OK. But for once Beth wasn't confident everything *was* going to be OK.

Michael swung his chair round now with his back to the girls and continued. 'Right girls, what am I going to do with you? Do you want to continue working in this business?' he asked staring out of the window.

'Yes Michael of course we do' they blustered, nodding furiously at the back of his head and squeezing each other's hands even tighter, unaware that Michael was watching their every move in the reflection of the window. Suddenly, Michael whipped his chair back round to face them again, lunged forward and grinned at them with what they later decided was a dirty old man's grin.

'Well my dears, I think it's high time you proved to me how talented you obviously think you are.' He leapt to his feet and walked over to the drinks cabinet.

'I won't offer you a drink as you've got a hard day's rehearsal ahead of you and anyway you look as if you could do with a week off the stuff.'

'Pompous bastard' thought Beth.

'Letchy Prat' thought Suzy.

He poured himself a scotch. 'I'm taking a show to Belgium and I need dancers who can also act.' He leered at them over his glasses with an even dirtier grin 'and I do believe that you two are very good at acting. So, what do you say? Interested?'

The last two weeks of the series passed without any major dramas and Michael began to think that his protégés were finally growing up at last, or if not at least heeding his warnings. They were on time for every rehearsal and seemed almost subdued. He heaved a sigh of relief; after all if the Belgium trip was a success, it could mean expanding to Europe.

The reason for this lull in their behaviour was in fact because they were so exhausted they had trouble speaking, let alone cause trouble. They kept a low profile, as they didn't want Michael to know about their celebrations. Well it *was* Christmas and they *were* going to Belgium soon, which meant the rent was covered until March at least.

'Do you realise Beth it's cheaper to stay out all night than come home' Suzy yawned as they staggered into their much-neglected beds at 5am one morning. 'We've hardly been to bed this month, so we ain't gotta change the sheets so often, *so* we save money at the laundrette, clever huh?'

Beth smiled at Suzy's hair brained logic as she snuggled down for what would only be about three hours sleep before facing another gruelling day's rehearsal.

They'd spent the evening at 'Annabelle's' nightclub and needing a lift home, but not wanting the usual groping that was expected in return, devised what they proudly claimed to be their most outrageous scam to date.

Choosing their unsuspecting victims who were to have the pleasure of transporting them home was easy. Obviously they had to have a car, that was top priority, but they needed to be relatively young, maybe only just having passed their driving test and keen to try out the back seat manoeuvres with two apparently eager playmates. Confident guys who'd been around a bit was out, they weren't so easy to manipulate. Convincing the two poor unsuspecting souls of their fabricated dilemma was easier than the girls expected.

'Do you think they really believed we were novice nuns?' asked Suzy lighting a cigarette.

'I don't know but it got us a lift home without any hanky panky didn't it?' Beth was reluctant to talk; she needed to catch up with her beauty sleep, but Suzy was wide-awake, keen to relive the events of the evening.

'They were a bit thick though, I mean there we were in full slap, dressed up to the eyeballs, *you* even had that see through crotchet dress on.'

'Yes well you weren't exactly the "Virgin Mary" in that 'Biba' creation' chuckled Beth from somewhere deep under the blankets, 'you didn't look too much like "Sister Suzy" to me.'

'Oh and I suppose you were *really* convincing as "Sister Elizabeth" with your "Star of David" in full view'. That was it;

Beth gave up trying to get to sleep. She sat up, lit a cigarette and together they spent the next half hour revelling in how they'd conned the two lads into dropping them at their local Church, telling them it was the Convent where they were about to take their final vows before retreating from the world forever. Eventually Beth dozily threw her dog end into the dried tea mug lying by the side of her bed and snuggled down again, this time determined to get some sleep. Suzy walked over to where Beth was now drifting off, threw her cigarette in Beth's mug and chuckled as she crept back into her bed.

Christmas was only a few days away. The series was finally finished and what with the prospect of Belgium in the New Year, Beth and Suzy were determined to enjoy the break. The only fly in the ointment was that they couldn't spend it together.

'Oh Suz please come to us for Christmas this year, you don't mind do you mum?' Joan who'd only popped in for a coffee, now found herself in a quandary. As much as she wanted Suzy with them she understood that her parents expected her home for Christmas.

'Well dear I think it's up to Suzy, she knows what's best.'

'You know I'd love to come, but all hell will let loose if I don't go home.' Suzy gave a halfhearted laugh 'Huh, I don't know why I bother though; Dad's idea of Christmas spirit is a bottle of Jack Daniels. She hated Christmas; it was always so full of aggravation, like the year when she was about ten. She remembered having sneaked a look at the bundles of badly wrapped presents under the tree and was so excited because for the first time in her life there was more than one present with her name on. But the excitement didn't last long because on Christmas Eve the police had barged in and arrested Sam for receiving stolen goods, not only taking her father away, but all the presents as well. It wasn't the first time she'd cried herself to sleep, and as she'd lain huddled under the covers she'd prayed that the police would lock her father up and throw away the key.

Suzy brought her thoughts back to the present and put her arms round Beth and Joan, planting a kiss on each cheek.

'I'll be all right' she smiled, I've only got to put up with my rotten family for a couple of days and then if it's OK with you I'll see you for the New Year.'

EIGHT

By mid January Beth and Suzy were in full swing, rehearsing for the Belgium trip. Michael was feeling relaxed and tanned having spent the Christmas break at his villa in the Canaries and he was looking forward if not slightly apprehensive about working with the girls again.

This trip was important to Michael, as for a while now he'd seen great potential in the European market. It would be a tight schedule, recording a two-hour special pilot in just ten days. He wanted the right choreographer, who would be prepared to dance in the numbers as well, and decided on Frank Martine. He'd known Frank for some time and liked his work, besides that he was straight, not a screaming queen, which meant not too many dramas.

Frank had come into the business at sixteen and now at thirty-two was well respected for his creative work. Unlike most male dancers his diminutive height hadn't held him back and the girls found his dark continental looks appealing. He fell instantly in love with Beth and she likewise loved the attention. Guy the only other male dancer was missing Bridget, his girlfriend in Yorkshire, but he was a game lad and after only two days with Beth and Suzy decided to make the most of his freedom.

The girls found the rehearsals very demanding, having for the first time in their lives learning lines for the sketches as well as the dance routines. Frank was an excellent jazz choreographer and Suzy loved his style. Beth wasn't quite so keen, but because of the mutual attraction, went along with it.

'He really fancies you; it's sickening watching him drool all over you!'

'Who? I don't know whom you mean,' smirked Beth. It had been a hard day's rehearsal and back at the flat Beth was pouring bubbles into a hot steaming bath.

'Who? You know damn well who I mean. 'Beth sweetie don't worry about the step, you *look fabulous*' mimicked Suzy.

'Well I'm struggling with the work Suz, you know I'm more tits and arse.'

'Hmm, you make that obvious; he can't take his eyes off yours!'

After a week's rehearsal in a freezing cold dingy church hall, the time came for flying to Antwerp. The whole group got on well, but Suzy sensed a change in Beth. She was in love! Of course this wasn't the first time, she fell in love almost every week, but this time it was different. Beth didn't make fun of Frank, and spent most of her free time with him, sightseeing and most evenings in romantic restaurants, returning to the hotel not drunk as she usually did, but dreamy and vacant. One night she crept into their room at 3am and gently shook Suzy awake.

Suzy pulled her head out from under the bedclothes and blearily squinted at her friend. 'Shit, whatever time is it?'

Beth sank onto the bed, put her head in her hands and moaned.

'Oh Suz what am I going to do? He wants me to sleep with him.' Suzy groaned as she switched the bedside light on and pumped up her pillows. 'Christ here we go again. Everybody you come into contact with wants to sleep with you and we decided that if they didn't then they must be poofs.' She looked into Beth's eyes, 'Oh no, you want to don't you? Have you told him you're a virgin?'

'Of course not.'

'Well I think he might find out sooner or later' Suzy smirked as she shivered her way across to the loo, 'won't be a mo, Snow White.'

41

It was 8.30am two days later and Suzy was pacing the floor, puffing on her third cigarette. Ever since they'd arrived in Belgium Beth had spent all her spare time with Frank and she was feeling neglected. Besides they were supposed to be going on a sight seeing coach trip that day. They'd already bought the tickets and now it was too late, the coach had left half an hour earlier. Suzy was in two minds whether to go on her own, just to serve Beth right, but deep down she was worried sick. She'd never stayed out all night before. She was down to her last fingernail and chewing it furiously, when suddenly Beth sheepishly poked her head around the door.

'Hello it's me,' she whispered guiltily, tiptoeing towards Suzy, attempting to hide her tights and shoes behind her back.

'Where the hell have you been? We've missed the coach you know' sulked Suzy refusing to look at Beth.

'I'm so sorry, but wait till I tell you what happened' said Beth throwing her shoes under the bed and stuffing her tights into her bag.

'I don't want to know, I'm having a bath leave me alone.' Suzy stormed into the bathroom, Beth followed, but the door was slammed in her face.

'Please Suz don't be like that.'

'Sod off Beth, you know I wanted to go on that trip, I've hardly seen you all week. I've been stuck in this bloody hotel room while you've been out with 'Frank the Wank' you selfish cow.'

'But Suz I saw his *willy*, actually Suz I *touched* his willy…in fact…' There was a silence from the depths of the bathroom, when suddenly the door was flung open.

'Oh My God, did you actually do it?' giggled Suzy, all anger forgotten, and flinging herself onto the bed demanded Beth tell her everything. Beth collapsed onto the bed next to her and relished in explaining every grope and sweaty detail of her first taste of lust with Frank, while Suzy listened with admiration and envy. When Beth had finished telling how she'd quite enjoyed it once she got the hang of it, she jumped up from the bed, and with hands on hips shook her 36DD in Suzy's face and purred.

'Listen you tart just because you've had a bit doesn't make you Marilyn Monroe,' laughed Suzy. 'So what now, is he going to whisk you off into the sunset?'

Beth flopped onto the bed, threw her legs in the air and reassured Suzy that as good as her 'Opening Night' was, she still needed a lot of rehearsing before signing a contract for a long run. 'Anyway I've missed you mate, come on let's do some sightseeing, we've only got two days left before we go home.'

NINE

Back home at last, Beth dragged her case through to the bedroom while Suzy dumped hers in the living room and grabbed the mountain of mail, which had clogged the front door mat, forcing them to charge the door at full speed landing them predictably in a heap on the hall floor.

'Not exactly Batman and Robin are we?'

Suzy shuffled through the letters, throwing most of them unopened across the carpet, went into the kitchen and put the kettle on.

'Has this weeks 'Stage' been delivered yet?' Beth asked, launching herself onto the sofa.

'Yeah, I'm reading it' shouted Suzy from the kitchen. 'There's a few auditions in for summer season. Where d'yer fancy lying on the beach this year?'

'Ooh! I think The Seychelles sounds good.' smiled Beth closing her eyes and stretching her long legs along the sofa, 'or maybe Barbados would do?'

'In your dreams sunshine' laughed Suzy as she brought in the steaming mugs of tea. 'You've got Blackpool, Morecambe and Bournemouth, take your pick.'

'Well, it depends which dishy hunk is starring in it. Come on Suz, if you had the choice between Bournemouth with Harry Worth, or Blackpool with Tom Jones which would you choose?' Suzy put the tea down on the coffee table and mockingly scratched her head. 'Hmm, now let me see. Well I'd be quite happy in Blackpool, as long as you were in Bournemouth.' Beth picked up a cushion and threw it at her.

'Charming, why would you want that?'

'Because, you tart, I wouldn't stand a chance with Tom Jones if you were around.'

'But he's not my type, my taste is more sophisticated. Now Sammy Davis Jr, there's a real man!' Beth anticipated Suzy's reaction and dived for cover under the remaining cushion, avoiding the deadly aim with the 'Stage'.

But the girls didn't have to audition after all, for among the pile of bills was a letter offering them both a place with the Tillers in Westcliffe on Sea for the summer. They jumped at it, although Suzy was a little disappointed. She loved Frank's modern style of choreography and was hoping to do more of the same, but agreed that they needed the work, because Michael hadn't heard how the pilot had gone in Antwerp, and the rent was due soon.

Excited at being back in the theatre and seeing some of the girls again, they made their way to the changing room, which was packed as usual.

'Oh no, Suz I forgot to shave!'

'Let's have a look.' Beth stood back as far as the space would allow and bending over, Suzy was now eye level with Beth's crutch.

'It looks OK to me, just your usual 6 o/clock shadow.'

'You should be so lucky; my crutch hasn't had that much attention for months' muttered someone from behind Beth.

Suzy stood up slowly and mouthed to Beth. 'Oops, lezibum at 10 o/clock' which sent them both into fits of giggles.

After a week of learning two killer kicking routines, Suzy was looking forward to getting down to some *real* dancing with Tommy Coast the choreographer, who was impatient to start work. He informed them that they only had one week to learn ten routines before the rest of the company would be joining them. On this particular show there were twelve girl and six boy dancers, which according to 'The B and S Manual' guaranteed fun and maybe a few dramas.

After the initial introductions they were sorted into groups. Tommy made it obvious from the start that he liked Suzy, but took an instant dislike to Beth. He kept her at the back for the whole routine and deciding he really liked the cute blonde, made Suzy his featured dancer for the first number.

The coffee breaks were usually spent huddled together with the other dancers, comparing notes on who had worked with who and who had slept with who and even more importantly who would be sleeping with who by the end of the season.

It was soon established that Tommy preferred his dancers blonde to brunette and definitely men to women, but where the connection was nobody could fathom out.

'I've worked for him before' whispered Lucy, a petite freckle face girl with laughing green eyes and a strong northern accent, 'he'll have us pirouetting down from the circle, landing in an arabesque and God help anyone who can't do it.'

'Oh well good luck Little Miss Popular' laughed Beth poking Suzy in the back, 'I'm quite happy being a tree up the back.'

As the week progressed it became clear that Suzy enjoyed Tommy's choreography where as Beth continued to struggle. Suzy offered to help her with the routines, but Beth was beginning to realise that maybe this just wasn't her style, but she wasn't sure what was.

They were both becoming fond of Lucy with the bubbly blonde curls. She was organised, hated being late or left out of any gossip, so when she suggested the three of them share a flat during the season they jumped at the idea, especially as she offered to find a place and pay the deposit. This suited Beth and Suzy, as they were broke as usual, but offered to pay her back as soon as they got paid.

The rest of the cast joined the rehearsal the following week and the atmosphere became a lot tenser, but a lot more interesting as far as Beth and Suzy were concerned. Billy Dainty was great fun, helping Beth to regain her confidence by complementing her on her assets, and everybody was looking forward to a great summer.

At the end of a gruelling fortnight, listening to Tommy screaming at the dancers and arse licking the 'stars,' the three girls caught the train to Westcliffe.

'So what's this flat like Lucy,' asked Suzy once they were settled on the train, taking up most of the carriage with their three suitcases and hundreds of carrier bags.

'I don't know, I rang the theatre and they gave me a list of digs. This was the only one left available. I know we've got to share a bedroom but apparently it's huge.'

'Oh well that's our sex life out the window then,' groaned Beth. Suzy gave her a quick look wondering where Beth's sudden sex life had appeared. But Beth was beginning to worry about this new found friend, after all they had only known her a couple of weeks and knew very little about her, only that she was from Manchester and smoked like a chimney, which at least was in her favour. Was she a rampant nymphomaniac, or maybe into S&M? Beth began to panic, imagining her and Suzy spending half the summer sleeping under the pier while Lucy was tied up back at the flat!

When at last they arrived at the station they bundled into a taxi and chatted excitedly during the short drive to 35 Cavendish Road. The flat wasn't exactly a palace; consisting of a small kitchen with a tiny window overlooking next doors brick wall, a scruffily furnished living room and a bathroom, stinking like a sewer. The biggest disappointment was the bedroom. Lucy was quick to claim the very creaky single iron bed in the corner, leaving Beth and Suzy sharing the double. This didn't bother them and decided the flat was adequate, especially as they weren't planning to spend too much time there anyway. One agreement was made, and that was if anyone of them wanted *privacy* for an evening, the other two would disappear. As they were to find out many times over the following weeks, this would mean spending an uncomfortable night curled up on the two shabby armchairs in the living room.

TEN

The summer of '67 was a particularly busy one for the girls and it didn't take them long to organize the cast party to be held on stage every Friday, to celebrate payday, not that they held onto theirs for long. Cooking at the flat wasn't even considered, especially when there was a perfectly good café right opposite the theatre that did a great egg and chips! They didn't waste any time at establishing themselves as regulars and working their sickly charm on Nigel, the owner, they were allowed to put all meals on the slate. So no sooner had they got their wages, Nigel was insisting on payment for his week's worth of fry-ups. And so it went on, pay the debts, start a new slate.

The flat became the meeting place for everybody including most of the stagehands. Paul, the lighting tech was becoming fond of Suzy, but kept it to himself. She was so blunt that he was sure that any approach he might have made would be entertainment for the whole theatre at the next Friday night party. So he made do with being just friends and ogling in secret. His brother Nick who worked the spotlight had better luck with Lucy, which pleased Beth and Suzy as their new flatmate was beginning to irritate them. It turned out that Lucy suffered from "clingyitus."

'Why does she have to copy *everything* we do?' moaned Suzy as the pair of them curled up for yet another night in the shabby armchairs, waiting for Nick and Lucy to finish whatever they were doing in the bedroom.

'I don't know but I've got an idea that'll teach her a lesson' grinned Beth.

The following Friday, as soon as they paid their due's to Nigel and with the pittance left over, the girls went straight into town, only this time Lucy was invited to join them and as they entered their favourite boutique, Beth's plan got under way.

'Ooh! Suzy look, don't you just love this?' she smirked, holding up a dress that neither of them would be seen dead in.

'Oh Beth I love it, but it's not fair, green doesn't really suit me and flowers are cool, they're all over Carnaby Street! Why don't you try it on?'

'I'd love it, but I'm broke this week, maybe they'll hold it for me till next Friday!' And true to form Lucy, who'd been shadowing them all round the boutique barged in and snatched the monstrosity from Beth.

'Our mom's sent me some money down, so I think I'll try it on.'

'Oh no I really liked that,' sulked Beth avoiding Suzy's eyes.

'Don't worry you can borrow it any time you like.'

'Ooh thanks, Lucy, I suppose you're going to wear it for the party tonight?'

And wear it she did, with Suzy suggesting cruelly that she looked like a cabbage patch, as she downed yet another martini and flirting outrageously with Derek, the magic act in the show, who Beth kept reminding her, was old enough to be her dad *and* married. Derek's wife Serena seemed oblivious of his roving eye.

'You be careful Suz, you're playing a dangerous game!'

'Don't be an old fart Beth, It's only a laugh, anyway you're just jealous because he fancies me and not you.'

'I thought we'd agreed to steer clear of married blokes. They're only after one thing, and he's not likely to get that off you is he...is he?' Suzy screwed up her face and insisted that she was just having a bit of fun, but then sheepishly added that she had a confession to make. They were standing downstage by the drinks table with The Stones complaining loudly that they could 'Get

No Satisfaction' over the sound system, so Suzy took Beth by the arm into the wings to explain.

'Well,' she started uncomfortably, making sure they weren't being overheard, 'I told Derek we were sisters!'

'*What?*' shrieked Beth in disbelief.

'I know, I know' whispered Suzy defensively, 'but I *feel* like your sister and your mum and dad love me like a daughter, in fact I think they prefer me to you, so it didn't seem that big a lie! Anyway it's gone too far now he's told Serena, so we've got to go with it, otherwise I'm gonna look a right Prat.'

Beth suddenly fell about laughing. 'Don't tell me he believed you, is he blind?'

'Oh, that was easy' smirked Suzy confidently; 'I told him our mum had an affair with an American singer, while she was at the Hippodrome, quite romantic actually.' She began drifting off into a dream, imagining some handsome star sweeping Joan off her feet, until Beth tugged at her arm.

'Did you say *who* your so-called 'Daddy' was? Not Billy Eckstein I hope?'

'Ooh, I don't think so, and they'd definitely be 'Passing Strangers' by now! Anyway, that's the fun bit. Everyone will be trying to guess who I look like.'

Beth stared at Suzy, stunned.

'Oh come on Beth, it'll be a laugh, we can keep them guessing all summer!'

Suddenly Suzy caught Derek's eye. 'Right, I'm off for a dance, keep your eye out for Serena for me' and off she wiggled to the centre of the stage where most of the party were dancing to 'Sam and Dave' but Suzy only had eyes for Derek, who was obviously enjoying her performance. '*My God who'd believe she was still a virgin,*' thought Beth watching Suzy putting her all into crutch bumping her way round the stage.

The 'sister act' didn't take long to spread through the company and the two girls enjoyed creating their 'fantasy family', their imaginations running riot at times. Inventing stories that were too outrageous to be believed, but the bigger the audience the bigger the tale, until one night they realised they may have gone too far. Les Collins the theatre manager was putting on a Sunday concert for charity and asked if any of the company would give up their time to perform in it. Beth and Suzy jumped at the idea of showing the world or at least the population of Westcliffe their amazing talent, and decided on a comedy routine with an unforgettable if not outrageous performance of "Doin' What Comes Naturally." They rehearsed surreptitiously every night for a fortnight and created their blatantly sexy costumes from whatever they could scrounge from the other girls. The local press were invited to attend the performance with interviews after the show.

Suzy and Beth sat in the dressing room doing their make-up. 'What if they check up on our story and ring home to find out more? Then we're in for it!'

'Hmm, can't imagine how poor mum would explain that one away to dad. 'Oh, so sorry Peter darling, I forgot to mention I had a mad passionate affair with Johnny Ray and by the way Suzy's my real daughter! She popped out one night while you were at the pub!' The two girls giggled nervously and carried on getting ready.

What they didn't know was that Joan had made a last minute decision to surprise the girls with a visit. She hadn't seen them for ages and missed their company. Arriving at the flat Lucy was quick to tell her of their special performance.

'Go to the Stage Door, tell them who you are and they'll let you in, you should just make it in time to catch the opening.'

'Thank you Lucy I'll do that' and as she went through the gate she turned, 'they'll be so surprised to see me!'

'Won't they just!' smirked Lucy as she watched Joan walk away.

Zipping up each other's costumes Suzy and Beth were unaware that Joan was being ushered into her seat in the theatre.

The show was going well and after the interval everyone settled back into their seats for the second half. Beth and Suzy were nervously waiting in the wings, when Billy walked out on stage and announced. 'Ladies and Gentlemen "The Carson Sisters!"

The girls came out, did their routine and brought the house down. They bowed, waved and ran off the stage, but were pushed back on to take another bow while the applause was still going strong. Beth and Suzy relished the spotlight and milked it for all it was worth.

'Oh God, I don't believe it,' hissed Suzy as they took yet another bow.

Beth stood up abruptly. 'What?'

'Keep bowing and get off stage I'll tell you later' whispered Suzy through a stage smile.

Derek who'd been ogling Suzy from side stage was first to congratulate them. 'Well done girls, I told you they'd love you.'

'Yeah, thanks,' but Suzy wasn't listening and pushed Beth down the hall.

'Oh by the way' Derek called after them, 'we heard your mum's in, she must be so proud!'

'What did he say?'

'You heard! Mum's here, that's what I was going to tell you. I saw her as we took that second call. She's about eight rows back, dead centre!'

'Oh shit, I don't believe it.' Beth pushed open the dressing room door and sank down into a chair. Suzy, slamming the door behind her, slumped cross-legged on the floor, all the excitement of the performance forgotten. Beth, lighting two cigarettes and passing one to Suzy, jumped as a knock on the door was followed by an unwelcome familiar voice.

'Come in Lucy' said Suzy half-heartedly. Lucy sidled into the room and with a blatant grin leant against the open door. 'Just thought you'd like to know your mom's here Beth. She wanted to surprise you.' She was disappointed at their response.

'Yeah thanks, we know, now if you don't mind we would like some privacy.'

Lucy eyed the two suspiciously. 'By the way Suzy you had a big hole in your tights!' She flounced out slamming the door behind her.

'Come on, we'd better go up for the finale and face the music,' said Beth pulling herself together. But little did they know the worse was still to come.

After the final curtain call, Billy stepped forward to the mike. 'Ladies and Gentlemen, in the audience today we have Mrs Joan Carson, mother of Suzy and Beth our talented singing sisters. Please come up on stage Mrs Carson.' Applause echoed throughout the theatre as the bemused Joan made her way onto the stage. The girls couldn't tell if she was in a state of bewilderment or ready to kill her little darlings, but she kept her composure as she was asked what it was like to raise two such outrageous daughters.

'Well they're always full of surprises!' Beth and Suzy visibly squirmed as the audience applauded and the curtain came down on a successful show.

Beth and Suzy quickly hurried Joan into the dressing room and made a space for her to sit down. Beth tentatively put her arms round her mother. 'It's so good to see you' and planted a kiss on her cheek. Joan ignoring her daughter stood up and turned to face them both. 'So, before we go any further, is there anything else I should know about?'

'Er, well there was that thing with Johnny Ray, but you don't want to hear about that.'

'I'm sure I don't Suzy!' Joan eyed them suspiciously. 'OK then, I think my *'daughters'* owe me a dinner, don't you? Nigel's café, isn't that the place you were telling me about? I could do with a nice juicy steak.' Joan walked ahead and Beth turned and whispered to Suzy.

'Phew that was close, she's not such a bad old girl, maybe she'll pay for dinner tonight if we behave ourselves.'

'I heard that, and as for dinner, we'll put it on your slate.'

ELEVEN

Del Flately, the reporter from the local Gazette, although interested didn't delve too deeply into the 'sister' story, and made an appointment for a photo shoot the following Wednesday. So after their usual Friday off loading of funds to Nigel in the café, they were into town again for new photo gear, which meant the shortest and most revealing dresses they could find.

Passing the pet shop in the high street on the way home, Beth noticed a new sign in the window "Puppies for Sale." She stopped suddenly and grabbing Suzy's arm dragged her into the shop.

'I have just had *the* most brilliant idea!'

'What the hell are you doing?'

'Just think Suz,' poking her fingers through the cage where eight sandpaper tongues and wagging tails clambered for her attention, 'we could have one each, look they're so cute.'

'Have you completely gone off your trolley?' Suzy was trying hard to ignore the masses of fur, which were now taking chunks out of Beth's hand. 'How the hell could we cope with two dogs? We have a job looking after ourselves.'

Beth yanked her hand back. 'We could train them and they could travel with us, they'd be real theatrical dogs!' As she spoke, Beth realised that Suzy wasn't going to need too much convincing; she was already smiling at one particular little bundle that had gotten bored and was amusing itself, chasing its own tail. Rubbing her sore hand Beth seized the chance. 'I can see the headlines now!'

"Talented Sisters Doing What Comes Naturally, Rescuing Puppies from Certain Death!"

'It *will* be certain death if we look after them,' laughed Suzy who was by now totally besotted with the spinning top. Beth had already taken the next stage into her own hands and was asking the assistant to let her hold one of them.

'As long as I can have that one,' mused an infatuated Suzy, pointing to the now exhausted and giddy bundle. Ten minutes later the girls staggered out with their prize bundles, plus accessories, struggling to contain their excitable new 'toys'.

'Beth, have you noticed anything?' The two of them were walking back along the seafront.

'Yes, this little sod's peed on me!'

'Oh I thought it was your new perfume 'Urine my Heart.' Beth screamed with laughter and Suzy broke into fits of giggles, both dropping their new furry purchases. Beth was now on all fours, circling Suzy in pursuit of the puppies, which were lapping up this newfound freedom. At last with the puppies retrieved, Suzy resumed the conversation.

'So, have you noticed that you picked the dark haired one and I chose the blonde one?'

'Does this mean you'll be telling everyone they're our cousins?'

'Well, now *there's* a story.'

Walking back to the flat they chatted non stop about names for their new "toys", and more importantly how they would sneak them into the theatre past Ernie the stage door man. They came up with a plan. With Beth's boobs bigger than ever and Suzy in the first stages of pregnancy, they swept straight past Ernie and down the hall to the dressing room.

'Psychedelic' and 'Freakout' proved popular playmates with the rest of the cast, which was just as well because that very first night, leaving them for just five minutes on their own in the girl's dressing room, while they went on for the opening number proved disastrous.

The sight and smell that greeted them after the routine without doubt surpassed the usual chaos of a dancers dressing room. Shoes were strewn across the floor. One girl barged past Beth and screamed at the sight of her Charleston costume, precariously hanging on for dear life to its few remaining sequins. The other dancers followed, throwing verbal abuse at the little 'shits' who had just had the most fun they'd ever experienced in the whole of their short lives. The culprits oblivious to the hate that was being thrown their way were exhausted and had collapsed, unfortunately for Carole, on her finale cloak for some very urgent shuteye.

'Do you want the good news or the bad news girls?' announced Suzy scrambling to rescue the remaining debris. But judging by the glares thrown her way she didn't give any of them a chance to answer.

'The bad news is they've pooed on this leotard,' cautiously dangling it well away from her nose. 'The good news is it's Beth's' and threw it across the room. Beth jumped away and let it fall at her feet.

'What's so good about that?' she screamed, kicking it away.

'Well it's your bloody dog' insisted a grumpy voice from under the clothes rail trying to retrieve her bedraggled feathered headdress.

'How do you know it was Psychedelic? It's not a stick of rock with his name running through the middle. It could have been Freakout.'

But for once, none of the girls were amused.

The second half opened with a scene from South Pacific. The dancers posed in different positions around the stage, while John and Tony the two male singers were slowly fanning them with giant palm leaves. Stacy the principle singer made her entrance to sing 'Bali Hi'. Softly the orchestra played her intro as she approached the microphone. The set gave the illusion of gentle south sea isles and tropical breezes, but as Stacy opened her mouth to sing, the heat from the stage lights was making the smell of the costumes unbearable, and the wafting stench of dog poo engulfed her. The dancers had made great efforts to rid their various costumes of untrained puppies, but failed, causing Stacy to miss her cue as she inhaled the putrid odour. The dancers looked at each other unsure of what was going to happen next. The orchestra played the intro again, while Stacy improvised by turning slowly, grimacing at everyone on stage and turned back again to face the audience with a smile. With effort she started to sing, just barely holding her notes. Suzy glanced across at Beth knowing something had to be done and quickly. As John and Tony continued to waft the fans, she signalled to Beth tilting her head toward the singers and glaring at their fans. She stood up slowly and Beth followed suit. The pair of them moved with hips and arms swaying towards John and Tony, who now both looked like they were ready to vomit. The girls grabbed the fans and swayed their way down to Stacy, who was still trying to get through the second verse. The singer glanced at Suzy and Beth standing either side of her with relief as they started to fan madly. Freddie the musical director was confused, but not surprised as they both gazed down at him with huge guilty smiles.

Fortunately Stacy managed to finish her song and the South Sea's breezes didn't waft into the stalls leaving the audience clapping enthusiastically and none the wiser.

Luckily for 'Psycho' and 'Freaky', the rest of the cast were putty in their paws and shared 'Poo Watch' while the girls were on stage. But how long the novelty of getting up early for 'walkies' after heavy drinking nights nobody was sure, but bets were being placed round the theatre on how long before the poor little things were 'accidentally lost'.

TWELVE

A warm gentle breeze greeted the girls as they walked along the seafront to the funfair where they'd arranged to meet Del for the photo shoot. Jan the head girl had given permission, providing they didn't embarrass themselves or the good name of the troupe. Beth and Suzy knew exactly what that meant and Jan was ever hopeful.

Del was surprised as the girls strutted towards him, Beth in a pink crotchet mini with a blonde nylon wig falling over her face and Suzy in a matching blue dress, attempting a Cleopatra impression in a long black wig. His editor had briefed him on the background of the troupe and the reputation for discipline, so the girls' appearance and attitude seemed totally out of sync with his information.

His job as reporter on the Gazette for the past ten years in the seaside town hadn't exactly been fast paced and full of action, and as he watched the girls fussing and giggling over their outrageous outfits he prepared himself for an unusual day. Setting up his camera he walked around the merry go round and found two motorbikes side by side.

'Right, get your bums side saddle on one bike and prop your legs up on the other.' Beth and Suzy arranged themselves as instructed, struggling to stay decent in their minis. Del seemed unaware and more interested in setting up the shot.

'Stay there, back in a mo.' He ran off and came back with two huge chocolate and vanilla ice creams, handing a cone to each of them.

Del shouted 'smile' and at the same time waved his arm in the air. Without warning the roundabout slowly came to life, but as it quickly gained speed all that Del could see through his camera was a whirling blur. In seconds a mass of black nylon hair, followed by a lump of ice cream flew straight from the merry go round landing at his feet. With camera dangling around his neck Del shouted for the ride to stop.

A crowd had gathered to see what the commotion was, and as the ride slowed down and came to a halt the reason became apparent. Suzy had not only lost her wig and ice cream but also her dignity. She'd slipped off the bike, with her new dress now ridden up to her waist. Struggling to re mount she realised she'd also lost Beth. She looked down and there was Beth flat on her back, wedged between the bikes, blonde wig completely covering her face, legs spread eagled straight up in the air. Suzy, suddenly noticing the growing audience, lost control.

'Don't laugh, I'm laying in something wet and cold.'

'So that's where my ice cream went, pity I was looking forward to that.' Suzy helped Beth to her feet, trying to hide her giggles until Beth noticed Suzy's hair and face, smothered in chocolate.

'Hmm, very sexy!'

Del was full of apologies to Bert the owner of the ride, who assured him that this was the best publicity he could ever hope for. Del shook the man's hand and promised free tickets for the show.

Deciding a clean up for the dishevelled pair was in order, Del drove them back to their flat where they changed into clean outfits. The photo shoot took place under a tree in the front garden and appeared in the newspaper the following week.

Much to the girls dismay it wasn't as glamorous as they had planned, however Jan was delighted with the results and thought the girls did a smashing job of keeping the reputation of the troupe intact.

'Well done girls, you look quite charming and don't the puppies look cute?' Beth and Suzy smiled in agreement, and as

59

they walked upstairs for the next number Suzy turned to Beth.

'Charming! That's what we are Beth, Charming!'

Beth and Suzy succumbed to Lucy's tagging along who was keen not to be left out. Well it was handy when they needed a couple of bob to buy fish and chips, or if they ran out of cigarettes.

It was 2am as they staggered home from yet another party. The girls flat was situated on the first floor of a typical seaside Victorian terrace, with Miriam the landlady on the ground, a nice enough old bird, but they knew she wouldn't tolerate any of their goings on

'Don't look at me I haven't got the key' whispered Suzy defensively.

'Well who wore this jacket last, it was in this pocket?' grumbled Beth.

'Ssh, keep quiet you two, I've got a key, but I can't see a bloody thing it's too dark.' Lucy fumbled in her bag blindly in the dimly lit street.

'Just hurry up I need the loo' piped up Beth impatiently and without warning grabbed Lucy's bag, tipping the contents onto the grass. 'Oops sorry it fell out of my hands.'

Seething, Lucy was down on her knees trying to retrieve her belongings. 'It's no good, I can't see it anywhere.'

'Hang on you two, I've got an idea' hushed Beth excitedly. 'Suzy's the strongest, so you stand on her shoulders and then I get on yours and climb through the bedroom window, look it's still open.'

'You've got to be joking' screamed Lucy, her eyes scaling the wall. But Suzy, never one to shy away from a challenge ignored Lucy's whingeing and immediately set to her task. She faced the wall, hitched her mini skirt up even higher and grabbing the windowsill for support, spread her legs and did the deepest pliée she could.

'Told you all those ballet lessons would come in handy.'

'Shut up Beth and get her up on my shoulders, I'm freezing.'

Beth cupped her hands and hoisted the reluctant Lucy onto Suzy's bare shoulders, hanging on for dear life to the drainpipe.

'For Christ sake Lucy, take your bloody shoes off, they're digging in my shoulders.' There was some major wobbling as Lucy flicked her shoes across the grass. Beth stood back eyeing the situation; she started to see the funny side of it, but controlled herself. It wouldn't take much to start Suzy off and then it would turn into a disaster.

'My God I'm going to break my neck,' shrieked Lucy, looking down and picturing her impending death.

'Not if I do it first' gasped Suzy in a strangled tone.

'Ssh you two, if we make a racket the old bird will wake up. Now for the Grande Finale' announced Beth ducking under Suzy's strained arms.

'Whatever you do don't make me laugh Suz, promise?'

'Promise... Drum Roll Please.'

'Suz!'

'I promise.'

Beth with her back to the window and facing Suzy, climbed onto the windowsill then onto her shoulders coming face to face with the now terrified Lucy.

'Now, if I can just get onto your ...ouch... shoulders, I can turn myself round. There, made it...'

Beth was a few inches away from fully opening the window and the safety of the bedroom when Suzy broke her promise.

'Lucy have you farted? Aah! It's disgusting, what on earth were you drinking tonight?'

'I can't help it, I'm scared.'

Beth could feel it coming from the pit of her stomach, but managed to control herself.

'Well as long as it's just wind, don't forget I'm in the firing line!'

It was no good. Beth's bladder gave way and she let go.

'Oh my God, she's...'

'Has it started raining?' piped up Suzy aware of spitting in the air.

'She's peeing and it's all over me, get me down it's making me sick,' pleaded a now very wobbly Lucy.

'She's not? Oh Beth you dirty cow.' Suzy, suddenly getting the gist of what was going on above her head, couldn't hold on any longer, her legs buckled and she crumbled to the ground, followed by Lucy and last but not least Beth. The three of them lay in a heap on the ground laughing uncontrollably. Lucy wasn't sure why she was laughing, she smelt of stale wee, was bruised and tired, but she was alive, just!

'Ouch something's digging' in me bum.'

'Move over Suz, lets have a look.'

'At what, me bum?'

'Will you two give over?' Lucy had stopped laughing. She'd just about had enough.

'Guess what I've found?'

Lucy snatched the key out of Beth's hand, 'so this was all for nothing?'

'Oh Lucy it was a laugh, and we didn't wake anyone up.'

'*A laugh?* You call this a laugh? I'm freezing cold, been peed on and I nearly broke my neck and you call this a *laugh,* God you two are sick' she snapped and stomped away to the front door.

THIRTEEN

One night after the show, Beth and Suzy had the bar to themselves. Everybody had either gone home or to the new club in town, but the two girls had responsibilities now and unaware that the bets were shortening on the dogs disappearing before the end of the week, they begrudgingly stayed behind. Lucy had invited Terry, who'd been overly interested in Beth's crutch problem at rehearsals, back to the flat for a coffee, so while Psychedelic and Freakout ran riot in the bar, the two friends took the opportunity to catch up. Beth didn't realise that Suzy was already on her third vodka, so it was a bit of a shock when she suddenly declared she felt sick and rushed to the loo. Beth quickly followed her.

'You haven't got a bun in the oven have you?'

'No, I haven't eaten all day that's all.'

Eventually Suzy staggered out and splashed her face with cold water.

'Blimey you look rough, whatever's wrong?'

'Nothing, come on let's get a drink before they shut the bar.'

Pat the barman was none too pleased to be left with the dogs that had made themselves at home by the crisps. 'It's about time they housetrained these two' he grumbled mopping the floor yet again. But seeing Beth propping Suzy up as they staggered out of the ladies, decided now was not the right time to tell them that the dogs were barred. Anyway he'd put a fiver on them being gone by the end of the month, so there didn't seem much point.

In the time it took Beth to drink her martini Suzy had downed two more vodkas and was definitely drifting.

'Easy you'll be ill again. He's not worth it you know.'

Suzy waved her empty glass at Pat, slumped back in the chair and spent the next half hour trying to reassure Beth that it was all a game, that the presents were great and the secret meetings were fun, but of course she didn't believe a word Derek said, of course she knew he was only after one thing. It had started out as innocent flirting, with the provocative dancing at the parties, but slowly Beth sensed that Suzy was beginning to believe the lies. She even read the notes that he left under Suzy's makeup tray in the dressing room, but could do nothing as Suzy wasn't confiding in her any more, and she was drinking more than usual.

'Have no fear Beth, the dogs are getting their exercise, but he's not!' Beth managed a feeble laugh, but deep down knew Suzy was in turmoil. They staggered home in silence, Beth sensing Suzy didn't want to talk, and as usual Psychedelic and Freakout were demanding their attention.

Suzy was quite happy to do the early morning stint with the pups, as it was the perfect opportunity to secretly meet with Derek. Still unconfident and insecure she relished in the attention. Beth was less impressed. She didn't trust him and was worried that Suzy would get hurt, apart from the fact that Serena was beginning to suspect. After all, this wasn't the first time she'd had problems with Derek and pretty dancers.

Derek and Suzy met most mornings at their pre- arranged spot, which Derek had found quite by accident while on a picnic with Serena. Suzy would walk the dogs over the cliffs and into surrounding woods, where Derek would be waiting in his car. He'd convinced Serena that he was probably going through a mid life crisis and at 44 needed to get fit with regular early morning runs.

Although besotted with Derek, Suzy had been relieved that the opportunity to take the relationship one stage further hadn't materialised, but she knew that time was running out, for there were no excuses now that they were able to be alone.

The alarm under Suzy's pillow blasted her out of a fitful sleep. She crept out of the bedroom, leaving Lucy and Beth to waste what promised to be another blisteringly hot day in bed. At the sight of Suzy, the dogs ran riot round the kitchen. They knew the routine by now. First, the long run across the cliffs and then along the winding path into the woods where that nice man gave them biscuits! Derek always brought them food, which Suzy saw as a kind gesture, but ultimately it was to keep them busy while he got busy with her. The dogs eager for their 'walkies' clambered excitedly at the door while she was still pulling on her shorts and tee shirt. Sneakers on, a quick check in the mirror and she closed the door quietly behind her. Normally she loved the heat and her ideal day would be sunbathing on the beach. Her skin tanned easily, which not only gave her confidence, it was an excuse not to bother with makeup. But this morning she had a monster hangover and the already stifling heat was making her feel sick. So she clambered down the cliffs onto the beach, where a warm sea breeze cooled her face. It was still too early for tourists and she was grateful to have the beach to herself. As the dogs chased in and out of the water, she kicked off her shoes and lay in the soft still damp sand. She needed time to clear her head before meeting Derek. She closed her eyes against the glare of the early morning sun and tried to sort out the muddle she seemed to have got herself into.

Who was she trying to kid? All that rubbish she'd told Beth in the bar last night about just playing games, pretending she didn't care. Of course she cared, he made her feel good, and she needed that more than anything. Ever since childhood the constant ridicule her father had inflicted on her had created a far more complex character than the world saw in that big smile.

She'd often dreamt of a time when she would be famous, when her parents and those who'd dismissed her as nothing more than a dreamer, would have to admit that she was special. But she was forced to keep her steely determination to herself, for any indication that she *could* rise from the depths of inadequacy and Sam had always been there to knock her down, reassuring her that she was worth nothing.

So what a strange business for someone so insecure to enter, where so much relies on looks, and although Suzy's confidence and talent grew, with her ego being fed by her contemporaries, it was still not strong enough to ignore a casual derisory remark from her parents. But each snide remark would reinforce her will to succeed and to prove everyone wrong.

She craved the love of others and with this man she got it, until the doubts set in again. She wanted to believe everything he told her, but he had to be lying. She wasn't beautiful; she knew that, because for years she'd listened to her father take great delight in entertaining his friends with his cruel humour.

"Look at those teeth boys, she can eat an apple through a tennis racket" and *"you should see her friends! They are gorgeous, how come I got the ugly duckling?"* But the worst of all and Suzy hid her face in her hands as she remembered her father's favourite saying. *"She wasn't born, she was the afterbirth."*

So however much she wanted to believe Derek, she knew it couldn't be true. Then there was Serena, tall, glamorous, with that sexy Italian accent and obviously used to her wayward husband. Suzy was convinced he would never leave Serena, although he often promised he would.

She lay there for a while longer, and having convinced herself that she was in control of the situation, jumped to her feet, brushed the sand from her backside, ran to the waters edge and as she splashed playfully with the dogs she shouted. 'Right, if he wants to play games that's fine by me! Come on boys, let's see what treats Uncle Derek's brought us today.'

As soon as she got back to the flat she was impatient to find Beth.

'You said *what?*' screamed Beth as soon as Suzy had finished telling her of her plan. It was lunchtime and she and Lucy hadn't been up long.

'Well I think you're a cruel bitch' snapped Lucy as she lit a cigarette without offering them round.

'Oh serve him right for stringing me along.' She certainly didn't need Lucy's approval.

'Let me get this straight Suz. You've told Derek that you'll go away with him after the seasons finished? And he's agreed to wait for sex until then? But you've no intention of going?'

'Of course I'm not going with him.'

'But Suz, Lucy's right, that *is* cruel.'

'Look you two; do you really think he's going to leave Serena? Of course he's not. He tells me all these lies just so he can say he's had a virgin and I think that's pretty cruel, but now I get all the treats without the constant groping. I think it's a brilliant idea.'

As the season progressed, so did Suzy's drinking. She was stringing Derek along for all she was worth, but needing the vodka to stop the guilt trips and the confusion that was still swimming in her head. She so nearly believed him, but then the old doubts would surface and she continued with the game, just to teach him a lesson.

Beth realised that Suzy had a major drink problem, when she arrived at the theatre one night to find her asleep on the dressing room floor. Shaking her awake she knew she was in no fit state to go on stage. With only a short time before the other dancers arrived, she panicked and dragged her into the showers, threw the cold tap into action and shoved Suzy under. The shock caught Suzy's breath, who stood fully clothed under the freezing torrent, but the furious expression on Beth's face made her fall about laughing and without warning broke into her own version of "Singing in The Rain" singing at the top of her voice, kicking and splashing about ensuring Beth got soaked as well.

After two verses Beth had had enough and managed to turn off the shower with Suzy seemingly calmed down, but only just. She still had a fit of the giggles and Beth wondered how she was going to get her through the show without anybody noticing. It would be instant dismissal if Jan or Les Collins saw her in this state. They had about half an hour left before the others would be arriving, so back in the dressing room, whilst Suzy sipped on her black coffee, Beth dried her hair and got her costumes ready. Suzy was now feeling drowsy, which at least was better than 'Gene Kelly' on drugs.

Floating around in feathers and sequins, introducing the principle acts in the opening number was a piece of cake, thought Beth with one exception, the high heels! Thank God she was working next to Suzy for most of the routine.

The girls made their entrance, one at a time behind each other from the back of the stage, to the tune of 'A Pretty Girl Is like a Melody' and with a slight shove Beth managed to get Suzy on stage. This routine had never been a favourite of Suzy's, complaining most nights that she felt like a drag queen in the bikini and feather headdress. All was going well until Suzy raised her arms and stood in position. Her fingers weren't in the gloves properly and her hands looked as if they'd had an accident with the bread knife.

The posing bit over; they crossed the front of the stage and were heading into their final positions when Suzy's shoulders start to shake; her headdress was slipping to the side and the feathers were following. Beth knew the giggles had set in, so did a quick step and closed in, pushing the 'dead ostrich' back into position. Suzy seemed oblivious and kept going, if a bit unsteadily till she reached her destination on the top of the podium at the back of the stage, to the side of the staircase. The principals and stars made their entrance down the stairs and nearing the end of the number, Beth standing one step below Suzy felt a sense of relief that this nightmare would soon be over. But then disaster struck. Just as Billy Dainty made his entrance, Suzy made her exit, disappearing with a loud thump behind the podium. Beth could do nothing but stay in her pose until the tabs closed and when at last they did, she ran to the top of the stairs, but Suzy had vanished, so dashed to the dressing room where she sat nursing her knee and a bump on her head, complaining to the girls she didn't feel well. Beth catching the tale end of the conversation came to her rescue.

'I told her earlier she wasn't looking good'

'Yeah, well you know me, the show must go on!'

Beth gave her a quick wink, while reassuring Jan she would take her straight home after the show. Once again they walked home in silence, without discussing the fiasco. Beth knew it wasn't the right time and hoped before long, things would get back to normal for Suz and they'd be able to look back and laugh about it.

FOURTEEN

Suzy kept Derek dangling from a great height for the rest of the season. The drinking slowed down, although the odd swig behind closed doors eased her guilty conscience. Convinced that he was playing with her emotions, she relished the thought of teaching him a lesson at the end of the season. But in fact Derek for once in his life was genuine about his feelings for her, and the poor unsuspecting romantic was in for a shock.

Without Beth and Suzy's knowledge a meeting was held in the 'Green Room' three days before the end of the run, with Pat the barman making the biggest profit on the dogs staying the course longer than anyone had expected. Nigel's aunt had promised to find homes for them and although the girls were sad to be saying goodbye to their willing playmates, they were secretly relieved to be rid of the responsibility. It was becoming more and more difficult keeping them out of trouble and under control. And if they were perfectly honest, they were bored with the constant need for early morning and late night exercise, something that certainly didn't fit in with their lifestyle!

One of the bigger local hotels opened its doors for the shows last night party. The manager had enjoyed the fun and had profited from their late night drinking during the summer and wanted to show his appreciation.

After a few drinks at the bar, the action soon moved to the indoor pool, where the heat was intense. It wasn't long before two of the boy dancers stripped off and jumped in, and after a few more glasses of bubbly were downed the girls joined them. A few completely naked, some topless, but Beth and Suzy as usual surprised everybody, disappointing a few by keeping their essentials under cover.

Derek declined the invitation, he wasn't sure he could trust himself after slyly watching Suzy strip to her underwear at the waters edge, revealing a slim nubile body before expertly diving in. Serena also declined to join them having been to the hairdressers that morning she had no ambitions to be remembered as a drowned rat.

Even Lucy stripped naked, revealing what Terry already knew, that she wasn't a true blonde! There was much groping under the water as the built up frustrations of the summer proved too much for some of the cast.

At 5am everybody was back in the bar, wrapped in towels sipping hot chocolate provided by the generous hotel management before the inevitable goodbyes with promises to stay in touch. But for the majority this would be just another pleasant memory.

Four hours later, and not for the first time that summer, the three flatmates were suffering major hangovers. Gingerly and silently throwing clothes and worldly goods back into the cases and carrier bags that had been stuffed to the back of the wardrobe some twelve weeks earlier; they faced the task of cleaning up the flat before the landlady made her pre- vacating inspection.

Confident all would be well, Lucy ordered the taxi for 12.30, and by one o'clock they collapsed onto the train heading back to London and bed.

As the train pulled into Liverpool Street station, they swapped phone numbers, and as Beth and Suzy waved goodbye to Lucy, who still had a long journey onto Manchester they heaved a sigh of relief to be free from their shadow.

A week later, with the flat in total darkness and curtains tightly shut, the girls stood either side of the kitchen window.

'What time did Derek say he'd pick you up?' whispered Beth, gently easing aside the curtain just an inch, giving her a clear view of the street below.

'7 o'clock and why are you whispering?'

'I don't know I'm just a bit nervous.'

'*You're* nervous; I've got my bike clips on!'

'Are you sure you didn't give him our address? I don't want some frustrated sex maniac barging in here throwing you over his shoulder and whisking you off on his white charger into the sunset, only to find out Snow White has turned into Lady Macbeth.'

'Of course I didn't' snapped Suzy 'and anyway his white charger's a boring green Volvo.' Beth went back to the window and peered at the café across the street where Suzy had agreed to meet Derek and although she didn't altogether agree with Suzy's little game, she decided she didn't have a lot of choice. It was either fall out with her, or go along with the charade and pick up the pieces whatever the outcome. She decided on the latter.

'What's the time?' whispered Suzy becoming more and more agitated as the minutes ticked by.

'7.15, it looks like you were right mate,' suggested Beth nervously, knowing that Suzy was going to be upset whatever. If he did show his face she'd be beside herself with guilt, and maybe even wondering if they could have made a go of it. And if he didn't, she'd be gutted because he really *had* lied to her all summer. Either way Beth was in for a tough time with her vulnerable friend.

'See I knew he was lying, the bastard, he was having me on the whole time. Good job I didn't fall for...Oh my God Beth, look that's him, there in the brown coat at the counter…Oh shit he's only gone and done it!'

They simultaneously jumped back from the window and stood in the dark with their backs to the wall, hearts pounding.

'What the hell do we do now?' giggled Suzy nervously.

'Nothing you twit, unless of course you want to run into his arms and disappear into the night!'

'Aah, no thank you, look at the state of him.' Beth joined her through the crack in the curtain. 'He does look as if he needs a good bath' sniggered Beth, 'maybe Serena's kicked him out.'

'And I bet he's got all his smelly washing in the car, expecting me to stand at a sink in some sordid little bed sit scrubbing and delighting at the mere touch of his underwear.' Beth openly laughed at Suzy's reaction and in fact saw it as a healthy option to the floods of tears she was expecting.

Twenty minutes later, having finished his second cup of coffee, Derek made his way back to his car, relieved and not surprised that Suzy hadn't turned up. He wasn't looking forward to explaining that he wanted to give his marriage another go, and although Serena still had no idea of his plans, she'd noticed he'd been distracted ever since they'd got back from Westcliffe. But once back home in Luton, Derek realised that Suzy was just a fantasy. He'd been flattered by the attention, but having got his feelings in proportion, decided to let her down gently. He knew she'd be hurt, but felt explaining to her face to face was kinder than over the phone or just leaving her waiting in the café.

FIFTEEN

For the following eighteen months job offers came thick and fast for the girls. TV variety was at its peak, and being in the right place at the right time proved successful for them both. Suzy welcomed pre- recorded shows after a painful incident during a live show. It was a clown routine and the final shot as the credits rolled was to be Ken Dodd surrounded by the clowns in given positions. Suzy, not wanting to mark her white gloves had left them off for the dress rehearsal and happily performed the required handstand. During the recording, she went into her position and the gloves slipped on the studio's shiny floor, shooting her arms straight out to the side landing her on her chin. Blood spurted out as she lay in a crumpled heap, but being a true pro, she lay still until given the 'All Clear'.

Beth had her problems too. During a run at the Victoria Palace she suffered a bad dose of food poisoning, but having a solo spot insisted on going on, with a polythene bag stuffed in her pants under her leotard in case of accidents. She got away with it, apart from the rustling that could be clearly heard when the music died down as she made her grand exit.

But Beth's favourite story, which she dined out on for years, was when Suzy was in the Wimbledon panto with Roy Hudd. She had a quick change out of a crinoline dress into a skimpy leotard and saved time by going naked under the crinoline. In the scene, she had to stand completely still in a position with Daniel her partner, while June Shand sang her heart out. At the end of the particular song, their exit was to be a simple arm movement and drift unobtrusively off stage together. Daniel and Suzy would relieve the boredom by trying out different ways to exit, each night becoming more and more outrageous.

One night Suzy went too far. She lay back in Daniel's arms and slowly kicked her leg. But as she brought her foot back down, her heel caught in the heavily weighted hem, and she slipped forward landing flat on her face, causing the heavily boned crinoline to go right over her head. She could do nothing but lay there in the dark helpless, with her bare bum exposed to the world. Daniel panicked as roars of laughter came from the audience, so he grabbed her arms, which were waving wildly in the air and dragged her off stage.

The year passed quickly and they spent many nights at the flat over a bottle of wine exchanging stories and gossip. In September they were offered a Christmas season in Glasgow, with the Tillers again and Beth had to work hard at persuading Suzy to join her. Eventually she agreed, secretly looking forward to working with Beth again. But it was still two months away and once again the rent was looming.

The job as usherettes at the Odeon cinema on Shepherds Bush Green wasn't exactly going to further the girls ambitions for fame and fortune, but hunger and a roof over their heads seemed top priority for the next two months until they started rehearsals in November.

As Betty Frampton the Supervisor produced their oversized uniforms, Beth wasn't sure whether to laugh or cry, as Suzy posed in her size sixteen limp white blouse, long black pleated skirt and huge brown wrap around jacket.

Although not ideal, they decided the job would have its perks. The hours of 3pm −10.30pm suited their fondness for lying in bed all morning, plus they got to see all the best films for free! The odd drawback with the strict staff restrictions didn't seem to put them off either. After all, once they'd shown the public to their seats, what was to stop them sneaking off for a cigarette, which was absolutely against the rules?

Smoking became even more hazardous to Suzy's health one afternoon, when she thought the coast was clear and lit up in the foyer. The first film had started and she had about an hour before the intermission. Enjoying the forbidden treat, she couldn't believe her eyes as the supervisor appeared from the office and headed straight for her. Quick as a flash she turned her back, exhaling as fast as she could, blowing the smoke away, turned back to face her boss, held her breath and threw her arms behind her back stubbing the butt out in the palm of her hand.

'Hello dear just thought I'd check out how my new recruits are doing.'

'We're fine,' squeaked Suzy hardly daring to breathe and with beads of sweat pouring down her face from the pain, she bit her lip, dying to scream.

Betty turned to see if Suzy was making this strange face at someone she might have recognized coming into the cinema. Seeing no one there she looked at Suzy again who had managed to put out the cigarette.

'Are you sure you're all right dear? You're perspiring and … well…your cheeks are very red.'

Suzy nodded slowly, wondering how much longer she could endure the throbbing pain, when a miracle happened.

'Ah! There's your friend Oh! My goodness what has she got on?' Suzy, still flinching, turned with relief to see Beth strutting across the foyer in what resembled the uniform but with a few changes. The brown jacket or skirt was nowhere to be seen, which left the oversize blouse pulled in at the waist by a leather belt just covering her backside. Her long legs accentuated by the four-inch heels.

For a split second Suzy forgot her agony and watched with admiration as Beth approached them beaming from ear to ear.

'Slight improvement don't you think?' She stated as she turned and posed for her captive audience. Betty was speechless for at least a minute, until she found her voice and circling Beth she boomed. 'What the hell do you think you're doing? This isn't a fashion show, where's your skirt?' Beth was surprised by the aggressive response; she thought it was a great improvement. 'Well it *is* 1969 not '59, why, don't you like it?' she twirled and posed again, demonstrating her catwalk skills. 'By the way what's that awful smell, it's like burning flesh? What's up Suz? You look a bit pale.'

Suzy near fainting point, with beads of sweat trickling down her forehead, clenched her fist, trying to dull the pain and shrugged her shoulders as if all was fine. She needed to get Beth's attention, so shot her hand up in the air waving frantically into the distance. While Betty looking more confused by the minute turned her head, keen to see whom Suzy was waving at, Suzy quickly shot her throbbing hand in Beth's face, who gasped in horror. 'Get to the loo and wash it'. Walking away Suzy blurted, 'Betty, I'm just going to wash my torch!'

'Going to wash her torch, what is she talking about?'

'Oh she means she's going to wash her hands and *get* her torch.' Beth was trying to stay ahead of things and sensing Betty's confusion, which of course was the whole idea, changed the subject. 'So, you don't like my uniform then?'

Keeping a watchful eye on the toilets, Betty turned her attention back to Beth, insisting she wear the uniform as intended. The next day Betty agreed that Suzy could be excused from ice cream duties in the interval due to her 'sprained' wrist, which was heavily but not too professionally bandaged. Sitting in her office she thought about the previous evenings shenanigans. Feeling something wasn't right, she decided just as many had before, to keep an eye on them!

The following two months seemed an eternity for Beth and Suzy, but to break the monotony they came up with their own ideas for usherette duties. Their favourite trick was embarrassing groping couples in the back row by 'accidentally' shining their torches on them, with looks of mock disgust! This worked particularly well one night when Ron from the chippie was sitting in snoggers row with a pretty blonde, and it *wasn't* his wife. The girls had caught sight of him before the lights went down, and waiting for the right moment they stood at the back, torches at the ready.

'After a count of three,' whispered Suzy, and that was it for poor Ron, who was in heavy petting mode with his leggy friend. The guilty pair stared into the torchlight like startled rabbits. 'There you are Suz it *is* Ron, I thought it was.' Beth whispered trying to keep a straight face.

'Allo mate' grinned Suzy mischievously. 'I said to Beth no, it can't be, Ruth's got brown hair, I suppose Ruth doesn't like James Bond then, so you brought a friend instead?'

'Yeah. Er… that's right,' replied a nervous Ron removing his hand from the 36DD's.

Suzy bent down and whispered in Ron's ear, 'well enjoy the film, and say hallo to Ruth for us, maybe we'll pop in for some fish and chips one night!' She stood up and the pair of them gave him a little wave as they left Ron to sweat.

The afternoon showings were usually quiet, so Beth would often sneak into an empty row for a well-earned snooze and Suzy who was a sucker for a good old love story would stand at the back of the stalls polishing up her acting skills, performing scenes word for word, imitating characters, pre- empting their lines. *Casablanca,* with all its emotion brought her to an academy performance one afternoon.

The tension built as Ingrid Bergman made her way over to the piano, but before she spoke, a voice was heard from somewhere at the back of the cinema stalls.

'Sam, where's Rick?' Then Suzy deepened her voice. 'I don't know I ain't seen him all night.'

Grumbling noises were heard and one or two people shifted uneasily in their seats as Ingrid caught up with her lines, Suzy well into the part continued.

'Play it Sam for old time's sake, play "As time goes by".' Now it was obvious that some nutter at the back had to be reported, and a woman who was losing her patience made her way up the aisle to the manager's office as Suzy was taking a necessary loo visit, humming a couple of bars and finishing with "Sing it Sam". Betty Frampton went to investigate the complaint, but a quick patrol of where the mystery voice was heard showed nothing untoward and returned to her office. Back with the film everything seemed normal again, until ten minutes later when the 'voice' returned from the loo, and before Humphrey Bogart could speak Suzy came in loud and clear with her rendition. "Of all the Gin Joints in all the towns in all the world she walks into mine". She was impatient now for a cigarette and as she walked across the foyer a man grabbed her by the arm and told her about the nutcase at the back of the cinema, imitating everyone in the film. Suzy grinned, assuring him she'd see to the matter straight away. The man marched back in to find his seat. 'I'm glad you find it funny, I paid good money for this film.'

Having sneaked a quick puff in the 'ladies' Suzy went back, not wanting to miss the end of the film. As Beth returned from having her sneaky ciggy in the back alley she heard about the commotion and knew immediately who the culprit was; she went to find 'Ingrid' and as her eyes became accustomed to the dark she saw the familiar figure walk towards her. Smiling they linked arms, making their way to the exit with Suzy performing her last line 'Louis I think this is the beginning of a beautiful relationship!'

But the incident which finally ended their career in the film industry occurred during the interval as Beth stood at the front of the circle, overlooking the stalls, selling refreshments from a tray draped round her shoulders. It was so heavy the straps were digging into her shoulders, so she lifted the straps over her head and placed the tray precariously on the ledge. It wasn't long before the inevitable happened. With one clumsy nudge of her elbow the tray started to topple. She grabbed it, but as if in slow motion she had to watch helplessly as the contents cascaded over the top of the balcony.

In dread she peered over to see ice cream landing in row D, choc-ices and cartons of drink splattering across rows E, F and G. One woman went screaming up the aisle, followed by someone covered in chocolate fudge. All four rows were in bedlam with people trying to avoid the attack. The rest of the audience were shouting and yelling for someone to stop the film.

Luckily it wasn't a full house so serious injuries were avoided and not being a particularly popular film the refunds were minimal until the theatre could be cleaned up.

Fortunately for Beth and Suzy they were instantly dismissed, but only two weeks before they were due to leave anyway, and they weren't the only ones heaving a sigh of relief as they said their farewells.

Betty Frampton was sure that she would be scrutinising hopeful employees with more care in the future!

SIXTEEN

Rehearsals for the Frankie Vaughan Show at the Alhambra Theatre Glasgow took two weeks and once they'd learnt the kicking routines, the girls anticipated some fun with Malcolm Goddard the choreographer. Malcolm was in his late forties with soft features and dark, now flecked with grey hair. He was always immaculately dressed even in his rehearsal gear and with the added bonus of a wicked sense of humour, had been the main feature in many a fantasy for hormonal dancers over the years. Although he demanded respect he was known not to take life too seriously, resulting in a soft spot for Beth and Suzy.

Most of the other girls didn't seem bothered, and as far as Suzy and Beth were concerned they were delighted to be once again the centre of attention. However out of the sixteen dancers' one, Jackie Taylor wasn't amused by their antics. Having led a predominantly sheltered life, she kept her distance from Beth and Suzy whom she thought crude and rowdy show offs. Unfortunately for her, circumstances arose that forced her into their company for the next eight weeks. She hadn't particularly made any effort to be pleasant to any of the girls during rehearsals, therefore wasn't included in the arrangements for accommodation in Glasgow.

Sensing Jackie was increasingly out of things, Beth and Suzy sympathised and offered for her to share with them.

'It's only one room Jack, but it's got three beds and it would help us out with the rent. So what d'yer reckon?'

'Thank you Suzy, but there won't be parties and men coming back all hours will there?'

'Don't be daft, we're not like that' replied Beth, wondering how she could be so ungrateful. After all she didn't see any of the others offering!

After coming to the same conclusion Jackie managed a tight-lipped smile, realizing she didn't have a lot of choice.

'Fine then, but I'd rather you didn't call me Jack if you don't mind, it's Jackie.'

The first week passed by quickly, taken up with last minute changes to routines, lighting and dress rehearsal with the principle artistes. Everything went smoothly and the opening night had great reviews. Meanwhile back at the flat the revues weren't so good.

'She had the nerve to tell me we're too noisy when we come in at night, we can't help it if she's asleep by eleven thirty, we're not nuns are we Beth?'

'We were once, remember?'

When the call came over the tannoy, eight of the sixteen dancers made their way on stage for the opening number of the second half. 'Dancing in the Dark' was one of Malcolm's more romantic routines. He'd chosen four dark haired girls and put them in long flowing pale blue chiffon dresses, while four blondes were in short sexy royal blue. Once on stage, the girls still had at least five minutes before curtain up. Pat and Maggie sat on the floor chatting; Sara was on all fours with June sitting on top of her trying out some chiropractic work on her back. Towards the back Liz was on her third pirouette, with Rosy slouched against a pillar rearranging her tights. Centre stage was Beth and Suzy who had decided to try out a trick they'd seen 'The Three Bizzarro's' a tumbling act, perform in the show. Suzy went down on one knee while Beth climbed on and sat astride her shoulders, her long flowing dress falling over Suzy's face. Suzy, struggling to her feet in the dark didn't hear Maggie's warning that the intro was about to be played.

'Now see if you can spin with me up here.'

'I can't see a thing never mind spin and don't fart you'll ruin me make up!'

Then without warning the curtain started to rise!

'My God, what's going on? The curtains going up too early' shouted Liz from the back and immediately struck a pose with her arms above her head. June sat frozen on Sara's back and the two of them turned their heads to the front and smiled. Pat and Maggie quickly kneeled trying to look balletic and Rosy used the pillar to create a sexy position, while Suzy clueless to what was happening under Beth's dress was still turning.

'Keep turning Suz, whatever you do don't stop.' Beth pleaded quietly, flinging her arms out to the sides, thighs clamped onto Suzy's head and smiling in preparation to face the audience.

'What's going on? Your thighs are cutting my circulation off.'

'Keep your voice down and keep going, the curtains gone up.'

'Bloody hell'

'We're almost facing front...oh here we go.' Beth smiled at the audience and through gritted teeth whispered 'Suz I can't gelieve this, you OK? Ny thighs are nung.'

'My head's numb, I can't hold on much longer.'

'Oh thank God it's going down again, blimey, they're applauding!'

Instantly, all the girls relaxed, along with Beth and Suzy who had collapsed in a heap of blue chiffon on the floor. Suzy came clambering out from underneath and the girls helped the acrobatic team straighten up. The orchestra started the intro and from the wings came instructions to take their places. The girls moved quickly and positioned themselves in different poses, not wanting to be caught a second time. Just as the curtain rose again a voice was heard softly saying.

'My ears feel like cauliflowers!'

Harry the stage manager explained that the new lad on the curtain was at fault and went on to express his appreciation on how well the girls had handled the situation. Meanwhile back in one of the dressing rooms Fay the head girl wasn't so sure.

'I still don't understand why Beth was up on Suzy's shoulders in the first place.'

Frankie Vaughan was a joy to work with. His dry gentle humour definitely made him a firm favourite with the rest of the cast and seemed to encourage Beth and Suzy's antics. But even they were shocked one night during his opening number. With the dancers in boater hats, swaying with canes behind him he sang the first verse of 'Give me the Moonlight'. Suddenly, unrehearsed, he turned upstage to face them and with a twinkle in his eye and a big grin he unzipped his flies, revealing bright red and white striped pants, casually zipped them up and turned back to face the audience.

But it was The Clark Brothers that the two girls spent most of their time with in Glasgow. Suzy was in awe of their tap dancing talent and spent most nights watching their act from side stage, dreaming of one day being as good as them. She even persuaded them to give her a few lessons between shows and they invited her to join their classes at The Dance Centre in Covent Garden on returning to London. Beth although appreciating the act, knew her limitations and just enjoyed their company.

Scotland was the only place to be on Hogmanay and everybody agreed to contribute to the party to be held on stage after the show. Once the opening number was over, popping corks could be heard all over the theatre with champagne generously provided by Frankie and having not bothered to eat before the show meant Beth got into the spirit of it all a little too early. The bubbles went straight to her head and she decided it was time to play a New Years trick on Suzy, who'd been given a part in a sketch with Frankie and Moira Anderson.

With their dressing room on the top floor, Suzy had to take the lift to stage level and like any other night Beth walked with her. The lift, used for moving scenery and costumes had heavy double iron gates and as Beth closed them she pointed out that the hem on Suzy's dress was coming down at the back. With Suzy distracted, Beth slid her hand through the gates and pressed the basement button. 'See you later' smiled Beth as her friend descended to the depths below. Suzy didn't even bother to look up; she was too busy inspecting the hem.

'Yeah see you later.'

Suzy couldn't work out why the lift went straight past the stage level and onto the basement. She cursed the ancient mechanism and thumped the stage level button impatiently. But nothing happened, so tried it again with more weight. Suddenly hearing her cue way above her, she began to panic. Rattling the gates she called for help. But the basement was only used for scenery storage, so no one could hear above the music blasting over the tannoys.

Up on the third floor Beth had the gates wedged open, but deciding the joke was over slammed them shut. Immediately it sprung to life, allowing Suzy to dash straight to the side of the stage, missing her entrance.

She cursed as she watched the sketch struggling to get the intended laughs, so judging the dialogue; she took a deep breath and timed her entrance at the next available spot. The glares she got from Frankie told her maybe her acting career could soon be over, while Fay gave her a verbal warning.

Beth kept quiet about her little 'joke'; she didn't think it would help matters by telling them what really happened, they probably wouldn't believe her anyway. After all Frankie was keen to get back into the spirit of the New Year celebrations and had forgotten about it. Fay's reaction was inevitable, but Beth had sensed for some time that this would probably be Suzy's last show with the troupe. She knew she felt frustrated and stifled by the discipline and style of dancing, so there didn't seem much point.

Anyway she didn't mean for Suzy to get into so much trouble, it was supposed to be a joke!

She'd wait for the right time to tell her. ......Or maybe not!!

'Five..Four... three... two... one!! 'Happy New Year' Major tongue sandwiches, groping and snogging continued way past the accepted two minutes of the usual New Year celebrations. Suzy eventually found Beth who was scanning the crowd for Brian, another potential victim. 'I'm going out for some air Beth.'

Brian Campbell loved his job as manager of the Kit Kat Club. A popular disco situated close to the theatre. With a late licence, it was a favourite haunt for many of the cast to unwind after the show. As an amateur boxer he regularly trained at the gym, using his intimidating physique and experience in making sure that any potential trouble at the club was soon squashed. He was smitten with Beth from the first moment he saw her on the dance floor. The cast had come in to help celebrate her birthday and had been coming in regularly for the past three weeks. He enjoyed the theatre crowd; they drank plenty but were never any trouble and the girls were gorgeous. But for Brian, Beth stood out, he thought she was the most stunning girl he'd ever laid eyes on, but Beth soon quashed any hopes of the relationship getting serious. Brian, not one to give up easily, had given Beth a spare key to his flat in the hope that one day she might change her mind and find him irresistible enough to charge in declaring if not undying love then a night of undying lust.

At nineteen Beth and Suzy's sense of humour hadn't progressed passed nursery stage and after an incident that nearly landed them in jail, they decided that maybe they should confine their victims to those with similar humour.

It hadn't taken long for the girls to come up with a plan they thought was funny and imaginative. What could possible go wrong with breaking into Brian's flat and taking all his clothes? Just for a laugh of course and Beth having her own key made getting in rather easier than the usual climbing of drainpipes and scaling walls.

They'd agreed on a Friday evening after the show, knowing Brian would be at the club until at least 2am. It was a ten-minute walk to the ground floor flat, situated in a quiet cul de sac. Once inside they scooped all his clothes from the drawers and suits from the wardrobe, including his shoes, flinging them into two suitcases they'd found on top of the wardrobe, which as Suzy pointed out was a bit of luck, as they hadn't exactly worked out any of the finer details. Fortunately Brian's upstairs neighbour Albie had seen off half a bottle of scotch at the pub that evening, which made their slightly clumsy getaway a lot easier. Back at the flat, experience allowed the girls to tip toe unheard up the stairs, along the landing and safely into their room. Jackie's heavy snoring enabled them to store the swag under the beds undisturbed. Tired but pleased with the results of their robbery, the girls congratulated each other, got undressed and fell into bed.

The next day was spent mostly in bed before heading off to the theatre. All seemed quite normal until they turned the corner and saw Brian standing at the stage door. Suzy nudged Beth and mumbled to keep a straight face.

'Watcha mate how's things?'

'Funny you should ask Suzy, I was robbed last night.'

'Brian that's awful, what happened?' Beth tried to sound concerned.

Brian took his time before speaking. He wasn't sure, but he had a niggling feeling that these two knew something. Beth could feel his eyes on them. 'So what did they take?'

'They?'

'All right then *he,* what did *he* take?' Beth didn't like his attitude.

'It was quite strange because who ever did it was very thoughtful.'

The girls glanced quickly at each other then back at Brian. 'Thoughtful?'

'Yes thoughtful, but slightly warped. You see he or *they* left me socks, underpants, a shirt and shoes, I'd say that was thoughtful wouldn't you?' he waited staring at the girls, 'but nothing else!'

'Huh?'

'Yes Beth, you see whoever it was didn't leave me any *trousers!* And I was wondering if you two knew anything about it?' The girls looked shocked at the mere idea.

Brian still not convinced, thought he'd give them one more chance to confess.

'Ok, well in that case I'd better call the police.'

'The Police!' Beth blurted, losing her usual composure, but Suzy staying calm, agreed that he should. Beth still in shock could only manage a nod. Fortunately some of the girls were approaching, which seemed an opportune time for Beth and Suzy to make a swift exit.

'Come on Beth we've gotta go or we'll be late.' She took hold of Beth's arm and opening the stage door pushed her inside the theatre. Heading toward the dressing room Beth regained her senses; 'you were fantastic Suz, so cool.' Suzy swished ahead, spun round and curtsied for Beth, who in turn applauded while Suzy blew kisses and thanked her appreciative audience of one.

An urgent meeting was called in the prop room after the opening, where they agreed to return Brian's belongings that night before the police became involved.

It was freezing cold and the streets were quiet as they made their way on foot with the two heavy suitcases. They turned the corner and feeling the weight of their loot, stopped to catch their breath. Beth nodded to Brian's flat across the road, pleased to see their final destination. They stepped off the pavement and were half way across the road when car headlights suddenly blinded them!

'Bugger I think we've blown it Suz' said Beth shielding her eyes and dropping her suitcase, as she watched a silhouette walking slowly towards them. As it came closer Suzy saw the uniform

'Oh my God it's the...'

'So what's this then a coppers dream?' The officer asked with a hint of a smile. 'We had a report of a burglary in this street just last night and the gentleman who was robbed asked us to keep an eye out, so may I ask what you two are up to?'

'Constable let me explain,' cringed Beth, while Suzy resigned herself to a night behind bars.

'It's Sergeant!'

'I do beg your pardon, Sergeant. You see...,'

'What's in the suitcases? It's a bit late to be going on holiday, or were you doing a moonlight flit, can't afford the rent ay? I think you two had better come with me to the station.'

After the minor interrogation in room B, the two would be convicts were told to wait in the hall.

'I think we've done it this time Beth, if the others gets wind of this we'll be sent to Siberia for the next winter season. Have you got a ciggy?'

'You're right, we might end up in Siberia, but then it's better than Cleethorpes.'

The sergeant couldn't believe it when he found them sprawled all over the bench sharing a joke. 'Follow me you two' he demanded sternly.

Beth and Suzy solemnly got up and were led into the office.

'Brian!' cried Beth and rushed over to greet him.

'Hello Brian fancy seeing' you here' was all Suzy could say.

'So I was right after all, it *was* you two I knew it, I just knew it.'

Beth took a step back; she didn't like the tone of his voice. Didn't he think this was funny?

'Thank you for all your help Sergeant Cooper, I won't be pressing charges, I will however take my clothes if that's all right with you?'

'Certainly sir, they're at the front desk.' Sergeant Cooper gave Brian a quick wink as he left the room, then turned to Beth and

Suzy and with a straight face told them they could go. Walking home Beth couldn't understand why Brian hadn't enjoyed the joke.

By the end of the eight-week run, the girls were pleased to be back on home ground. Brian had kept his distance from Beth after the 'robbery' and Jackie had pushed Suzy to the point of planning her murder.

'If we'd stayed another day I swear she would have come to a sticky end!'

'Well I thought you'd got your wish the night of that storm. How on earth did she sleep through all that thunder and lightening?'

'She was a junkie on those sleeping pills remember? And you did smack her face a bit hard."

'Well I thought she was dead' chuckled Beth remembering Jackie's rude awakening.

'We should write a book on all our adventures' suggested Suzy unpacking her suitcase. 'And we'd be whisked away by our agent to a hidden destination, while the shit hit the fan, probably the Seychelles and when we got back they'd be queuing up for autographs and interviews.'

Suzy smiled, 'well we'd better do a few auditions otherwise it'll be a bloody short book!'

SEVENTEEN

It had been threatening for some time, but the girls were finally going to have to accept that their careers were heading down different paths. Beth was disappointed that Suzy wasn't going to join her at the Victoria Palace with the Tillers, but understood she wanted to move on. Then out of the blue Tillers offered Suzy a three-week run at the Palladium with Tom Jones and all ambitions to be the next Shirley Maclaine was put on hold, although her high spirits were short lived.

'What the hell are you moaning at?' shouted Beth, losing her patience; you haven't had to audition, you're at the Palladium, *and* you'll be working with the guy you've been fantasizing over for years.'

'Oh I know I'm really lucky' retorted Suzy sulkily 'but it's only for three weeks' and realising how peevish she sounded, flung herself across the unusually clear kitchen table, rolled on her back, threw her legs in the air and opened them into a side split. 'Gene Kelly can audition me any time he likes.'

'You are such a tart, now put some knickers on' giggled Beth forcing Suzy's legs together. 'You've got a month to kill before you start rehearsals, so why don't you do some classes and learn to dance properly?'

'You cheeky cow! Blimey have you noticed how filthy this place is Beth?' She was still laid flat out staring at the greasy nicotine stained ceiling.

Beth shook her head disinterested.

'Well it is, so why don't I do it up a bit, while I've got a bit of spare time. You'll be busy getting your legs in the air at the V.P. and it'll give me something to do.'

'But you don't know anything about decorating.'

'I know but I'll make it up as I go along. It can't be that hard slapping a bit of paint on.'

Suzy immersed herself in her newfound talent, creating as she saw it an ambience of psychedelic harmony with 'Sergeant Pepper' blasting around the flat helping create the mood she was aiming for. By the end of the first week the kitchen walls were bright orange, which was a definite improvement on the greasy grey, but Beth was convinced 'Rembrandt' must be on the 'funny fags' when she staggered in after a gruelling days rehearsal one evening to find Suzy standing in the hall grinning from ear to ear.

'What's going on?' she asked irritably.

'I've got a surprise for you' said Suzy jumping up and down excitedly. 'Close your eyes.' Beth not in the mood for games went to protest, but seeing Suzy's eager face obeyed. Suzy grabbed her hand and led her into the living room 'OK you can open them now.' It took a few seconds for Beth's eyes to adjust to the darkness and it took her brain a little longer to digest the vision before her.

'Blimey Suz' she was lost for words, but when she did find them they weren't exactly what Suzy had expected. 'It looks like a brothel!' The somewhat bland cream room that she'd left that morning was now a deep blood red, including the ceiling. Purple tie dyed sheets were thrown over the tatty and ancient floral sofa and at the window hung what looked suspiciously like Indian sari material. A dozen candles flickering from every available surface enhanced the sultry atmosphere.

'Oh no, you don't like it! Suzy wailed. 'I haven't stopped all day, I wanted to surprise you.'

'Oh you've certainly done that,' laughed Beth tiptoeing round the room still trying to taking it all in. Suddenly she spun round to face the now tearful Suzy and threw her arms round her.

'You are a genius, I love it, *it's fantastic.*' Relief swept over Suzy as she proudly told Beth how she'd found the sari material in a sale in the market a week earlier and hid it under the bed. How the walls really needed another coat but she was too impatient and wanted to finish it for when Beth got in.

'Ah! I've just realised, that's why the bath had purple scum marks round it last week.'

'Yeah, I dyed the sheets in it but ran out of cleaner.'

Beth suddenly forgetting all her aches and pains of the day ran to the off licence, returning with two bottles of sparkling wine and fish and chips. 'Procol Harem' played quietly in the background, as they lay sprawled across the floor of the candle lit room, which still reeked of fresh paint. By the time they'd seen off the second bottle, Beth was explaining to her interior designer how she wished the bedroom to be turned into a pink passion palace.

'You want pink? I'll give you pink and it'll be a palace, but the passion, I'm afraid I can't guarantee. There's only so much one can do with a pot of paint!'

Three weeks later, Suzy was exhausted but pleased with her first attempt at decorating. Beth got her pink bedroom, the walls, ceiling, door, skirting board, windows, chest of drawers and wardrobe, in fact every object in sight was various shades of pink, and even the mirror and bed legs had been victims of Suzy's sense of humour.

'Suzy Noden you're a very sick woman' was Beth's initial reaction. 'You are completely warped and I think you need help.' Suzy accepted the compliment humbly and ran for cover in the kitchen, knowing Beth secretly loved her new boudoir!

EIGHTEEN

Suzy started rehearsals for the three-week run at the Palladium, and once the show opened, spent every night on side stage watching her idol, fantasizing that every thrust he performed was just for her. So at the end of the first week when he invited all the girls for a drink in his dressing room, Suzy was beside herself with excitement, but was one of only five to accept. Most of the girls were wise to his reputation and steered clear, but Suzy wasn't going to miss an opportunity like that.

Quickly touching up her lipstick and undoing just one too many buttons on her dressing gown she heaved her boobs up to create an impressive cleavage.

The star dressing room was surprisingly small and as the five girls nervously filed in, Suzy giggled at the sight of the two huge sofas placed opposite each other dominating the tiny room.

'I bet they've seen some action' she sniggered as the girls squashed themselves onto one, which left Tom sprawled along the other, eyeing his prey. After the initial introductions they were all offered drinks.

'I'd love a gin and tonic, thanks' purred Suzy remembering Beth's successful flirting tactics, while the others accepted soft drinks. She hung on his every word and even made him laugh with her direct crude humour. In the dressing room later on, Jill demonstrated to the rest of the girls how Suzy had practically thrown herself at him. Suzy denied the accusation, but deep down was quite pleased with a good nights flirting.

The following night after the opening, Tom's P.A. Alan knocked on the dressing room door asking for Suzy, he had a message from Tom, inviting her to a party. Not wanting to appear too keen she thought about it for a whole five seconds then nodded vigorously, without realising what she was letting herself in for.

'Oh my God what am I going to wear?' she shrieked once the reality had sunk in. Ignoring the worried looks on some of the girls faces and envious looks from a couple of others, she held up her striped mini dress she'd worn to the theatre that evening and decided a quick spray with deodorant would do the trick.

'I shouldn't bother too much about your dress, it's your underwear you should be more worried about' smirked Anne eyeing Suzy's baggy faded blue pants and off white bra 'you know he's only after one thing don't you?'

'Well I'll just tell him he can't have it.'

'Don't be daft Suz, you were flirting outrageously last night in his dressing room, and with all your clever remarks he thinks he's onto a certainty. Why do you think he chose you?'

'Oh no! So what do I do? I can't tell him I'm still a virgin; I'll be the laughing stock.' Anne rolled her eyes and shook her head at Suzy's naivety, but came up with a suggestion that won waves of approval from the more experienced girls in the room.

'Well you could do what I've done in the past as a safety measure.' Suzy was all ears. 'Just tell him it's the wrong time of the month. So he won't invite you again, but at least you'll get a night out with no strings attached! She burst out laughing at her own pun and the rest of the girls joined in.

'Oh! Very funny.... but what if he doesn't take no for an answer?' But Anne only laughed, assuring her that one glimpse of that blue string and he'd run a mile.

'You mean I've got to actually wear one?' Suzy asked incredulously.

'Well you'd better be prepared in case it gets that far, I know what you're like after a drink! Unless of course you *want* to go the whole hog?' All eyes were on Suzy not convinced she would be able to resist the man that millions of women fantasize over.

'You be careful!' warned Jean giving Suzy a hug on her way out after the show.

'Be careful, are you joking? More like lucky bitch!' Anne was feeling as jealous as hell. 'Doesn't he realise he's wasting a good night on her?' She snapped, 'now if I went, I'd make sure he had a good time.' She flounced out of the room and slammed the door.

'Yeah you've given many a welcome in those hillsides!' shouted Suzy after her.

Once alone Suzy frantically dressed, put her dirty fishnet tights in her tote bag and waited in the dressing room for Alan to come and fetch her. She felt like Cinderella, and Tom was definitely her Prince Charming. OK, so the striped football dress wasn't exactly a silk ball gown, and she'd probably have a job daintily slipping out of one of her purple Biba boots as she scampered into the darkness at midnight, well she might have to delay her departure if the party was really jumping, but this *was* like a fairytale! And there'd be plenty of "Oh yes she will! Oh no she won't!" later on hopefully.

The following three hours turned from a fairytale in to a full-blown pantomime!

By 3am she found herself standing alone in a very up market cul de sac, surrounded by smartly painted doors, brass knockers and window boxes somewhere in the middle of Mayfair. Shocked, stunned and completely humiliated Suzy shivered as she tried to focus on her immediate problem, which seemed to be multiplying by the minute. Refusing to recall how she had actually got herself into this abandoned state, her pride not being top priority, she stoically concentrated on how she was going to get home. She ran to the end of the cul de sac, following the sound of the traffic, which seemed to be coming from around the next corner. The Edgware Rd was a welcome sight, at least she knew the way and a good walk was what she needed to clear her head, which was just as well because she didn't have enough money for a taxi.

As she headed down the Bayswater Road towards Lancaster Gate, her mind started to recall the nightmare. Clutching her bag across her for warmth she kept her eyes on the pavement, too embarrassed to even face the passing late night traffic. How could she have been so *stupid?* 'Thanks a lot Anne!' she shouted, her pace quickening with rage, remembering Toms reaction to her untimely female problem. 'What did you expect Suzy?' she ranted on, oblivious to odd looks from the occasional pedestrian, sidestepping the obvious drunken mad woman, 'him to run to the chemist for some aspirin and spend the evening rubbing your back for you? God Suzy you are so stupid!' As she approached Holland Park tube she practically broke into a run, sensing the safety and sanctuary of home and Beth. Not far now, just across Shepherds Bush Green and she'd be home. She ran two at a time up the stairs to her front door, where she paused to catch her breath. Glancing at her watch, 4.15am, she suddenly realised that Beth would be fast asleep, but as she quietly fished around in her bag for her keys, the door suddenly flung open and there stood Beth, grinning knowingly, or so she thought until she saw Suzy's face.

'Don't you dare ask' threatened Suzy barging into the flat before Beth had a chance to speak.

'I'm freezing cold, run out of fags and *that* must have been *the* most embarrassing night of my life.' She flung herself down onto the sofa, threw her head in her hands and rocked backwards and forwards moaning loudly.

Beth looked at Suzy in bewilderment as she lit a cigarette and wafted it under her nose. Suzy shot her head up, craving for that first puff, but Beth snatched it out of her reach.

'Sorry mate,' Beth teased. 'All I got was a message from Jean that you were off to some posh party and not to wait up, so I want all the sordid details or no ciggy.' She took a drag and blew the smoke in Suzy's face.

'So you little hussy,' I take it from your mood you didn't see his "Green Green Grass of Home"?'

Suzy looked up with a wry smile 'I did actually, but I wouldn't let him see "My Delilah".' Beth deciding she deserved the cigarette, lit another one for herself and waited. After explaining Anne's great safe sex plan, Suzy went onto describe the rest of the evening in minute detail, from the cream leather seats of the Silver Cloud Rolls Royce, to the smooching at the party. She got to the part where after a couple of hours they were invited for coffee at a friends mews cottage, but when they got there the place was empty, and Beth burst out laughing.

'Oh, Suz you are so naïve, what did you expect?'

'Coffee!' insisted Suzy. 'With cream of course.'

'So what did you do?'

She shook her head and started giggling as she explained how she excused herself and dashed to the bathroom and when she eventually came out ready to give him the excuse, he was standing by the window stark naked, glass in one hand, cigar in the other.

'And believe me he was *smokin'!* So I took a deep breath and told him I was really sorry, but oopsy these things happen, but maybe next time.'

'You said *what?* Maybe *next* time?'

'I know I know, but I was nervous.'

'So go on, what did he say?'

'Well he was furious, asked why I hadn't told him before we came, said it was a waste of time and told me to get a cab home, because he was going back to the party. I think he felt a bit of a dick…. I didn't though.'

'What?'

'Feel his dick.'

By the time Suzy had finished telling her tale in the dressing room the following evening, Anne, Natasha and a couple of others were sniggering among themselves, not believing her story for one minute.

'Are you saying you actually refused him, after spending the whole night smooching with him at a party? Come on Suzy you're not normal.'

'Oh shut up Anne, it was your bloody idea in the first place' defended Jean.

'Well I'd have had him in the back of the car, those cream leather seats would have got a right bashing!'

Suzy had heard enough. 'Yes you and hundreds of others probably, at least I'll be famous for saying NO!' Cath and Jean suggested that she should at least have asked him for the taxi fare. Suzy agreed but had already planned her tactics with Beth the night before.

As Tom took the whole of the second half, the girls said goodnight during the interval, leaving Suzy nervously choosing her moment. She packed her bag and made her way downstairs.

The orchestra struck up the overture for the second half and Suzy positioned herself in the passage between his dressing room and the stage door. She wanted everybody in the theatre to hear what he'd done to her, and she was going to make a quick exit as soon as she'd said her piece! Her heart was pounding as the overture came to an end and suddenly his dressing room door opened. She had to do it now, before he disappeared on stage!

'Tom!' she shouted as loud as she dare. He looked round in surprise. She took another deep breath. 'Thanks for last night, it took me nearly two...' she stopped mid insult as out of the same door followed...his *wife!!!!* Tom glared at Suzy, his wife glared at Suzy and then Alan popped his head round the door and glared at Suzy. She froze! Then they were gone, round the corner and onto side stage. She could hear the screams of adoring fans in the audience as he made his entrance, which meant it was time for her to make an exit! She flew out of the stage door and ran down the steps into the darkness of the underground. 'Oh, shit shit shit, what have I done?' she was sweating and her head was spinning as she practically fell into a near empty carriage. '*Oh no, I can see the headlines now'* her mind was working overtime. *"Virgin named in divorce proceedings!"* She lit a cigarette and puffing furiously closed her eyes as she went over and over the look of horror on his face. Suddenly the reality of having to face everybody at the theatre the following evening gripped at her stomach like a week old madras curry. She stubbed out the cigarette with a fury on the carriage floor and immediately fumbled in her bag for another, shaking as she lit it. This time she shouted out loud 'Oh my God what am I going to do?'

By 2am, Beth and Suzy had decided that her only option was to shave her head, change her name to Dominic and join a monastery in the Italian Alps. A convent had been ruled out due to the fact that Suzy couldn't sew, which as a nun was compulsory and black was such a harsh colour without makeup. Anyway monks were into wine growing, which probably meant quite a lot of wine tasting goes on as well! This decision like all major life changing decisions was encouraged by the two wine bottles, which now lay empty across their living room floor. It may not have been the most sensible way to sort out a problem, but it did guarantee them both a good night's sleep!

The following evening as Suzy walked through the stage door, she'd decided to take whatever punishment was due to her. She'd spent most of the day, blaming everyone apart from herself, but that same old expression that Michael Walsh had used, "prick teasers" kept coming back in her head. Hadn't she only gone out with him to feed her ego, to impress the rest of the girls? Yes, he had chosen her over the others, but she wasn't stupid, it wasn't her wit or her flashing smile that had won him over, more like her flashing boobs!

She nodded sheepishly at the stage doorman and rushed up the stairs to dressing room 11. As soon as she opened the door she was stopped in her tracks by an immediate hush in the room. All eyes were on her. Then Anne broke the silence.

'And what did you get up to last night then?' she bellowed with an overdose of sarcasm.

Suzy searched for a friendly face. 'Why, what do you mean?' she asked innocently.

'Well, rumour has it you made a bit of a fool of yourself in front of his wife! And you've obviously blown it *because* "little miss get a load of this, but don't touch" you have been summonsed to report to the Sex God downstairs as *soon* as you get in. Of course he didn't come himself, he sent his lackey boy Alan and he didn't look too happy.

'How did you know?' asked Suzy cringing.

'Oh, *everybody* knows,' laughed Anne 'but then wasn't that the idea?'

She resigned herself to a life of ridicule, as she bravely made her way back out of the room and down the stairs to face probably instant dismissal.

Standing outside number 1 dressing room, Suzy took a minute to make sure all blouse buttons were fastened to the top and her skirt was at least covering her bum. It didn't occur to her that maybe it was a bit late for modesty. She timidly knocked on the door and jumped back startled as it was flung open immediately by Tom who stepped aside, inviting her to sit down. Confused but relieved she declined the offer of a gin and tonic and keeping her knees tightly squeezed together, with her hands clasped firmly on her lap, she took a deep breath and keeping her eyes glued to the carpet she made her apologies for the ugly scene and hoped it hadn't caused too many problems at home.

But as she was just coming to the end of her grovelling speech and she finally lifted her head from the depths of the tuft pile she was greeted with a smug smile that made her snap. She jumped up and faced him head on.

'Oh, you find this funny do you? Well while you were lining up your next victim and I hope *she* wasn't a waste of time, I had to walk home in the freezing bloody cold, because unlike you 'twinkle twinkles' us dancers don't earn enough to pay for taxis, let alone have chauffeurs running us round in big flash cars. Just because you couldn't get your leg over, doesn't give you the right...to....' Tom had heard enough; he stepped forward and gently put his hand over her still busy mouth.

'Ssh!' He insisted and without actually biting a chunk out of his hand, which did momentarily flash through her mind, Suzy had no choice but to shut up. Confident he'd got her attention; he held her by the shoulders and guided her to the sofa where she fell reluctantly.

'Now young lady' he started 'I actually asked you to come and see me so that I could apologise to you. I was way out of line, but as you so delicately put it, I'm used to getting my own way.' Suzy blushed. 'So if I promise not to pounce on you, would you like to come for a meal tonight? Alan has invited Jane, so there'll be safety in numbers and I promise to take you straight home, if that's what you want?' she nodded a little too furiously and he burst out laughing.

'Right then my little virgin' Suzy shot a look, but said nothing, how did he know?

'Ooh I'm far too experienced not to see through your little act' he was teasing her now. 'Just promise me one thing, if you've anything to say, then you come and see me, don't shout it around for the entire world to hear, because believe me the only person you're embarrassing is you. OK?'

'OK' she croaked.

She started to make for the door, when he suddenly took a small bunch of flowers from the sink at the far end of the room and offered them to her.

'Here, something to show your friends, maybe it's not so bad being a good girl heh?'

She took them and shyly thanked him, apologising once more. As she ran up the stairs panicking now that she'd miss the opening number, it dawned on her the significance of the flowers. These would wipe that smile off Anne's face. She burst through the dressing room door, where again the silence cut in and waved the flowers above her head. 'Look at these girls' she bragged 'and I haven't got to open my legs for them, just put them in a vase like everybody else!'

It wasn't the only embarrassing interlude for Suzy during the run.

'Overture and Beginners' had been called, but Suzy was as usual nowhere near ready. The overture had already started as she rushed down the stairs to take her place in the line-up. But disaster struck. In her rush to get there before the curtains opened she tripped, slipped on her backside and with legs sprawled, her heel ripped through the backcloth and smashed a lamp. 'Oh bugger!' was all she could mumble as she pulled her foot out of the gaping hole and straightened her headdress. With the stage now in partial darkness and only seconds to go she instinctively scrambled to her feet and practically threw herself into the line as the curtains opened. Shaking with nerves, she managed to hold a fixed smile as she went through the motions of the first sixteen bars of the regimented routine, until the line turned upstage and she let out a muffled scream as she caught a glimpse of the shattered broken lamp laid strewn around the stage. Her legs continued kicking, but her mind was racing and for a split second squeezed her eyes shut, trying to blank out the gasps and sniggers that seem to wave down the line from the other girls, with Diane pinching her arm and adding to the drama by whispering 'You're in the shit now!'

That was the final straw and failing to control her nerves, the giggles set in.

Now they were kicking round to face the audience and the troupe switched on their luminous smiles again, but Suzy was losing the battle to control her bodily functions, forcing tears of suppressed laughter to stream down her face, her suspect bladder control finally let her down. As the routine progressed and the girls formed a circle, the look of horror on the other girl's faces didn't help as they caught sight of the puddles trickling across the stage. But there was nothing Suzy could do, but carry on kicking.

Russell Wright, the Musical Director poised in the pit conducting the orchestra, couldn't believe his eyes, as drops of water seem to be flicking off the end of one of their shoes. As the sixteen girls kicked their way down to the front of the stage before finishing the routine down on one knee, his eye followed up the flicking leg and was confronted with Suzy's convulsed contorted face desperately trying to hold everything together.

At last the routine was over and the curtains, seemingly taking forever to close, finally allowed Suzy to rush to the dressing room before the inevitable interrogations began. The bill for the dry cleaning of the sequined costume was negligible to the humiliation she faced not only for the duration of the season, but in fact haunted her, as the rest of the cast ensured her 'little accident' would be the highlight of gossip in every theatre bar and party for years to come.

But things were looking up on the professional front, when just three days before the show finished she got an audition for a BBC 2 series 'Colour my Soul' and Ralph Talbert's style of sexy jazz was right up her alley.

Beth on the other hand had finally found her forte at the Talk of the Town where she was a firm favourite with Bill Petch who promised her a great future.

In contrast to Suzy's work, the 'Talk' gave Beth an opportunity to wear lavish costumes and more make up than a drag queen! She was on cloud nine!

It surpassed cloud nine when one of her idols, Sammy Davis Jnr was appearing for the week. On his last night he invited everybody into his dressing room for a drink and Beth broke her own record for getting ready. The previous held was for a blind date, which didn't come close in comparison.

Once inside the star sanctuary and determined to speak if not touch her idol, Beth made a beeline for the empty seat next to him and for the next half hour Beth sat riveted to her chair, refusing to give up her front row seat at any cost. After four more martinis she was having trouble concentrating, but her ears pricked up when Sammy who had been entertaining everybody with his stories, told them of the time he was locked out of his hotel suite.

'…and she thought I was a porter, and I don't mean Cole Porter man.' Everyone fell about laughing, but with the room now swaying, Beth's mouth became detached from her brain and was keen to contribute. 'Huh, you think that's funny! Let me tell you about the time my friend Shoozy and I were locked out.' And she did, with slurred speech and hiccups setting in. Her voice becoming louder and louder the more excited she got.

'… and there we were laying on the ground in my pish, shmelling like two week old jockshtrapshs!'

The room filled with laughter, but as pissed as she was Beth realised she'd committed one of the worst sins in show biz. She'd upstaged the star! While Sammy found the story funny, his assistant and manager moved him away to the other side of the room, before the situation became embarrassing.

The drink was already beginning to wear off and she was feeling sick, so decided to take a taxi home rather than the stuffy tube. As she swayed on the edge of the kerb ready to pounce on the first orange light she saw, a man sneaked up behind her and spoke softly in her ear.

'I loved your story even if you did do a no no!'

'Oooah…' Beth jumped with fright and staggered to stay on her feet as she fell into the kerb. As the mystery man helped her back onto the safety of the pavement, she tried to focus on the handsome face, which was attached to the most gorgeous body she'd ever seen.

'Th…Thank you, I think I overstepped it though' and added coyly 'but at least I got to meet him.'

Trying to pull herself together for this vision in front of her, she took a deep breath,

'I'm going home now, it's late and I have a call tomorrow, it was nice meeting you …er?'

'Bobby… Bobby Brant, maybe we'll meet again?'

Beth managed a weak smile and nodded as she manically waved down a cab, praying she wouldn't throw up right there and then. Safely seated in the back of the cab she tried to remember the name of the man she'd just met. *'Bobby something, Bobby Brown? No can't think of it, quite dishy though, oh well probably never see him again'* and she dozed off in the warmth of the taxi.

NINETEEN

Everyone in the 'biz' knew Bobby Brant. Not only did he have the body of a Greek Adonis with a face to match, at twenty-nine he was a very successful choreographer.

Ambition was Bobby's focus and after ten years in the business he'd learnt that dancing wasn't his greatest gift, but creating fantasy was. He attributed his success not only to his obvious talent, but the skills he'd learnt in using people, which he did well and often. There were only two occasions that he would admit to using his sexual preference for "climbing the ladder".

He didn't have the usual gay giveaways; in fact quite the opposite, and the girls drooled along with the boys, nobody knew for sure because he kept his social life private.

Rumours had been rife for years as to whether he was in the 'Arthur or Martha' camp and he was often irritated at the whisperings that followed him everywhere.

Sitting in his Notting Hill flat one evening an idea came to him. If he had a wife, people would maybe stop discussing his sex life and start to have a little more respect for his work. He racked his brains for a suitable candidate. Of course she'd have to be totally independent and not the usual nosey female. Oh no he had far too many secrets for prying questions. Pouring another red wine, his ego assured him that some poor sucker would be only too grateful to be to be seen on the arm of the great Bobby Brant. In a flash he remembered Beth Carson.

'Of course' he said smugly 'she'd be perfect, attractive, outgoing and best of all probably a secret lesbian.'

After their initial meeting waiting for the cab, he'd met her again two weeks later at a party, and she was the only highlight of the evening. *'Made me laugh a few times and I know she fancied me, even though she spent most of the evening dancing with the blonde tart.'* Smiling to himself he went over to his aquarium and leaned over the top of the tank.

'OK cat food, what do you think about me getting married? Not a good idea? Well too bad, I'm going to get me a wife anyway.'

'Are you getting tarted up for that bloke again?' Suzy called out from the kitchen.

'Yes I am and I might add he's not just a bloke, he's Bobby Brant, choreographer extraordinaire' came the reply from the bathroom.

'Oh excuse me! So is this the real thing?'

Beth came out of the bathroom beaming 'Suz I'm in love with him'

Suzy smiled and hugged her friend, knowing that if this *was* the real thing she should be pleased, although she had her reservations. There was something about Bobby Brant she couldn't quite put her finger on.

Two months later Beth became Mrs. Brant and was head over heels in love with Bobby. They found a spacious flat in Chiswick, with three large bedrooms, three because it was understood before they got married that Suzy would be sharing with them for a while, until she could find a place of her own. It suited Bobby; not only did it convince him that his new wife was indeed a closet dyke, but it also meant he would have time for his "other" life without being missed, and Beth was delighted her friend would still be with her, but Suzy wasn't so thrilled. She still couldn't work out what it was about the man, but something wasn't right. Still for now it suited her to stay at the flat. One, it enabled her to be with Beth and two, she could keep an eye on Mr. Brant!

It was a cold and rainy Sunday morning and with Bobby at a meeting, the two girls made the most of their time alone.

'Oh Suz this is just like it used to be and we can smoke ourselves silly because Bobby's not here, I'll just have to remember to open the windows and light some candles.'

Suzy scoffed and rolled her eyes.

'Oh shut up, it just makes life a bit easier. Besides Bobby's so good to me, he doesn't ask for much, actually he doesn't ever ask for anything, know what I mean?'

'You mean the "oh be joyfuls"?'

'Indeed I do, I'm not sure if he's forgotten how, or he's just too busy thinking about his next show.'

'Blimey Beth, you've only been married four months, if it was me I'd be thinking there was something wrong with me.'

Beth raised her eyebrows, and as always the pair of them burst into fits of laughter.

With breakfast over, they spent the rest of the day smoking and watching old films.

'God it's 10.30 already, I'm off to bed, what time is Bobby coming home?'

'Don't know, he said not late whatever that means, but I'm not waiting up for him, so you go up, I'll clear up.'

Beth had just fallen asleep and Suzy was in the loo for the third time when she heard Bobby come home. Creeping into the bedroom and leaving the door ajar, he undressed and slid into bed, but Beth stirred sleepily.

'Oh Bobby is that you?'

'Who else were you expecting, Suzy?'

'Eh?' Beth yawned and turned over to face him. 'Did your meeting go well with, what was his name?'

'Charlie and yes it did thanks, how was your day?'

'It was smashing just like old times. It's been ages since the two of us have spent time together, we...'

'I know, I know, you chatted about the same old stuff and ended up in fits of laughter.'

Ignoring the interruption, but hurt by the innuendo Beth sat up, 'Bobby what is it with you?'

'Must I Beth? I'm really tired.'

'Yes you must' she insisted as she put the lamp on.

On her way back to her room Suzy heard Beth's raised voice; and hung around outside their door.

'Maybe it's my imagination but it seems that every time I mention Suzy you get upset.'

Bobby sat up, 'upset, about *her*, you must be joking.'

'No I'm not joking' Beth retorted sharply. They were about to have their first argument.

'Tell me the truth, don't you like Suzy?'

Bobby wasn't stupid; he knew he had to choose his words carefully. He had a good thing going with Beth and to make her chose between him and Suzy could be disastrous.

'My darling of course I like Suzy, I know how close you two are, but sometimes I feel well, sometimes you're distracted.'

'What do you mean, distracted? She's my best friend, but then you wouldn't know what that's like.'

He knew what she was insinuating, he kept his 'friends' well away from home, leading Beth to believe he had none, but he had to stay calm, he needed her by his side for the Charity Ball at the Dorchester next week. Everybody loved Beth and Bobby was under no delusion that without her social skills his diary wouldn't be as full as it was. He put his arm around her, but for once she didn't respond. Bobby tried a new angle.

'Darling, the first time I saw you I knew you had star quality with your personality alone, but the way you dance on stage, sweetheart you're incredible.' He kissed her on her head and waited. Beth wasn't expecting this, she was thrown off guard and a weakness of the old Beth, succumbing to any man's compliments meant the battle was over before it started.

'You really think I have star quality?'

'Yes, I wouldn't say so otherwise and believe me I know it when I see it. Now don't misunderstand me when I say this but,' he softened his voice, 'Suzy doesn't have it.'

Beth stiffened slightly.

'I know you love her and she's your best friend, but she doesn't have what it takes, God didn't give you tits and arse for nothing.'

She giggled and for the first time in a long time they made love. It was Bobby's planned finale. As for Suzy she slowly walked back to her bedroom with tears in her eyes and made plans of her own.

'What do you mean your moving out Suz?'

'Beth I've been here for five months and it's time for me to go. I appreciate you letting me stay but what can I say, three's company and two's a crowd.'

Beth smiled affectionately as Suzy plonked herself down in the chair, 'Oh you know what I mean, you're married and... well... things have changed, not between us, but you know me and Bobby never really liked each other and its getting harder every day to keep my mouth shut. He's always making remarks about how I dress or how I talk, it's said in fun but I know he means it. I haven't told you half of what's gone on, but I'm sorry to say this, I think he's a ponse.'

Beth sat down next to her

'Suz, I...'

'No let me finish, if I don't go now I'm afraid of what will happen to our friendship and I couldn't bear the thought of you not being a part of my life, there I've said it now. I'm so sorry

Beth, please don't be angry with me.'

Beth put her arm round her and squeezed her tight.

'Oh Suz I'm not angry with you, anyway we're more than friends, we're sisters remember?' She grabbed a tissue, passing the box to Suzy 'and don't think I haven't noticed when I've come home; I could cut the atmosphere with a knife. I suppose I ignored it because I didn't want you to leave, Suz I still don't, why don't you let me speak to Bobby, I'm sure we can work things out.'

Suzy grabbed Beth's arm.

'No please don't do that, it'll only make things worse. Beth, it's for the best you know that, besides I've got the chance to share a place in Notting Hill with one of the girls, cheap rent and close to the tube.'

She was feeling better now she'd got it off her chest, but one thing was clear; ever since she'd overheard Bobby that night in the hallway she would never trust him again and for the first time they had to face the fact that their lives were now going down different paths. Love and trust had sustained this incredible friendship, now it would take courage and fortitude to remain so.

TWENTY

Things changed for Beth after Suzy moved out and not particularly for the better. Everything in her career was going well, as lead dancer in a new show at the "Talk" Billy insisted she got a pay rise. But her personal life was not doing so well. Bobby had moved into the spare room, with a weak excuse that Beth's snoring was hindering his creative juices! Playing the part, he remained very attentive in other ways, still telling her she had *star quality* and he was doing all he could to promote her. So the arrangement suited her for the time being, knowing she would have to deal with it eventually. In the meantime her biggest concern was Suzy. They'd met for lunch as usual on Tuesday, with Suzy promising to ring the following day. Two days later Beth was getting worried; leaving three messages with Linda her flatmate, but Suzy still hadn't returned her calls.

'Suzy you must call Beth she phoned again tonight.'

Suzy agreed, but had other things on her mind. She'd auditioned for lead dancer in a new West End show. It was the topic of conversation, mainly because of the choreographer Melvin Havies, whose reputation was growing. Suzy was ecstatic; she'd danced really well and looked fabulous. Melvin and the producers were impressed and asked if she was available to start rehearsals right away. Melvin gave her a wink and said he'd call her for sure in the next couple of days. She knew this was a good sign and for the first time in her life felt confident. By the time she got home she was late for her date with Mark, the new man in her life, so it was a quick tart up before leaving the empty flat to tell him her exciting news. The phone rang five times, stopped and rang again, then fell silent. '*Oh bugger I forgot to ring Beth,*' thought Suzy as she ran down the stairs '*ne'mind I'll do it tomorrow.*'

Bobby arrived at the out of town restaurant for his weekly secret rendezvous with Melvin. The affair had been going on for sometime; unbeknown to Beth and he was shown to the table where Melvin was on his second wine. They ordered lunch and sat back, enjoying their drinks, exchanging the latest gossip and news. Only meeting once a week meant that there was plenty to talk about, but Bobby wasn't prepared for what followed.

'Remember that new show I was telling you about?'

Bobby nodded 'Yes but I didn't think it was going to happen for a while.'

'Well apparently with the show at the Adelphi closing early next year, they've decided to get things moving. The auditions were yesterday and we've got some good dancers.'

'I'm pleased for you Melvin,' Bobby said, but in fact he wasn't pleased. Why hadn't he been told about the auditions? He was planning to promote Beth for lead dancer, but he'd obviously missed the boat.

'Do you know Suzy Noden…?'

Bobby nearly choked on his drink. 'Hmm, name sounds familiar, why?'

Melvin looked concerned. 'Are you all right dear heart?'

'Yes, a bit of a dry throat that's all, so what's with this Suzy Noden?'

'She's fabulous, came yesterday to audition, we had a meeting today and decided she's perfect for the lead, I'm phoning her tomorrow.'

Bobby's brain was racing; he had to do something and fast. He made an excuse to go to the gents to give himself time to think. By the time he came back to the table he'd had a brilliant idea.

'Melvin I remember who that girl is now and you're not going to like this, but I care about you and I think you should know.'

'What ever is it Bobby?'

'I knew her name was familiar and I remember why. She has a serious drink problem!'

It was brilliant. He'd remembered Beth and Suzy laughing about an episode during a summer season in Westcliffe when Suzy got plastered a few times due to some guy she'd met in a show. With some exaggeration and lies Bobby spent the rest of the meal turning Suzy into an alcoholic with little hope for the future and by the time the waiter brought the coffees, Melvin's face was showing signs of desperation. Rehearsals were only three weeks away and where was he going to find a lead dancer as good as Suzy?'

Bobby, sensing his lover's predicament, continued the charade.

'I've just had a brilliant idea Melvin, why don't you use Beth as your lead? She'd be wonderful and looks great. She picks up really fast, I don't know why we didn't think of her before.'

'But isn't she at the "Talk" under contract?' He was taken aback by the suggestion; he cared for Bobby and didn't want to hurt him. Beth looked good, but her style was completely wrong for his show. Suzy on the other hand had everything he was looking for, but he couldn't risk his career and use her after what Bobby had told him.

'No problem there, I can pull a few strings and she can rehearse during the day with you until her understudy is ready to replace her at the "Talk", it'll work Melvin, she'll be great, trust me.' Bobby gave him a lingering look across the table and Melvin although still not totally convinced fell helplessly into the trap.

TWENTY-ONE

In room 205 of the Ascot Hotel, just a short walk from Paddington station, Bobby's lunch meeting was nowhere near over.

Melvin folded his arms behind his head and lay back on the pillows while Bobby phoned Beth with the good news. Ok, so she wasn't ideal, but she looked fabulous and Bobby had promised to work with her on her dance techniques before rehearsals started. Melvin stretched and felt the passion in his groin returning as he admired Bobby's perfect naked body standing by the window. He was confident that his lover would be eager to please him for the third time that afternoon. Bobby would feel eternally indebted to Melvin for securing his financial security by signing up Beth for his show, giving him the lifestyle he had always craved. He smirked inwardly imagining how Bobby would be explaining later that evening to the poor gullible bitch just how he'd managed to swing the deal.

Their eyes met as Bobby replaced the receiver and Melvin greedily grew impatient for the power game to commence.

Beth put the phone down and stood in the hall shaking with disbelief. Could it be true what Bobby had just told her? He'd said he hadn't time to explain, but promised to be home as soon as the meeting was over. She stared into the mirror and a smile slowly spread across her face. 'Melvin Havies wants *me* for his new show' she assured herself, as if her reflection doubted the news. '*Me, Beth Carson* is going to star in *Melvin Havies* show,' she repeated. Glancing up at their wedding photo, she blew her husband a kiss. This proved he really did love her and all doubts that had been plaguing her since Suzy left were swept away by a surge of passion for Bobby. Suddenly she raced into the kitchen, grabbed her cigarettes and poured herself a much-needed glass of wine. She spent the next four hours, smoking and pacing the floor impatient for the divine Bobby to walk through the door and tell her all the details of her newfound stardom.

Bobby couldn't believe his eyes as he staggered into his flat later that evening. He was quite literally shagged out, with the 'meeting' going on longer than he'd expected and was looking forward to a long soak in a hot bath with a gin and tonic. Beth on the other hand had other ideas. Knowing her husbands distaste for her usual exuberance, she slinked across the candlelit lounge in bright red silk pyjamas, inviting him to join her on the sofa. She handed him his G&T and controlling her growing urge to jump on him, excitedly demanding to be told every single detail of the meeting, she gazed into his somewhat bloodshot eyes enticing him to explain. Not realising that what she was about to hear was a pack of lies.

It turned out to be one of the longest nights of Bobby's life!

Beth had been sulky and difficult ever since Suzy had moved out, and was asking too many questions about the problems he'd had with Suzy, but he was damn sure he preferred her moods to what she had planned for him that evening.

His ego wouldn't allow him to play down his part in the deal, but at the same time wishing Beth wasn't quite so keen to show her gratitude. They eventually fell into bed at 2am with Bobby just staying awake long enough to apologise to his eager playmate for the drink affecting his performance! Beth, almost relieved that Bobby was unable to perform was far too excited to sleep. She lay on her back in the dark, reliving what Bobby had told her. How he'd persuaded Melvin to come and see her at the "Talk" and how he'd fallen instantly in love with her, confirming she wouldn't need to audition. She dreamt of her opening night, the standing ovation and then the speeches, plus there'd be TV interviews. 'Oh my God there's so much to do' she whispered to herself, wriggling her feet with excitement, 'I *must* have a new dress for the opening night party! And I *must* ring Suzy.' She eventually fell into a deep sleep dreaming of that Jamaican beach!

Linda hearing the crying tapped lightly on the bedroom door and walked in. In between sobs Suzy told her about the phone call from Melvin.

'He said I'd got the job, but because of my condition they couldn't use me after all, I asked what condition and he went on to say that I should get help.'

'What condition Suzy?'

'Don't look at me like that; I'm not up the spout if that's what you're thinking.'

'Well what the hell did he mean?'

'He said that he's found out about my drinking problem!'

'Drinking problem?'

'Yeah, I couldn't believe it.' She reached for another tissue and blew her nose for the umpteenth time.

'Did you deny it?'

'Of course I bloody did, but the more I did the worse it sounded. But that's not all, he then tells me...' Suzy started crying again; Linda sat on the bed and tried to calm her down.

'Tell you what?'

'That they'd found a new girl for the lead and who do you think it is?'

'Who?'

'Beth!'

It took Suzy the rest of the week to find out the truth. Angry that unfounded lies were being spread about her flatmate, Linda willingly phoned Melvin's office on the pretence of being Suzy's non-existent agent. Melvin's assistant confirmed very curtly that Mr Havies would certainly not be using Suzy Noden and added that he was indeed grateful to Mr Brant for bringing it to his attention. She also suggested that as Suzy's agent she had a responsibility to her client.

'Cheeky bitch' snapped Linda slamming the phone down. She slid down the wall and sat on the floor next to Suzy who was dejectedly staring into space. Almost to herself Suzy muttered. 'Oh, it doesn't surprise me one little bit, he always hated me,' swivelling round on her backside to face Linda, she looked puzzled and hurt.

'But do you know what really gets me? It must have been Beth who told him, and I can't believe she'd do that, not Beth surely?' Linda put her arm round her.

'Why don't you ask her? Honestly Suz, it's no good ignoring her, she rang again today, just talk to her. At least you'll know where you stand.'

'I don't ever want to speak to her again OK?'

'But…Suz'

'Look, she tells him I'm an alcoholic, knowing he's friends with Melvin and that's that, she's in!' She shook her head violently, not wanting to believe the obvious. 'He must have brainwashed her'

'Who'

'Flobby Bobby, he must have, because my Beth would never have done that willingly.'

'Oh, Suz, people change when they get married, their brains go soft, it's the regular sex.'

'Well I know for a fact she wasn't getting that, which is another thing that doesn't make sense. Ever since we were kids, blokes have committed murder to get in Beth's knickers, you've seen her, she's gorgeous, but the one bloke she marries who can get it any time he wants ain't interested, don't you find that strange?'

Linda laughed 'Suzy, Beth's sex life is the least of your problems at the moment, which reminds me, when are you seeing Mark again?'

Suzy flicked her hand nonchalantly in the air, 'Ooh I don't know, I said I'd ring him sometime, when I'd got over the flu and anyway I'm not ready for that love stuff.'

'Flu? What flu?'

'Well every time he rang I was bunged up from crying, so I just thought it would be easier to say I had the flu.'

'Maybe you should tell him, he might be able to help.'

'Would he cut Bobby's balls off for me? I don't think so.'

'Maybe he hasn't got any and that's why Beth's not getting her nooky.' It was the first time Linda had seen Suzy smile all week. 'Anyway Pam Devis is auditioning next week for that new club in Wakefield, why don't you go? It'll do you good to get out of London for a while.'

'Yeah, I know it's just that.... oh I don't know, I just wish...'

Linda didn't question what Suzy was wishing, instead she suggested a drink down the pub to take her mind off things.

'Only orange for you though, don't want you back at the AA do we?' She ran out of the front door with Suzy in hot pursuit.

Beth was getting fed up with leaving messages for Suzy to ring back and Linda was running out of excuses.

'For goodness sake sweetheart, will you come away from that phone, you've got more important things to think about than sulky Suzy.' In fact Bobby was terrified that if they did eventually talk, the truth might come out and that would spoil everything. There was only one way to make sure those two never spoke again.

'Darling come into the lounge, here have a drink I think you might need it.'

'Why whatever's wrong my sweet?' Beth followed him in, sat down and took a swig of her drink, 'come on Bobby what's happened, has Melvin changed his mind?'

'No, don't be silly my angel nothing like that, but I have got something to tell you which you're not going to like. Believe me my love it breaks my heart to say it, but I can't bear to see you hurting, she's just not worth it.'

'What am I not going to like? Who's hurt me? Who's not worth it? Come on Bobby what the bloody hell are you talking about?' Beth was frightened.

Bobby went to his wife, knelt at her feet and stroked her hand as he explained that the reason Suzy wouldn't ring back is because she's embarrassed.

'Embarrassed, about what?' Beth asked incredulously

'Hush my darling girl let me explain. Beth, she's jealous of you, always has been, but you were too loyal to see it.' Bobby could tell that Beth wasn't taken in by his lies; he knew stronger tactics were required.

'I know you don't want to believe it but to be honest that's why we didn't hit it off when she lived with us.'

Beth tried to defend her friend, but was shot down in flames by the next statement.

'Beth I promised Suzy I would never tell you, but I think it's time you knew the truth.' He continued before Beth had a chance to jump in.

'About two weeks after she moved in, while you were out shopping, she came to our bedroom and, well I'm embarrassed to even talk about it, but she sneaked into our bed while I was asleep.' He eyed Beth's reaction carefully before continuing.

She didn't move, just stared him and nodded for him to go on.

'Well my darling, I woke up to find someone fumbling under the covers and my whistle being gently blown, but of course I knew it wasn't you' he smiled knowingly into her dumbstruck eyes.

'I threw her out immediately of course and she begged me not to tell you. She said she was desperate to be in one of my shows, even offered to 'service' me if it would help, slightly tacky even for Suzy's standards I thought, but have no fear my love I refused all her advances with the promise it would go no further as long as she left me alone.'

The thought of Suzy or in fact any woman servicing him actually repulsed him, but he was proud of his little charade and was keen to share the ludicrous joke with Melvin, whom he'd arranged to meet at the usual place in precisely one hour. He had to get a move on if he wanted this little production to be put to bed before he left.

Beth didn't know what to think. She was stunned into a rare silence. *Suzy*, no, it wasn't true! It couldn't be true! Why was he lying? Bobby clearly nervous replenished their drinks and sat back down beside her.

'But Bobby she was still a virgin' informed Beth eyeing him suspiciously 'she turned down Tom Jones for Gods sake, are you saying she's suddenly turned into a nymphomaniac and with *you, my* husband? Oh come on Bobby I don't believe a word of it. She doesn't even know what a blow job is.' She jumped up from the sofa and stormed across the room, glaring at him accusingly, demanding an explanation.

Bobby was losing his patience; he didn't have time for childish loyalties.

'Oh grow up Beth' his voice becoming aggressive. 'Do you honestly believe all that rubbish? Who does she think she's kidding? Jesus even *I* would have jumped into bed with Tom Jones.'

'Don't be disgusting'

'Well don't be so naïve; he probably screwed her lights out and then dumped her because she got a bit trappy. Huh! I bet she wasn't even that good at it! Her pride was hurt, so she made *him* out to be the bastard. Come on Beth think about it. Would you or anyone you know turn down the chance of a night with Tom Jones?'

Beth had thought about it many times, privately. Suzy *was* a terrible flirt and at the time thought her story somehow too incredible. Could she really have been so ashamed of what she'd done that she invented that cock and bull story? She always did have a vivid imagination. Was this why she wasn't answering her calls? Maybe she realised that Bobby would tell his wife eventually and couldn't face her. Beth's mind was in turmoil.

She needed time to think, alone. She downed her drink and turned to Bobby.

'Go to your meeting Bobby, I need to clear my head' and dragging her hands through her hair despairingly she disappeared into the bedroom closing the door behind her.

Relieved to be let off the hook so easily, Bobby tucked Beth into bed, reassuring her that he loved her so much that he couldn't stand by and allow Suzy to hurt her anymore. He gently reminded her that all childhood things should be put away as her loyalties were now with him. He then escaped, confident in the knowledge that Beth still as gullible as when he first met her would in due course agree.

Beth hardly slept that night. She tossed and turned, trying to sort things out. They'd gone through so much together; she would never forget the fun and dramas, but Suzy was ambitious; would she *really* do *anything* to further her career? She was also insecure, had been ever since she'd known her and desperate to be loved, but was she so jealous of Beth finding happiness that she would jeopardise their lifelong friendship? Beth didn't get any answers before drifting into a fitful sleep.

Bobby woke her at 10.30 the following morning with a tray of tea and twelve red roses. He kissed her gently and suggested that after a steaming hot bath, which he'd prepared for her, they take a day off and drive to Brighton. He thought it would do them both good to spend time together and even promised he wouldn't get bored if she wanted to browse round the 'Lanes'. Bobby could always manipulate Beth, and Beth was feeling too fragile to realise it. She gratefully accepted all his proposals, keen to put yesterday's events out of her mind.

TWENTY-TWO

Suzy was pleased that Linda had nagged her into going for the Wakefield audition. She became more and more depressed as the week had gone on and Linda was becoming increasingly worried about her. Beth had stopped leaving messages, which in a way was a relief, so although reluctant, Suzy dragged herself along. But as the audition progressed and the hundreds of girls were slowly whittled down to the last twenty or so, Suzy suddenly realised that she really wanted the job.

As Pam asked her to step forward into the final line up of the ten successful girls Suzy burst into tears. Confused by all the emotion, the other girls looked away in embarrassment, but Pam immediately stepped up onto the stage, put her arm round her and took her aside. Suzy pulled herself together enough to explain that she was just so thrilled to be chosen.

'Well, my dear I'm flattered, I didn't realise I was so popular.' She said kindly.

Pam Devis had been in the business many years and her dancers were her family. She was their friend, their mum, and their confidante, but always their boss! She ran a tight ship with kindness and a sharp wit, which put paid to anyone who wasn't prepared to work.

There was an added bonus for Suzy too. Fred Peters, Pam's assistant choreographer from Glasgow was the only male dancer in the show and they got on like a house on fire. His wicked and crude sense of humour instantly appealed to her and they spent the next twelve weeks building up a friendship that was to last for the next twenty years.

The Wakefield Theatre Club was a new venture with no expense spared. Stars from America were invited to appear, with the Jazz Expo Show, the highlight of the season. Tony Bennett, Johnny Ray and many others were great crowd pullers and although impressed with the wealth of talent on the stage, Fred and Suzy's favourite entertainment was a competition as to who could pull the best looking man who dared walk in the club. Suzy would dance with a guy, flirt outrageously and report back to Fred whether there were any stirrings in the cellar. He of course would be watching for any sign of movement in the area. One night while Suzy was smooching with a particularly handsome victim, she signalled to Fred with a sneaky thumbs up that there was definite progress being made. But Fred seated at a table on the edge of the dance floor wasn't convinced the gorgeous hunk was enjoying all her lusting and sexy teasing, so while Suzy dreamily nestled into his broad chest, Fred took a chance and winked at him. The six-foot dreamboat responded instantly with a smile and winked back! By the end of the song Suzy, although finding her dance partner as dull as ditch water was confident she had him in the bag if she'd wanted him, which she didn't, but she was way behind Fred on points and needed this one to catch up. She thanked the brain dead body beautiful, kissed him politely on the cheek and strode back to join Fred at the table.

'Definitely an 'Arthur' she stated with confidence, I think you owe me a drink.

Fred gloating at having once again won the night's prize grinned.

'Oh I'm sorry hen, but I can assure you he's definitely a 'Martha', he was winking at *me!* Mine's a large scotch!'

And so it went on for the rest of the season, until the time came when they had to say goodbye. Fred was beginning to find the limited social scene frustrating and couldn't wait to get back to London. He understood Suzy's reluctance to return, having enjoyed many a drunken night after the show swapping tales of woe. So when she happily accepted Pam's offer to go to Coventry for eight weeks in the Cilla Black Show, he waved her off at the station with a final bet that it would be less than a week before she'd be phoning him out of boredom or with one of her major dramas.

It was a full nine days before the phone call came.

'Fred he's gorgeous, you'd love him.'

'I'm sure I would hen? Do you want me to come up there and see if he's up to it?'

'Oh, no problems there, he can't keep his hands off me.'

'Oh don't tell me you've finally let a man into those iron knickers?'

'Don't be disgusting'

'Well it's about time I suppose' agreed Fred. 'You owe it to Queen and country to go forth and fornicate.'

'Well as long as I keep my queen happy! You are happy for me aren't you?'

'Cheeky bitch! Go and get laid and when he gets bored with you, send him down to me. I'm free all day tomorrow.'

'No chance, I'm hanging on to this one and anyway I'm getting the hang of all that dirty business and I think with a few more rehearsals I might be quite good!'

'So what's the poor suckers' name?'

'Richard,' she said dreamily, 'but you can call him Dick.'

'Everyone's a dick to me hen! Byeeee.'

It took Suzy a full three weeks to realise that she was completely and absolutely head over heels in love with Richard. She would watch him from side stage every night as he and the other four guys in the act had the audience in stitches with their musical comedy. A couple of the other girls had worked with them before and tried to warn her off, telling her they were all ravers and it would end in tears. But Richard was different, he was attentive, often commenting on her appearance and wanting Suzy by his side at all times. She made him laugh and was a lively contrast to his quiet personality.

Four weeks later Richard and Suzy had their first row. She had been offered a TV series, which meant her going back to London as soon as the season finished, but Richard wasn't impressed.

He was sat in his dressing room, quietly strumming his guitar when she burst in and as she jumped up and down, flinging her arms about excitedly telling him all the details, he remained still, fixing her with a steely stare.

It was one of the features that had first attracted Suzy, not his steely stare, but his vivid blue eyes, contrasting wildly with his shoulder length black hair, bringing an Italian Romeo air about him. Many a night as he lay asleep beside her, she would gaze at him and visualise them on a gondolier floating through Venice, with Richard serenading her in the moonlight. His broad Norfolk accent would have shattered other less romantic souls, but not Suzy, for she could switch easily from a Venice canal to a haystack in the middle of a Norfolk field, as long as she was with Richard.

She finished telling him her good news and waited for his reaction. She so desperately wanted him to be proud of her.

He shrugged his shoulders, which was as emotional as Richard could get.

'So, that's it then!' he said 'we might as well say goodbye now.'

'Wha...what do you mean? I don't understand. I thought you'd be pleased for me.' Suzy was confused. How did this affect their relationship?

Richard carefully put his guitar down and pulled Suzy towards him.

'Darling I'm thrilled for you, but I'm in Blackpool with the boys this summer and if you're in London we'll never see each other.'

'Yes we will' panicked Suzy. 'I'll come up every weekend and you can come down to see me. It'll be fine. I'll ring you every night.'

'I'm sorry Suzy, but it won't work, you either want to be with me or you don't.'

Suzy pulled away and stared at Richard who hadn't moved from his chair. Tears were streaming down her cheeks. 'So what are you saying?'

'Well it's up to you' he said calmly 'if you want to go back and do your series, then that's your decision, but you could come to Blackpool with me, you'd easily get into a show there and we'd be together.'

Suzy couldn't believe what he was suggesting. 'So you're saying if I don't come to Blackpool it's all over?'

'Well it wouldn't work otherwise, but Suzy I'm not telling you what to do, it's up to you.'

'Well for Christ sake Richard, show some emotion, you sound like you don't give a shit what I do.'

Richard threw his hands up in the air and laughed.

'Of course I want you to come, but it's got to be your decision.'

Suzy shook her head defiantly, folded her arms and straightened her back.

'So you're saying if I don't give up my career, it's all over?'

Without answering, Richard shrugged his shoulders, picked up his guitar and continued strumming. 'But why should I give up my career? Why can't you give up yours?' She screamed, realising the whole idea was totally irrational, but he was after all giving her an ultimatum.

What he said next knocked her for six.

'Well I can't give up mine now can I? What would we live on when we're married?' He tilted his head to one side and grinned as Suzy froze into a rare silence, with a gormless look that made Richard burst out laughing.

'Well, what do you say?'

'Eh? Oh ... err...thank you...'

'No you idiot, what do you think about getting married?'

When it finally did sink in, Suzy rushed forward and jumped on him, knocking him backwards off the chair and landed on top of him. As he lay pinned to the floor she screamed in his ear.

'Marry you? Oooh! Yes, yes, *yeees!*' Then she smothered him with kisses until he couldn't breathe. 'Oh Richard I love you sooo much.'

As he struggled to sit up Suzy pushed him down again.

'Oh no you don't' she teased 'you're not going anywhere till you've asked me properly.' She sat astride him, pinning his arms above his head.

'Come on ask me' she insisted, grinning from ear to ear.

She was too happy to notice his irritation at being forced into saying something remotely romantic.

'Suzy, get off you're hurting me' and he struggled to free himself, trying not to show his impatience.

'Well say it then. Go on...Suzy.... my... darling...'

Not wanting to burst her bubble, he gave in and repeated through gritted teeth. 'Suzy... my... darling...'

'Yeah, yeah, go on' encouraged Suzy excitedly

Richard had nowhere to go, 'Will...you...marry...me?'

'What do you say?' She was pushing her luck now.

'Pleeeeese!'

Giggling she scratched her head, 'Oh, OK then!' and she attacked him again with more kisses. 'Oh Richard I'm so happy I could wet myself!'

That did it. Richard pushed her off and struggled to his feet, leaving Suzy spread-eagled on the floor, grinning at him feeling happier than she'd ever felt in her life.

She gave into Richard's demands and went to Blackpool for the summer, but found herself at a loose end at the end of the season when in October he went on tour.

Back in London Linda hadn't got a new flatmate, so was happy for Suzy to move back in, who seemed a different person to the sad girl she'd kicked out the door months earlier.

'Well you might as well pay me rent if you're going to keep me up all hours telling me about this new man of yours' she laughed helping Suzy carry her cases to her old room.

'Any news from Beth?' asked Suzy casually as they sat round the kitchen table catching up with all the gossip. She'd thought about her often while she'd been away, but time and falling in love with Richard had helped heal some of the wounds.

'No not a word since you left.'

'Oh, I just thought it would be nice if she could come to the wedding, but I expect Bobby's got her starring in some porn film,' she added bitterly.

TWENTY-THREE

It was three months into the show and Beth had a major decision to make. She had struggled to cope with the work, even though Bobby had driven her into the ground rehearsing her day after day as if his life depended on her success!

She knew she was out of her depth, and Melvin had shown his contempt on more than one occasion. So when her contract came up for renewal she was reluctant to sign.

Bobby was furious. He had taken control of their financial affairs and had squandered most of their earnings on his sordid other life. Melvin had long since gotten bored with the charade and had moved onto less demanding playmates, which left Bobby seeking his perverted expensive pleasures in tacky hotels in Kings Cross and Soho.

'You've got to sign Beth, we need the money.' He had his back to her as he poured himself a large scotch. She realised things had been tight since Bobby had lost the contract for a TV series and knew he was feeling sensitive about not being able to secure any other work, but she'd had enough of the barbed comments from the other dancers in the show. 'Oh Bobby please don't make me, they're so cruel to me, I can't take much more.' She whined, not daring to mention the vicious rumours that were flying round the theatre concerning her husband. Mostly that the only reason she got the part was because Bobby was screwing Melvin Havies. It was all getting too much for her and she wanted out! Bobby, aware that rumours were rife within the industry, realised that something drastic had to be done, and after all he couldn't hide those unpaid tax demands from Beth forever. Reassuring her that he would think of something and not to worry, he sent her to bed refilled his glass and spent the rest of the evening mulling over his future.

The next six months were frantic for Suzy. On Richards's insistence she was turning down any work that kept her away from him for too long, convincing everybody including herself that it was her decision. She was determined to be the perfect wife, even moving to Norfolk she saw as an adventure, even though when Richard had first told her of the move she'd had her reservations and Fred hadn't helped, throwing his arms up in shock horror when she told him of their plans over lunch one day.

'Oh hen, don't do it, you're too young to die! He'll have you in a floral apron up to your armpits baking bread and flower arranging for the church.'

'Why Fred you sound quite jealous, can't you just be happy for me? I love him and he loves me.'

'Christ you're such a romantic. You see it as all roses round the door, don't you? What about when he's away? You'll go out of your head stuck up there on your own, I give it three months!'

'I'll be fine' laughed Suzy determined not to let Fred spoil her dream. 'The cottage we're buying needs loads of work, so I'm gonna be too busy to get lonely.'

'So you're willing to give up everything here, career, friends, *everything* to be a *fucking builder* in some god forsaken derelict hole in the middle of nowhere. And look at you you're like a skeleton where have your tits gone?'

Suzy blushed, she knew she'd gone a bit too far with the diet and didn't need Fred rubbing it in.

'Well I was putting a bit of weight on and I don't want to look like Besse Bunter for the wedding do I?'

'You mean *Richard* thought you should lose some weight.' And by Suzy's defensive reaction knew he was right. Fred grasped her hand and squeezed it, only then noticing her near skeletal fingers. 'Suz I'm really worried about you, how dare he criticise you, you looked fabulous as you were.'

Suzy reached across the table and hugged him. 'He only wants me to look my best; I promise you I'll be fine. I'm gonna miss you like crazy, but you can come and visit anytime, it's not that far.' She sat back in her chair and grinned, willing Fred to be pleased for her.

'No thanks darling, wouldn't trust those sheep'

'You mean you don't trust yourself with the sheep!'

With still three months to go until the wedding and Richard away most of the time, Suzy was getting bored, so when she was offered a pantomime at the Palladium, she rang Richard to ask if he minded. He flatly refused, insisting that she spend her time preparing for the wedding. Even suggesting that she did some exercise, to prevent getting flabby. 'And for God sake do something with your hair, it's getting far too long. I want you at your best on our big day.'

Suzy was incensed and immediately rang Fred for reassurance. Fred went into a rage, after she'd finished telling him of Richards bullying, but realising he was only upsetting her all the more, gently persuaded her to take the contract, after all, Richard didn't own her, not yet anyway! Suzy felt stronger when she put the phone down, and with renewed courage, and before she had time to think about it, immediately rang the choreographer, accepting the job. Richard made inane threats over the phone when she told him of her decision, but eventually realised she was determined to undermine him. 'Make the most of it Suzy, because you won't be flying off to London when we're married.'

Suzy's tummy lurched at being reminded that very soon she would be leaving everything and everyone she loved behind, but readily agreed. Nothing was going to mar her dream of the perfect marriage in the perfect cottage with her perfect man. But first she had a show to do.

The Aladdin panto played to packed houses most nights, and Suzy as usual found the boy dancers' dressing room a lot more fun than the girls, who apart from the odd one or two she thought aloof and bitchy. Most of them had worked for Irvine Wells before and seemed to think that doing a pantomime was way beneath them.

Over the years Suzy often found this to be the case. The more successful and high profile the show she was working on, the less friendly and more ambitious the dancers seemed. She of course had always been ambitious, with shared dreams of her and Beth being discovered and whisked off to Hollywood, but having fun along the way was always high on their priority list. This was more prevalent now that she was about to embark on a new life with her darling Richard. She wanted to have fun with fond memories of her last show, before she became Mrs Richard Parker.

Most of her spare time was spent swapping dirty jokes with the boy dancers and listening to their sordid sometimes gruesome, but always dramatic love lives. They saw Suzy as one of the boys or one of the girls depending on their sexual preferences and she loved them.

One night when Suzy barged in their room complaining loudly about the atmosphere in her dressing room, they encouraged her to get it off her chest, insisting on all the details of who said what about who, and she happily obliged with accurate impressions of all the girls. As the call came over the tannoy for the finale, she went to dash out to get changed, when Vince called her back. 'I think you'd better listen to this darling' and he produced a tape recorder from under his dressing table. All the boys in the room fell about laughing, except Suzy who immediately realised what they'd done.

134

'You bastards, you've stitched me up. Oh my God what have I said?' The room suddenly went quiet as her voice boomed out from the machine. "...and Annie said that Louise's tits are so droopy she has to lift her skirt up to..." 'Oh, stop the bloody tape' she screamed, charging across the room, trying to snatch the machine from Vince who held it over his head, way out of her reach.

'OK, what do you want? I'll give you anything, you rotten bastards, just give me the tape.'

'Don't worry we won't play it back to them; it's our little secret. Isn't it lads?'

'Oh yes of course' they all agreed, grinning, but not all that convincingly.

'So, what do you want?' She eyed them suspiciously.

'Nothing, honestly, it was just a laugh. Here have the tape, it'll remind you of us when your swede bashing in Norfolk and anyway we think they're all bitches too, it's just that you're impressions are so funny, you're wasted just dancing, you should try comedy.'

'Oh shut up' protested Suzy embarrassed.

'No really' added Tim, one of the few straight dancers who Vince had once told her had a soft spot for her.

'Well that's no good to me is it?' she'd replied

'What?'

'Well it's no good to me if Tim's spot is soft!' And they had both laughed.

Suzy glanced round and smiled affectionately at the boys, flattered by their comments, she couldn't stay cross with them for long.

They had one more trick up their sleeve before she turned into a swede basher as Vince had so gently suggested.

In the finale, the dancers were positioned around stage, and as the curtain opened they'd welcome the stars of the show, who would run down the sweeping staircase to take their bow. Suzy's position was centre stage at the foot of the staircase, which meant she was constantly in the spotlight. Every night she would under dress, having her jeans and T-shirt on under her Chinese Coolly costume, ready to make a dash for the tube before all the crowds came out of the theatre, the Velcro on the costume making it easier for her quick change. This particular night the boys had a surprise for her. A split second before the curtain opened, four of them rushed at her, ripping off her costume and threw it onto side stage, before jumping back into their positions. Before she realised what was happening, the curtain had risen and there she was in full spotlight with rolled up jeans and bright blue T-shirt. She could do nothing but stand there, glares from some, quizzical looks from others and even the odd giggle as the principles made their descent.

She didn't even mind the telling off she got from the stage manager, for the memories she would take with her were worth all the embarrassment of that night.

TWENTY-FOUR

Beth peered nervously out of the plane as it made its descent into Pearson Airport, mesmerized by the metropolis below where her new life was about to start.

She'd spent the last eight hours trying to sort out her thoughts, but her mind had kept going round in circles. Reflecting on how a month earlier Bobby had suddenly announced that he needed to change his life, convincing her that a drastic move was necessary due to their financial problems. But it was his reputation for hard drinking and excessive sexual perversions along with growing rumours of heavy drug use that was the real problem. His lifestyle was becoming a liability and work had been drying up.

Everyone in England was shocked at their announcement of emigrating and Bobby's sudden departure with practically all their savings on the pretence of arranging suitable accommodation, leaving Beth to sort out the finalities in England, gave her parents cause for grave concern. But no amount of heart rendering chats with Joan and Peter could persuade her to change her mind, although confused by the urgency of his departure she was desperate to save their floundering marriage and felt she had no choice.

So here she was half way across the world, alone but excited at the thought of a new adventure. Suddenly she was brought to her senses by the sudden jolt of the plane landing.

'Thank you for flying with Air Canada, we hope you enjoy your stay in Toronto' enthused the ever-smiling airhostess. *"She's putting on a good show,"* thought Beth sadly.

Bobby didn't meet her at the airport, insisting that the sooner she stood on her own two feet, the sooner she would feel at home. Beth loyally agreed to the cruel demand, determined to make a go of her new life! She enjoyed the cab ride, noticing immediately the different attitude of the friendly driver proudly pointing out places of interest in his city compared to London cabbies. Beth was amazed at the cleanliness and gasped in awe at the towering skyscrapers. She felt like a child on a great adventure. Suddenly she thought of Suzy and how she would wet herself with excitement if she were here. But as they pulled up outside her new apartment she was brought back to reality.

Her excitement was soon diminished and her heart sank as Bobby greeted her with an indifferent peck on each cheek. He took her suitcases, handed her a glass of wine and showed her around. She was impressed with his choice of spacious apartments, overlooking High Park with a large bedroom, living room and galley kitchen. There was deep brown fitted carpet everywhere, which Bobby explained was the latest thing called Shag Pile.

'Oh Bobby surely not a mass orgy tonight I've only just arrived!' she was trying so hard to keep the atmosphere light and keen to know more ignored his impatient glare. 'Oh anything I should know about in case I put my foot in it?'

'Well the humour isn't the same and discussing any bodily functions is definitely out.' Was this a warning? She wondered, eyeing his obvious contempt.

'Bodily functions! Do you mean peeing or…'

'Beth!' Bobby shouted, 'I know it's strange but you'll get used to it.'

'Will I?' she asked cautiously 'or will they get used to me?'

The next month proved difficult for Beth, discovering only too soon that indeed things were very different. She decided to look for a job that she felt confident with until she got on her feet, and was soon signed up with two somewhat conservative modelling agencies that loved her London fashion sense nearly as much as her cute accent.

On the first day of a show she rushed into the changing room, stripping down to her pants and crossing the room she felt all eyes on her. Glancing round she saw that the other models were facing the wall to undress. Beth couldn't resist it. Humming the 'Stripper' she nonchalantly rolled her shoulders and swayed her hips, swinging her boobs to and fro! The other models carried on changing trying to ignore her. After the show Pamela took her aside. 'Beth we don't flaunt ourselves here and would prefer it if you were a little more discreet in future.' Beth was incensed.

'I noticed,' she snapped tersely, 'but you see back home we don't have a problem with prancing around naked, we love it, in fact we positively insist on it.' She added sarcastically.

Bobby's career wasn't faring too well either. Struggling to make his mark, his so called major change of lifestyle was in fact even by Canadian standards, a third rate half hour weekly variety show at a local TV station. Beth refused his offer to be one of his dancers, preferring the old fashion modelling assignments to prancing around dressed as Annie Oakley. But the biggest shock for Beth was the weather. Never in her life had she experienced such cold, with winter starting around mid October and temperatures reaching at least -18c by December. She began to feel homesick and the deeper the snow fell, the deeper her depression became. Bobby, far from caring for her welfare was desperate. His career seemed to be floundering by the minute and needed Beth to continue earning the bucks, but her confidence and enthusiasm was reaching an all time low and Bobby was losing patience. Reluctantly accepting she was still his social passport to respectability, he needed her on top, which meant finding a way of dealing with her negative mental state, which seemed to be rapidly descending into the pits of total melancholy. Needing to get a grip of the situation and taking advantage of the fact that he could still manipulate Beth, especially when she was at her most vulnerable, Bobby chose his moment carefully.

They were having a rare evening in together and although not actually communicating, they were at least in the same room and for once being civil towards each other. From his sofa at the far end of the living room Bobby casually took from his shirt pocket a pouch and expertly began to roll a joint, keeping a watchful eye on Beth who, curled up on the other sofa, was staring vacantly out of the window at the blanket of white sky, which was promising at least another three days of heavy snow. Bobby licked the paper, pinched the end and lit it, inhaling slowly and deliberately, welcoming the desired effect, which almost immediately began to swim around his head. As Beth leant up on her elbow to pour her third glass of wine she became aware of an unfamiliar smell wafting across the room. Of course she recognised it, but never before in her own home. She turned, glancing at Bobby with an incredulous air. He nervously acknowledged her with a casual nod and a smile, drawing on the joint yet again. He'd relied on pills and dope for most of his life, but up until now had kept his habit well away from Beth knowing her apparent disapproval. As he exhaled, enjoying the gradual feeling of well being, he tentatively offered it to Beth. But without the energy or inclination to argue Beth shook her head, poured her wine, fell back onto the sofa and closed her eyes, drifting into a lethargic doze.

'Come on Beth, why don't you try some? It'll make you feel better.' Bobby swung his legs round and sat on the edge of the sofa. Without opening her eyes Beth shook her head. 'I don't do drugs thank you.' She replied sharply.

'Oh sweetheart, this isn't real drugs, it's no more harmful than that wine you're slugging back.' He smiled gently at her as she sat up and sighed deeply. Bobby persisted. 'Beth darling, you know I wouldn't let you come to any harm; it'll just take all those dark feelings away and I can have my funny happy Beth back.' Tears began to well up in Beth's eyes; she was feeling so low and hated herself for it. Smiling through her tears she watched Bobby as he came and sat next to her, offering the joint once more.

'Just try one puff and if you hate it I promise I'll throw it away and we'll open another bottle of wine and get pissed. How about that?' He put his arm round her shoulders as if protecting her from the evils of the world. Beth laughed quietly and nodded, feeling safe in his arms, she would do anything to shake off this blanket of despair that gripped her every waking hour. Tentatively she put the joint to her lips, dragging on it slowly just as Bobby had shown her, sat back and closed her eyes, allowing the drug to gradually dull any nerves or misgivings she may have had.

They remained slumped on the sofa well into the night, sharing another joint and finishing the wine. Beth was feeling more relaxed than she had for years, welcoming the numbing effect, obliterating all anxious emotions that seemed to be spiralling out of control and had been ever since she'd arrived in Canada.

The following morning Beth had an early fashion shoot, but when the alarm blasted her out of the depths of unconsciousness she silenced the over enthusiastic voice blaring from the radio, promising yet another day of blizzards. She lay on her back savouring the last few precious moments of slow awakening in comparative silence, broken only by Bobby's light snoring as he lay next to her still in a deep sleep. Reluctantly accepting she couldn't delay the inevitable any longer, she dragged herself into the shower, allowing the warm torrent of water to wash over her aching limbs and thumping head. Bobby was awake when she finally emerged clean, but still not refreshed enough to muster up any energy to face the day ahead and he followed her into the kitchen, almost delighting in her obvious suffering as she lit her first cigarette of the day.

'Wow you look like you had a good night' he laughed eyeing the dark circles under her eyes. 'Don't worry I've got just the thing to perk you up' and he disappeared into the bedroom, returning a few seconds later shaking a small bottle of pills in the air. 'Here take one of these and you'll feel a million dollars.' He said smiling, and taking a single pill from the bottle he offered it to

141

Beth. Beth eyed it suspiciously. 'Bobby the last thing I need right now is to be spaced out, I've got an important photo shoot for a magazine this morning and my brain feels like bloody candy floss as it is.' Bobby ruthlessly persuaded her that the magic pill would help her get through the day, and may even make her feel better and Beth reluctantly relented, washing it down with a swig of tea. It wasn't long before the dreaded drug did its job, not only helping Beth face her long day with unexpected enthusiasm and energy, but as Bobby predicted she was soon completely hooked and begging for more. At last Bobby finally had her where he wanted her, trapped in his seedy world giving him the power to control everything she did, and Beth unwittingly had become completely dependant on him.

TWENTY-FIVE

After six months of unemployment and overspending, things were brought to a head with a final confrontation between Bobby and Beth, one that neither of them expected.

It was Bobby's birthday and Beth had twenty minutes before her hair appointment. She raced to the department store and quickly found a blue silk shirt she was sure Bobby would love, but a suitable card wasn't so easy. An overwhelming sadness came over her as she read the sentimental words of love on most of the cards. After returning five cards she opted for a blank one, but the heavy cloud stayed with her and deciding she couldn't face the hairdressers, she cancelled the appointment and made her way home. Chances were that Bobby wouldn't be there and the thought of some time to herself, soaking in a long hot bath was just what she needed. In fact as soon as she walked in the apartment she felt better. Throwing her coat on the kitchen chair and kicking her shoes off, she danced down the hall flinging the bedroom door open.

'OH MY GOD!' She screamed, staring at the bed. 'Bobby what the hell is going on? Who's that, what are you doing?' Beth steadied herself against the doorframe, unable to take in what was before her. All at once she felt numb, sick, confused.

'Beth… Oh shit… Beth!' Bobby jumped up from the bed and quickly covered his naked friend who it seemed found the situation amusing by the smile that crept slowly onto his face.

'Well darling, if this isn't a perfect scene for "What the wifey saw".'

'Oh shut up Randy' Bobby shouted making a desperate attempt to get dressed, while Beth trembling fled into the kitchen to find her cigarettes. Tripping over his trousers Bobby stumbled after her, frantically reaching for her. 'Beth, sweetheart, it's not...' but she pushed him away.

'Don't you dare touch me and for God's sake get that....that....*thing* out of my apartment...now*!*' She screamed.

Randy appeared fully dressed and composed. 'Sorry I can't stay, it seems I've overstayed my welcome anyway, but I got what I came for' and he slapped Bobby on the backside.

'Piss off Randy' fumed Bobby, opening the front door and glared at his friend to leave.'

'All righty bye now, nice meeting you Beth' Randy smirked as he left, blowing Bobby a kiss. Bobby slammed the door and slowly walked back into the kitchen where Beth stood in a daze.

She turned to face him. 'You bastard, how could you bring him here? In my home...how dare you!' She grabbed his birthday present and hurled it at his face, 'here have this, although it looks as though you've already had your present.'

Bobby rubbed his eye as the shirt hit its target and fell on the floor. 'Beth let me explain, it's not what you think.' He was panic stricken, he couldn't think clearly. 'Is there any wine left? I need a drink!'

Shaking her head Beth seethed 'I don't believe you Bobby. What's to explain? And what do you mean it's not what I think? Oh you mean it was an audition, he's some hotshot producer, Oh I see, how silly of me. You were just showing him an idea for a routine using a mattress!'

Pouring a large glass of wine, Bobby softened his voice. 'Beth, don't do this,' he pleaded, touching her arm, but she shook him off.

'So how long has this been going on?...No don't tell me....yes tell me, I have to know.' A lump came to her throat and the tears began to stream down her cheeks. She sank into a chair and Bobby seized the opportunity to take advantage of her emotional state. He knelt beside her and wiped her eyes. 'You mean the world to me Beth, you know that, but I'm so depressed not having any work and Randy has been a very good friend to me. Remember how close you were with that friend of yours in England?'

She suddenly sat up and looked wide-eyed. 'You mean Suzy?'

Bobby poured a second glass of wine; he was treading on dangerous ground.

'Yes Suzy, that's right, I'd forgotten her name. Well darling it's the same thing, you were very close and I'm sure you two must have thought about it at one time or another.'

Beth sprang to her feet; she couldn't believe her ears. 'What the hell are you talking about Bobby?' Her voice was loud and full of contempt. 'How dare you suggest that Suzy and I slept together, are you out of your mind?'

Frustrated Bobby retaliated. 'Oh for Gods sake Beth it doesn't matter to me if you did, I still love you.'

Beth's anger rose to a new level. He was not only patronizing her but he was insulting Suzy as well. 'You know you disgust me; you haven't even got the balls to tell me the truth. Christ I've been so stupid.' She began to pace the floor, puffing furiously on her cigarette. 'All this time I thought the late nights were business and not wanting to sleep with me was just my imagination. I wouldn't listen to gossip in England because I trusted you and believed everything you told me. I came out to Canada to be with you and start again. How *could* you do this to me?' She fell into a heap on a chair and collapsed over the kitchen table, covering her face with her hands.

'Beth, listen, please.' 'No *you* listen!' Beth jumped to her feet again, pointing a finger at him.

'It's bad enough coming home to find your husband in bed with another man, but to treat me like a child and tell me it's nothing, it's 'just what friends do' is sick...and don't you dare *ever* bring my friendship with Suzy into it, just because your idea of friendship includes screwing them, *mine is not!*' Suddenly feeling sick to her stomach, she couldn't bear to look at him and ran into the living room, threw herself onto the sofa and sobbed uncontrollably.

Bobby was on his third drink; frustration and irritation were setting in. He followed her into the lounge, and as he watched her racked body heaving on the sofa, was thankful she'd stopped the verbal onslaught for two minutes. Beth, aware that he was watching, looked up, her eyes dark with anger. She wasn't done with him yet.

'So, the famous Bobby Brant isn't all he's made out to be is he? What else haven't you told me?' She asked coldly now facing him.

'Oh, wouldn't you like to know?' He was playing for time, unsure of how to deal with Beth's sudden aggression.

'Yes, come on spit it out, let's get everything out into the open.'

Bobby frantically ran his hand through his hair. 'OK, you asked for it. Beth, you stupid cow,' he snarled in her face, 'I'm a rampant homosexual, always have been always will be.' He stood back, took a swig of wine, tossed his glass across the room, shattering it against the wall and laughed. 'There, my precious wife, what do you think of that?'

Beth squirmed at hearing the words. She closed her eyes, but the pain didn't go away. She found her voice and almost in a whisper asked. 'Then why did you marry me Bobby?'

'I'll tell you why you silly bitch. Because I needed a wife to drape on my arm, someone to take to functions, someone to show off. And believe me dear Beth you're the best! Quite outstanding in fact and I thank you for that.'

'You bastard!' She lunged at him and made to slap him, but he was too quick for her, catching her arm mid air, he gripped her tightly and threw her back onto the sofa, hovering threateningly over her.

'Tut tut, nasty temper you have my love and your timing has never been that good.' He continued the tirade of abuse as Beth could only sit there and listen.

'Only things didn't quite work out quite as planned. And here I am stuck in this God forsaken country with no work, no money and a wife, who I might add is lousy in the sack.' He burst out laughing, his eyes wild. 'You should see your face Beth. This is a rare moment! What no funny one liners?'

The words were spinning around in her head, she didn't want to hear any more, she wanted to run out of the apartment and keep running, but where? She was so far away from home. Bobby bent down and put his face into Beth's 'there's even more Beth, do you want to hear the rest?'

'NO!' She screamed pushing him away and covering her ears with her hands, 'I want you out of this apartment. If you're not gone by the time I get back tomorrow night, I'll have to make some phone calls and inform a few people that my darling husband is nothing but a dirty little queen and probably a cheap one at that.'

'Don't you threaten me you talent less whore! Where would you be without me?'

'Probably starring at the Talk of the Town actually;' she quipped indignantly.

'In your dreams sweetheart, you...'

'Oh piss off Bobby, go and stay with Randy, I assume he lives up to his name, that is if he can tolerate your pathetic love making.'

'You self-righteous bitch!'

Bobby stormed into the bedroom, phoned for a cab and started packing. Beth collapsed onto the sofa totally drained; she needed something to calm her down and fumbling in her purse found what she was looking for. The drugs had become a part of her life, ever since that evening when she'd tried that first joint and now she relied on them more and more. She popped two in her mouth and struggled to swallow without a drink, sat back, resting her head on the sofa and waited. The following fifteen minutes seemed never ending as she listened to him crashing about emptying drawers and filling suitcases. At last he appeared at the bedroom door, red faced.

'I'll be back tomorrow for the rest of my things. I can't say I'm sorry it's over because quite frankly, it's been hell!' He dragged his belongings across the room, opened the front door and called back 'by the way I'm sorry you wouldn't let me tell you more, especially about your friend Suzy!' The door slammed hard and Bobby left with a satisfied smile on his face. It took Beth a couple of minutes for the words to sink in, but when they did, she shot off the sofa and ran to the door; Bobby was already in the elevator. She ran to the window and waited. The cab pulled up as Bobby ran down the front steps and threw his two cases into the trunk.

'Bobby' she screamed 'Bobby.... wait, what did you mean about Suzy?'

From the back of the cab Bobby could faintly hear Beth's desperate shouting, he looked up, smiled and blew her a kiss and as the cab drove off.

TWENTY-SIX

It was a miracle that Beth managed to get through the fashion show the next day. She'd woken with puffy eyes, having spent most of the night crying after Bobby had left. Using tea bags and other modelling remedies she looked quite presentable, although her mental state was questionable and by the end of the show she was grateful to go home and hopefully be alone.

There was a sense of peace in the apartment and Beth exhausted was overwhelmed with mixed emotions. Locking the door behind her she put the bottle of wine she'd bought on the way home in the fridge, hung her coat in the empty closet and this time she went slowly down the hall to the bedroom, tentatively opened the door and immediately noticed that Bobby's clothes had gone. As she lay in the bath she felt strange but at the same time relieved, and slipping into her favourite pink piggy pyjamas she began to relax. Bobby had always hated them and for the first time that day Beth smiled at the irony of it. She forced herself a small salad and with her glass of wine she climbed into her clean bed, having thrown out the soiled linen the night before, and although fragile she felt ready to try and sort things out. Lazing back on the pillows she stared at the wall opposite, letting thoughts of the previous day replay in her mind. Slowly she began piecing it all together.

The worst of it all was realizing she had been used, all their plans they'd made had all been a lie and she'd believed everything he'd told her. How could she have been so naïve? She desperately tried to recall whether there had been any signs that maybe she'd missed, any slight indication that the man she'd loved so much and who she thought loved her had in fact apparently found her repulsive. There had been rumours back in England, but it was normal for show business people to appear theatrical, almost camp and she'd put it down to jealousy and refused to believe any of them. Remembering his words made her cringe and sliding deeper under the bedclothes she forced herself to focus on more positive things, her future.

'Well, it could have been worse; at least he didn't take my jewellery and make up!' She was talking to 'Potty' a scruffy rag doll with one eye and blonde plaits, that Suzy had found in a charity shop years earlier on one of her treasure hunts. It was her wedding gift to Beth.

'But why is it called 'Potty' Suz?' Beth had asked

'Because you *are* potty and I should have one strapped to me permanently with my bladder control!' They had laughed so much and Beth had promised that 'Potty' would always be well looked after. In fact 'Potty' lived on Beth's pillow, often a comfort, but always a constant reminder of happier times.

Beth held the doll close to her chest, 'Where are you Suz?' She whispered sadly. Suddenly, remembering the last thing that Bobby had said to her before he left made her sit up. Feeling the sweat on the back of her neck she tightened her grip on the doll.

'What did he mean…what about Suzy?' There were still too many unanswered questions. Her head was swimming, but exhaustion, the pills and the wine was beginning to take hold, so she turned out the light, lay her head on the pillow and closed her eyes. Clutching her ragged friend tightly she drifted into a deep sleep.

After spending her second night alone, Beth was far from rested. She'd tossed and turned most of the night, trying to retrieve some sanity in the madness of the previous two days, but all she could confirm was that Bobby was gone. She could hardly drag herself from the security of her bed, her head was throbbing and every limb ached. She staggered to the phone with every intention of calling in sick and cancelling the day, even cancelling her life, but she only got as far as dialling the first two numbers when she slammed the phone down. '*No* come on Beth, the show must go on!'

Getting through the next few months were difficult, with her moods swinging from calm and accepting to sometimes completely irrational at the slightest thing. Since her supply of drugs that Bobby had inadvertently left at the apartment in his rush to leave was almost gone, she was depending more and more on the pills the doctor had prescribed to get her through. Christmas came and she spent New Year with friends, not that Beth remembered much of the festivities, spending most of the holiday in a drug filled haze, popping green pills to help her sleep and white ones to get her through the long days. On returning to her flat she listened lethargically to her messages. But she jumped with alarm and her tummy churned at the sound of Bobby's voice booming out from the machine, informing her curtly that the divorce would soon be finalised. Hearing his voice brought all the turmoil of confused and angry emotions to the surface again, emotions that she'd spent months trying to dull with the help of pills and booze. But as she sipped at her first drink of the day a welcome feeling of relief overwhelmed her, with the realisation that the nightmare would soon be over and for the first time in months she welcomed the sanctuary of sleep with only one bottle of wine to aid her.

Over the following few days she could think of nothing else but her impending freedom and the thoughts that she would soon be free to begin a new life brought an energy to her very being, an excitement that also fed a restlessness in her soul. Friends who were beginning to despair as they tried desperately to help her come to terms with the cruel truth of her sham of a marriage, were surprised but delighted when out of the blue Beth invited them to her apartment for a party to celebrate her new found freedom. While the party was in full swing, Carol took Beth aside and told her she was moving back to Calgary to be closer to her family and suggested to Beth that she go with her. Beth, keen to kick start her life again was fascinated by Carol's description of her hometown and readily agreed. Over the next three months the two friends planned their new adventure and Beth's confidence grew as the date drew nearer for her leave behind a life she was keen to forget.

TWENTY-SEVEN

September came and with the trees losing their leaves, by the end of the month winter had arrived. Beth had withstood the Toronto weather, but since moving to Calgary three months earlier she was finding it a real challenge. The temperature would drop to −27 degrees, with winds blowing in across the Rocky Mountains. These temperatures weren't to be taken lightly and Beth learnt to dress and drive accordingly. A far cry from her dreams of lying on a sun drenched beach, she resembled an Eskimo, as she cautiously manoeuvred the dangerous icy roads, in a down filled jacket, fleece lined boots, thick scarf, mittens and ear muffs. She was on her way to meet the new love of her life, David.

Determined that her new life would be drug free, she'd booked herself into the rehabilitation clinic almost as soon as she stepped off the plane and it wasn't long before David her counsellor with his soft green eyes and gentle manner became her lover. At first she'd worried that things were going too fast. Was she ready for another relationship? All those hours in therapy had helped her clean up her act, but he now knew all her innermost secrets and Beth feared he'd use this information to manipulate her, as Bobby had done. David sensing her anxiety, had spent hours talking things through, helping her to trust him, and as their love grew so did Beth's confidence, along with the fun which for so long had been missing in her life. She enjoyed many a night being serenaded under her bedroom window, in three feet of snow and at last she felt there was someone in the world that shared her madness.

By the following spring, Beth had plenty to keep her restless nature occupied and for the first time she sensed a calmness with the changes in her life. Now free to marry David, she happily took the plunge and they had a small ceremony in her friend Jackie's garden.

During the reception Beth felt sick and made a quick exit to the bathroom, putting it down to excitement, too much food and champagne. But two days later, not feeling any better, she saw the doctor who promptly confirmed she was pregnant! Never having thought herself to be particularly maternal, she was surprised at the sheer joy she felt.

Beth's parents had flown out for the wedding, and by the end of their stay were so impressed with Canada and with the news of a grandchild on the way, surprised the newlyweds by telling them that they were seriously contemplating emigrating! Beth couldn't believe it. She missed them so much and had made many emotional phone calls over the years.

On their way back from the airport after saying goodbye, she sat quietly with David in their new apartment.

'Darling do you really think they'll come to live here?'

'I don't see why not, your dad was crazy about the place and your mum wants to be near the baby' he smiled rubbing Beth's tummy, 'do you have a problem with it?'

'No' she frowned 'no, I'd love it, I'm just surprised.'

'Well, I guess life's full of surprises.' He smiled at her. No one knew that better than Beth.

Nine months passed and Christmas gave Beth and David the best present they could hope for, a healthy son. Beth was overwhelmed and surprised at the joy she felt, but before David could suggest, or friends hint that she'd better hurry up and produce number two before the body ticked into the dreaded menopause, she stated firmly that nine months as a blubber whale and 18 hours of screaming agony was enough for her in this lifetime.

Just three weeks later Joan and Peter emigrated from England and moved in until they found jobs and an apartment.

'Beth I can't do the washing up without a bowl, I'll buy one today.'

'Mum I've told you, we don't use bowls, dishes are done in the sink' Beth sighed.

'How ridiculous.' Snapped Joan 'well I don't care how they do it here, I'll get one anyway.' Beth carried on folding the diapers and smiled as she thought how brave her parents were, in their mid forties, starting a new life, with nothing but a few clothes and a trunk of sentimental treasures. She had to hand it to them; it took some courage, even if they weren't ready to give up some of their English ways, not yet anyway.

That evening Joan proudly produced her shiny new bowl and Peter grinning with delight, struggled through the door laden with packages.

'Go on Pete, try them on, give us a fashion show,' encouraged Joan as Peter disappeared upstairs. As soon as he was out of earshot, Joan whispered, 'I don't know what's got into him. Wait till you see what he's bought, but whatever you do don't laugh.' Ten minutes later Peter slowly strutted down the stairs and posed proudly at the bottom, while his audience managed to stifle their giggles. John Wayne had always been his lifelong hero and as he stood in the red check shirt, jeans tucked into cowboy boots, minus the spurs and a Stetson hat that sat easily on his ears, causing them to stick out, everyone was speechless, until.

'Uh... dad...um... You look great.' David was the first to speak.

'Ooh, yes dad, I can't believe you're wearing jeans, but are you sure that buckles big enough?' Beth teased, as Peter hooked his thumbs under the huge leather belt.

'It sure is' Peter nodded with a Canadian drawl, 'yer know what they say…when in Rome!'

'What *does* he look like Beth? I can't go out with him like that' Joan said, hoping for a little more support from her daughter.

'Well you better just get used to it little lady, 'cos I'm wearing this on our first visit back to England.' John Wayne was indeed alive and well, and they all burst out laughing.

Two weeks later life returned to some sort of normality when Joan and Peter moved into their own apartment. Beth soon got her figure back and returned to part time modelling, but it wasn't long before she felt restless again and ready to move on.

Over the years Beth kept trying to fill the void with different jobs and friends would make fun each time she chose a new career, which on average would last a year. She reminded them that if she'd stayed in England she could've been a famous star. But for now she found renewed enthusiasm for her latest venture with Lindsey, a girlfriend who'd come up with the brilliant idea of house cleaning.

The idea was that after six months they'd become managers, while others did the cleaning, but as usual things didn't quite work out and the average workload of cleaning three homes a day, meant that by the end of the week, hysteria would set in, along with total exhaustion and cracked hands.

Friday was here at last and as they unloaded the equipment into the last house for the week, they tossed the coin as usual as to who got to do the upstairs, with the loser getting downstairs, which included the usual greasy kitchen. Lindsay lost the toss, so Beth headed up to the bathroom. 'Scruffy', Mrs. Johnson's pride and joy lay by the living room window, unperturbed by the now familiar intruders. At twelve years old he was on borrowed time for Shiatsu's, stone deaf and with arthritic back legs, he spent his retirement enjoying the quiet life.

On her hands and knees scrubbing the toilet, Beth suddenly thought of Suzy *"Oh Suz what has it come to? Well I'm performing a beautiful cleaning job on this toilet!"* and muttered 'this one's for you Suzy.' Suddenly…

'Oh My God BETH! Oh please, for God sake get down here!'

Beth dropped her brush and flew down the stairs.

Following Lindsey's moans into the living room, Beth tried to control her laughter at the sight of Lindsey kneeling on the floor, clutching the end of the vacuum, with a yelping Scruffy attached. Lindsey looked up at Beth.

'I've sucked the dog up! BETH! Don't laugh, Scruffy's tail is stuck in the vacuum' and Scruffy moaned in agreement. Beth knelt down and patted the snarling dog on the head.

'What's the nasty cleaning lady done to you Scruffy? Don't worry we'll have you out of here soon.'

'Oh very funny… what the bloody hell are we going to do?' Lindsey desperately pleaded.

Beth rummaged in the kitchen drawer and approached the accident scene wielding a pair of kitchen scissors. 'I think a little surgery is in order'.

'What are you gonna do with those?'

'I'm going to punish you for being such a cruel cow vacuuming up animals, especially when they're still alive, it's not part of our service.'

'Get off the God damn stage Beth and be serious, you're not gonna cut him out are you?'

'We have no bleeding choice, now keep still' and Beth began to separate the dog from the vacuum. Scruffy whined, while Lindsey moaned, as large chunks of hair billowed into the air and landed on the carpet. Once freed, Scruffy shuffled off to a corner and lay down, licking his once beautiful fluffy tail.

'He looks like he's been through a shredder, what will Mrs. Johnson say when she sees that?' Lindsey said still slumped on the floor in disbelief.

'Hopefully she'll think he's got a touch of creeping Alopecia! You do you realize he'll be dysfunctional for the rest of his life with nothing to look forward to but years of therapy?' Lindsey glared at Beth as she brushed of the remaining hair from her sweater, stood up and stomped into the kitchen. Beth wasn't going to let this little tantrum stop her.

Don't forget you knocked the head off Mrs. Boldings Royal Dalton figurine and put it back on with the gum you were chewing at the time.'

'Forgot about that, she never hired us again did she?'

Lindsey scooped up the hair, hid the evidence in the garbage and made a coffee. They went outside for a cigarette and made a pledge never to tell anyone of their mishaps.

Later that evening while Beth was soaking in the bath, she reflected on the day and smiled. It reminded her of years ago with Suzy, although Lindsey didn't always understand Beth's humour, it had reminded her of the past when laughing and being childish was easy and felt so good.

TWENTY-EIGHT

At last the day had arrived that Suzy had been waiting for and in precisely two hours she would be walking down the aisle to start her new life with Richard, a new adventure in the depths of Norfolk and she was beside herself with excitement. It was early October and the blazing hot sun was helping to make this the most perfect day of her life. All her friends would be there, except of course for Beth whom Suzy so desperately missed. To be here sharing her special day would have made her happiness complete, but no amount of searching over the years had led to her getting any nearer to her friend's whereabouts. She seemed to have just disappeared. Even the new occupants at Beth's parents flat had no forwarding address, so Suzy had to finally give up on her search, reluctantly admitting that Beth was obviously getting on with her life. And here she was doing exactly the same.

She glowed in her Grecian low cut wedding gown, showing just a little too much cleavage for the vicars' taste, who felt compelled to suggest she wear a shawl to cover up. Sam and Barbara were happy to be rid of their daughter, although Sam kept asking Richard when he was going to get a real job, but at least they agreed to come to the wedding, even though Sam slipped off half way through the ceremony to watch a race at the betting shop. Barbara made the most of the free bar by getting so drunk she dominated the evening by insisting the band play for her while she performed a medley of Shirley Bassey and Judy Garland songs. She had always been a frustrated performer and wanted to show that Suzy wasn't the only talent in the family.

With the honeymoon over, Suzy settled into country life with ease. As with most people who live in crowded cities, living in the country was only ever a dream, but for Suzy it had come true. Richard was away most of the time performing, which suited Suzy, who'd always enjoyed her own company, it gave her a chance to catch up with her own thoughts and dreams, for when Richard was home her time was revolved round him. She made few friends as the village had just the one shop and pub.

'You sound like fucking Miss Marple' laughed Fred, during one of their regular catch up phone calls. 'What the hell do you do all day? I bet those sheep are busy!'

'Oh Fred, don't be so disgusting.' She scolded, pretending to be shocked. 'I love it here and you should see what I've done to the cottage, you'd be proud of me.'

'I'd be more proud of you if you got your arse back here and did what you're good at, getting those legs in the air....'

'Oh but I am, well when Richards home I am and I'm getting better at it!'

'You know what I mean, I'm doing a show in September and I need a partner, you'd be perfect.'

Suzy's heart leapt and then sank, 'Oh Fred don't, please, you know I can't, Richard wouldn't hear of it.' Then suddenly realising she'd opened the floodgates for more of Fred's character assassination of Richard she quickly changed the subject.

'Richard's got a TV show coming up soon, well not just him, you know the group has.' She bumbled nervously trying to sound positive.

'Well maybe then he'll become famous enough to buy you a car, so that you can get out of that hell hole.' Fred felt strongly about her leaving the business. He'd always had faith in her talent, the few comedy sketches he'd seen her do had confirmed to him she had a great future and wished she believed in herself as much as she believed in that bloody Richard.

Suzy put the phone down and felt a twinge of sadness. Fred would never understand how important it was for her to be part of a family. She had spent a long time alone, since her early childhood in fact, with parents who hadn't shown her love or attention. That was until she met Beth, whose family had treated her as one of their own. Now she had a chance to start again, to belong, to feel needed and loved and yes she would even give up her love of dancing for that.

Richard was busier than ever with the act since their appearance on the popular game show, which left Suzy on her own a lot more than she'd expected, but success brought a change of lifestyle that they both enjoyed.

Suzy found that her interest and flair for interior design increased as they afforded to have the tiny two-up, two-down semi extended into a four bedroom detached house. Suzy was in her element, surprising Richard every time he came home with yet another room transformed, working way into the night and spending every waking hour building their dream home. Not being allowed a bank account of her own, she would spend the housekeeping money that Richard had left her on paint and fabrics rather than food, after all she didn't want to get fat and Richard not love her anymore. She was thrilled at Christmas as she opened her presents, for along with the bottle of perfume was a screwdriver kit, hammer and DIY manual.

'Oh darling thank you, it's everything I put on my list.'

Richard was useless at DIY and was grateful that Suzy enjoyed it so much, besides it kept her busy while he was away.

As Richard sat at his desk, on one of his rare nights off, Suzy thought how drained he looked. 'Why don't I deal with the bills? I could do it while you're away and it'll give me something to do,' she offered, sneaking a kiss on the back of his neck. He swung round to face her and grabbing her round the waist he nuzzled into her breasts. Suzy tingled at his warm body holding her tight.

'Oh don't you worry about boring things like bills, you know you're useless with money, just concentrate on getting the house finished. Why don't you treat yourself to a haircut, it's looking a bit of a mess, ask them to thin it out, give it a bit more shape.' Suzy smiled, she was relieved, about the bills anyway, he was right, she didn't have a head for figures, but her stomach turned at the comment about her hair. It was one of the few attributes she was confident about.

People had often told her how lucky she was to have such thick hair and envied the fact that it was naturally blonde too. Suzy had worn it short from time to time when she was younger, but as she'd got older preferred wearing it long. She could hide behind it if needed and if not, she enjoyed the attention it brought. But Richard didn't like it; he wanted her to change it. She would make an appointment first thing in the morning.

It was about two years later and the act was going from strength to strength, with a succession of TV shows and Richard had agreed to let Suzy go with him to the studios in London for the latest recording.

'I wonder if Michael Walsh will be there today?' she said excitely as the security guard waved them through the gates of the television studios. Glancing up at the building that had been such an important part of her life, her heart raced as the memories came flooding back. But of course her life had changed so much in the past nine years since she had last skipped arm in arm with Beth out of those gates, probably cheeking the guard on the way.

'Of course he is, he's producing this week's show, but listen Suzy don't go pestering him OK?' Richard warned her.

Suzy swung round to face him, wide eyed. 'I don't believe it!' she shouted 'why the hell didn't you tell me?'

Richard got out of the car and impatiently slammed the door. 'Oh for God's sake Suzy don't start, I've got more important things to think about. Don't forget you're here as my guest, so just behave yourself.'

'*Behave myself!* Bloody cheek, what do you think I'm gonna do, flash my bum on camera... Hmmm, not a bad idea actually' she sniggered.

'*Suzy...*'

'Well honestly Richard, sometimes I think you're ashamed of me. Christ I feel you're doing me a big favour bringing me today' and she stormed off towards the revolving doors and into reception. But as they stood in the lift taking them to the dressing room, Suzy's anger soon disappeared. Nothing was going to spoil the day; she was going to enjoy every minute, reliving memories of all the fun times and hopefully meeting up with old friends. Suddenly she remembered Michael and rounding on Richard she asked eagerly, 'I wonder if he'll remember me, did you mention me at rehearsals last week?'

Richard was beginning to regret bringing Suzy; he could see she was going to be a nuisance. They were doing a new routine for the show and he needed to concentrate, she obviously didn't understand the stress he was under and decided there and then he wouldn't bring her again.

'Who Suzy, who are you talking about now?' he snapped

'Michael of course,' she smiled, ignoring his intolerance.

'No, why should I mention you? He won't remember you anyway.'

'Of *course* he will...'

'Suzy, however many dancers do you think he's worked with over the years, why should he remember you?'

'Because...' she smiled confidently 'Beth and I got into so much trouble and we always thought he was up for a threesome.' She raised her eyebrows and grinned, expecting him to return with an equally knowing smile. But he wasn't amused. Taking her roughly by the shoulders, he looked her straight in the eye.

'Suzy, you're going to stay out of the way today, this show is important and I doubt if Michael would want to be reminded of two silly little girls who obviously drove him up the wall, besides it won't do the acts reputation any good if we're associated with dancers who were, to put it bluntly a pain in the arse.'

'Ouch, let go Richard, you're hurting me.'

The lift jolted to halt and as soon as the doors opened, Richard pushed Suzy back against the lift wall and marched off ahead to the dressing room, leaving Suzy stunned and close to tears. The doors were about to close on her when she came to and jumped out. She slowly followed Richard, smiled politely at Keith and Barry who were discussing last minute changes and sulked into a chair.

Half an hour later they were called onto the studio floor, with Suzy trailing behind, determined not to miss anything. She made her way quietly to the back of the stalls and found a seat in an empty row.

After two tech runs, the boys were asked to wait as the producer wanted a word with them.

Suzy couldn't believe her eyes as Michael Walsh appeared in the studio. She sat up and leaned forward on the seat in front as if trying to get a better view. She smiled as she studied the man, who had been so prevalent in those carefree days, when Beth and she had enjoyed such notoriety.

"Hmm, put a bit of weight on I see" she thought *"and where's all the hair gone?"* Suzy giggled as Michael's practically bald head shone in the strong lights.

'Oh Beth, where are you? You should be here with me' she whispered. Suddenly her attention was brought back to the studio floor where Michael was staring straight at her.

'*Suzy Noden!*' he bellowed, 'I don't believe it. Come up here, it's not like you to hide in the dark!' Suzy instinctively jumped to her feet, and for a split second she was taken back to the day he roared angrily at her and Beth for being in that precise place. Soon realising she wasn't in trouble, she half ran to him and they hugged like old friends. Richard looked on, not completely confident that Suzy wasn't going to embarrass him with one of her clever remarks. Michael finally released his grip and held her at arms length, grinning affectionately and looking her up and down. 'Well, well, well, look at you, all grown up and married I hear.' He turned to Richard and without letting go of her he said 'do you know these two drove me to drink!' Richard smiled politely, not wanting to encourage this little reunion, just a polite hello would have been sufficient for him, after all they had a show to do and Suzy shouldn't even be here.

'So tell me' Michael continued 'where is she? Not far away I bet!' and he whipped his head round the studio frantically searching for Beth as if expecting her to suddenly jump out from behind a camera. Suzy lowered her eyes, unsure of what to say, 'she's…um…er….' she stuttered, but Michael interrupted 'listen, let me finish here and I'll meet you in the bar, we've got a lot to catch up on' and turning to Richard he said 'you don't mind us catching up with the old days do you? You're welcome to join us.' With a set jaw, Richard smiled and shook his head, 'no of course I don't mind,' and turning to Suzy added sarcastically 'I assume you know where the bar is?'

It wasn't long before Michael and Richard joined her in the bar and as soon as they'd got their drinks and settled down, Michael was keen to hear all Suzy's news.

'So where is she then?' but didn't wait for an answer 'joined at the hip they were' he said turning to Richard and added 'you must be quite a guy!' They were a pain in the arse for years, didn't take anything seriously' and leaning closer he whispered 'a right couple of prick teasers you know?' Richard gave an embarrassed smile and tried to change the subject.

'Er…Michael, do you think we need the lighting up on that last number…'

Michael smiled politely 'no it seemed fine to me, but I'll have another look when we go back…now come on young lady, tell me all, is Beth married as well?'

165

'Ooh yeah, she's been married for years,' then she had a brainwave, 'actually you might know him…Bobby Brant!' She searched his face for any kind of recognition. She didn't want to admit that she'd fallen out with Beth or that they'd not spoken for years, but if there was a chance that he or someone in the studio knew where they were, then maybe…just maybe…

Michael stared at Suzy with a startled look.

'What Michael…what is it?'

'Are you saying Beth married Bobby Brant?'

'Yeah why, do you know him?' Those old familiar tummy butterflies were having a party again.

'Know him? Oh yes I know him all right, a right little shit. He screwed a lot of people in the business and I don't mean just out of money.'

Michael stared into the distance as if trying to recall………. 'And Beth married him did she? Well I'd have thought she could have done better for herself. Oh no offence Suzy' and gave her arm a quick squeeze.

'Don't worry I hated him too, but Beth was besotted with him, promised he'd make her a star' she scoffed, not even trying to hide her contempt.

'But didn't he have to get out of the country?' Continued Michael, 'financial trouble I'd heard.'

Suzy's heart jumped at this vital piece of information.

'Abroad, are you sure?'

Michael looked confused 'what do you mean, you didn't know? I can't believe it' he said whipping his head round to Richard, who was feeling decidedly like a spare part in this cosy stroll down memory lane.

'Do you know Richard, I was expecting great things from these two, they were so talented' he eyed Suzy and grinned 'and I have to admit there was a time I would have…'

Suzy recognised that grin even after all these years, *"Bloody hell, so we were right, you did fancy a threesome."* She wanted to laugh, but by the stony look on Richards face, thought better of it.

'Michael, I don't suppose you know where they are now?' she asked, trying to get the subject back to Beth's whereabouts, 'you see Bobby and I didn't get on, and we lost touch.' She kept her voice calm even though she wanted to jump up and down screaming, 'BLOODY TELL ME WHERE SHE IS, YOU BALD HEADED GIT!'

'Ooh sorry no idea; I wouldn't have thought he'd have advertised where he was, too many people after his guts. Poor Beth, mind you she could always handle herself, that one.'

Richard had had enough. The whole day was turning into the 'Beth and Suzy Appreciation Society' and he was getting sick and tired of hearing how bloody wonderful they were. Of course he'd never met Beth, but he sure has hell felt like he had, quite tasty by all accounts, but this was supposed to be a business lunch and Suzy, once again was centre of attention.

'Excuse me; sorry to break up this happy reunion, but I'd like to talk about those changes we mentioned before lunch.' He glared at Suzy to make herself scarce and she understood immediately, recognising all the familiar impatience and excused herself.

'Yes of course' agreed Michael 'we'll chat again later huh Suzy?' and he pecked her on the cheek adding 'it's so good to see you again.'

TWENTY-NINE

The silence in the car on the way back to Norfolk suited Suzy. The show had gone well, but Richard had been decidedly frosty with her since lunch. He'd seemed almost jealous of her friendship with Michael, with snide remarks and put-downs during the rest of the day, so she stayed well out of the way, even during the recording she refused Michaels offer of watching from the VIP lounge sensing Richards's disapproval.

She watched his face as he drove north out of London, he was tense and obviously not in the mood for a chat, so she played safe by reclining her seat as if intending to sleep. Closing her eyes she smiled as she remembered how Michael had seemed genuinely pleased to see her. But it was what he'd told her about Beth that took up most of her thoughts.

So she had gone abroad, but where? Even with all the information that she'd been given by different people she'd spoken to around the studio, that had either known Bobby or had known somebody who'd known him, it still didn't make sense. Surely someone must have heard where they'd gone! But it was generally the same reaction from everybody, that Bobby was indeed a total bastard and most of them had a good idea of where they'd like him to go, and gave her detailed descriptions of what they'd like to do to him if they found him. But Suzy wasn't interested in which part of his anatomy they wanted to stuff, anyway they were too late, it was probably full, as she'd spent years imagining the lorry loads she'd like to ram up there.

If not the actual country, but a rough guide to say within five thousand miles would have helped. But nothing came to fruition and the initial pleasure of seeing Michael again was drowned by the disappointing feeling in the pit of her stomach, a feeling that was to repeat itself again and again over the next few years.

She must have dozed off because the next thing she knew was Richard shaking her roughly.

'Suzy come on wake up, we're home, have we got any food in, I'm starving?'

She tried to stretch in the confined space of the mini and glanced blearily at her watch.

'Oh darling it's three thirty in the morning,' she yawned, forgetting the threatening argument.

'I can't help that, I've been working all day while you've been having a good time with your friends' and he stormed off in a huff.

Richard had the next few days off and seemed more relaxed being back at the cottage. His mood lightened and he made the most of the warm summer evenings playing golf at the local course. But Suzy had felt restless since her day at the studio. She realised how much she missed London and her friends and she was becoming irritable. When she suggested to Richard that she got a job locally he pointed out to her that with no qualifications she stood little chance.

'But I could do waitressing or something like that; you don't have to be Einstein surely to serve food.'

'What do you want to get a job for anyway? You've got everything you need.'

'Oh I know and I appreciate everything, it's just that I want to earn my own money and be independent.'

'But you only have to ask,' he replied shortly.

'But I don't want to have to keep asking you every time I want some ciggys or chocolate. Besides you keep complaining about the phone bill, and as you say it's mostly me phoning friends in London, so I if get a job I can pay the phone bill. See, makes sense don't it?' She said cheering up at her unintentional logic.

Richard was losing his patience, 'well it's time you packed up smoking anyway, and then maybe the money I give you would last longer.'

'Oh don't keep on about my smoking, it's the only thing…oh there's the phone' and she ran into the hall to answer and lit a cigarette. 'Hello! Oh hi Lorna…'

Richard went back to watching the cricket, knowing that Suzy's ambition to be in the catering trade would soon be forgotten, she'd never cope, she hates cheese, doesn't know her camembert from her cheese spread and her maths is atrocious. He laughed to himself as he visualised Suzy adding up the diners' bill on her fingers. But it wasn't long before his peaceful afternoon was interrupted again as Suzy burst back into the room and stood directly in front of the TV blocking his view.

'Guess what?' she screeched excitedly, 'I'm not going to be a waitress…'

'Oh good now do you mind if I watch the cricket…'

'No no, I mean I've just been offered another job, that was Lorna, you remember Lorna Reynolds? A brilliant dancer, anyway she says Paddy Stone is short of a dancer for a Norman Wisdom Special.' She didn't think it wise to add that there may be a series afterwards; she'd worry about that at a later date. First she had to get him to agree to this.

Without taking his eyes off the TV, Richard made his feelings very clear and said icily. 'I thought you'd got over all this nonsense. Why can't you just be happy looking after me?'

Suzy jumped on his lap and flung her arms round his neck, 'Oh darling it's only for a week, besides you're away till next weekend and I'll be back before you, keeping the bed warm for when you get home.'

At last she had his full attention. 'What do you mean next weekend, when do they want you?'

'Tomorrow' she said excitedly 'a girl's let him down at the last minute and Lorna thought of me, isn't that great? I can't believe it, Paddy Stone is the best there is. Lorna says he's a hard taskmaster, but she's worked for him for years and reckons he's a pussycat underneath. Oh Richard I'm so excited.'

'Well it looks like you've already made your mind up' he said watching her jump up and dance round the room. 'Where will you stay?'

'Lorna's, she's got a spare room.'

'Oh I see, so it's all settled then?' he added bitterly. 'Well you'd better find out the train times, because you're not taking the car.' Suzy didn't need the car; she would have flown there on gossamer wings.

She planted a kiss on his cheek 'Oh thank you Richard, you wait you'll be so proud of me' and she raced upstairs to pack a bag.

The following week was the worst week of Suzy's life. Lorna was right, Paddy was a hard taskmaster, but she hadn't mentioned he used verbal abuse and fear to get the best out of his dancers. That evening after the first day of rehearsals Suzy threatened to go home, but Lorna reassured her that he did like her.

'But he totally ignored me.'

'Well that's a sign that he likes you, he only picks on the ones he doesn't like.'

Not totally convinced Suzy agreed to see the week out, if only not to let Lorna down, but an incident on the third day nearly changed her mind again.

Neil Diamond was the guest star and the dancers backed him as he sang his hit number "Rock Me Gently". This routine involved twelve rocking chairs placed around the floor, with the dancers expected to jump onto them, and with one foot on the seat and the other on the back of the chair, rock gently to the music. This was a task in itself, as the chairs had a life of their own on the slippery floor. After thirty two bars they had to push on the back of the chair with their foot, causing it to tip backwards and the girls were to jump over the top landing in given positions. This took a great deal of rehearsing and a lot of shouting from Paddy.

Suzy like many of the other girls were nervous each time they failed to clear the chair, with Paddy ranting and raving at the idiots he had to work with. She had managed to keep a low profile up to that point, but determined to make the jump; she pushed the chair a little too hard, went flying over the top, landing on her head and fell unconscious. As she came round she was aware of a crowd round her and a lot of noise, which caused a ringing sound in her head. The next thing she knew was cold water being thrown on her face and Paddy's voice screaming at her.

'Get up off that fucking floor and get back on the chair, we've got a show to do!' Lorna and Ali helped Suzy nervously struggle to her feet and quietly warned her not to get upset. 'He'll bury you if he sees you crying.' So Suzy swallowed hard and wiped the threatening tears away, but the headache was unbearable. She went back to the chair and shakily stepped on it ready for the rehearsal to continue.

The end of the week couldn't come soon enough. Suzy hated every minute of it, but had to admit when she saw the routines being played back on the monitor, that she was proud to have been a part of it, they looked amazing and even more proud to have survived the week, even though Paddy never spoke another word to her after her accident. So she had the biggest shock of her life when two weeks later she got a phone call from Lorna asking her if she'd be interested in doing the series for Paddy

'I don't believe it' Suzy said 'I thought he hated me'

'No, I told you he didn't; in fact he told me how much he admired you for not making a fuss when you fell off the chair, so do you want to do it? Come on Suz, it'll look great on your CV, dancers would die to work for Paddy.'

'You mean dancers *will* die when they work for him. No sorry Lorna, do you know, I never laughed once all that week? But thanks anyway.'

THIRTY

Babies seemed to occupy most of Suzy's thoughts over the next couple of years, with most of her friends on their second or third.

Richard had agreed that it was time for her to come off the pill some eighteen months earlier, but with work taking him away most of the time it seemed she would never get a chance of being a mum.

She tried to occupy herself by taking on bigger and more skilled tasks around the house. Having a keen eye for a bargain, she loved going to auctions, and spent hours stripping off the old chipped paintwork only to reveal a beautiful piece of pine furniture.

Richard had prodded her tummy, moaning about her weight gain, but no amount of dieting had made any difference, so she made an appointment with the doctor, imagining all sorts of nasty diseases or maybe a blockage. But it was the best blockage she could have imagined and drove the four-mile journey back from the surgery in a dream.

Pregnancy suited her and she blossomed, along with enormous boobs that she'd only ever dreamt of. Richard liked them too.

'This is more like it,' he commented, eyeing her impressive cleavage one day as they lay in the garden enjoying the sunshine. Suzy was proud of her growing bump and wore a bikini whenever she could.

'Do you know Suz, you lost so much weight just before we got married I was going to sue you under the trades description act!' He laughed.

'But if you remember Richard you *told* me to lose weight' She would never forget his words. 'Don't want to get flabby, just because you got me hooked', she shuddered at the memory.

'Well we don't want you letting yourself go, do we fatty?' He added, smacking her thigh hard enough to leave a red handprint. Suzy didn't want to continue the conversation. Aware that her hormones were playing havoc, she thought it best to ignore it and enjoy her little footballer practicing his skills inside her.

'I suppose a fuck's out of the question?' she whispered to Richard as they wheeled her into the operating room for an emergency caesarean. Of course Richard was terribly embarrassed, but had to laugh along with the nurses, who explained it was the effects of the gas and air.

Ben was born at the respectable time of 6.18pm. He was Suzy's little miracle and she fell instantly in love with him.

Ten days later Richard drove his new family home and for the next two years noticed a complete change in Suzy, who had never seemed more content. He was spending more and more time away from home, either working or catching up with friends down the pub, leaving Suzy time to focus on being the perfect mother.

When Ben was old enough for playschool, Suzy and Richard agreed to try for another baby, but a year later with still no luck Suzy became restless.

She read in the 'Stage' about auditions for the summer season at Cromer, which was only five miles from her village. She laughed at the memory of Michael Walsh, all those years ago threatening Beth and Suzy that Cromer would be the only place they'd get a job, as if it were the last place on earth anybody would want to work, and here she was phoning the director, excited at the prospect of appearing there.

Once Dick Condon had read her CV he was more than happy for her to join the cast without having to audition.

Richard was furious that she'd gone behind his back, but as she pointed out, he had been away for three weeks and if he'd rung her a little more regularly than once a week she would have been able to discuss it with him.

'Anyway the doctor suggested I find something to take my mind off babies and then maybe it'll happen.' She said determinedly.

The Cromer Pier became Suzy's second home. It was the perfect job for her, doing what she loved most and still able to spend all day with Ben, only leaving him during the evenings with a regular babysitter while at the show.

The short walk to the end of the pier where the theatre stood, defiant in the face of the cruel North Sea, usually meant battling against the harsh Norfolk winds, even in the height of summer. But once inside, the warmth of the old time music hall atmosphere was that of an era long gone. The unsettling groan of creaky floorboards as the waves crashed underfoot only added to the ambience of being part of real theatre, if somewhat dangerous at times during the occasional storm.

The rest of the cast were friendly and it was refreshing for Suzy to be working with people who weren't burdened with the huge egos that had been so abundant in London.

She became firm friends with the other three dancers and it wasn't long before the old Suzy surfaced with pranks and generally having a great time.

One of her less than hilarious pranks was to wedge a kipper behind the heating pipes under Ros's dressing table and the smell over the next couple of days caused Ros, who was particularly meticulous in her personal hygiene, to become more and more paranoiac. She began to shower after every number and overdosed on the deodorant. Even Suzy was beginning to regret the whole fishy episode, suffering along with everybody else in the theatre from the stench. She finally owned up and threw the shrivelled corpse over the side. It took a good week and gallons of disinfectant before things got back to normal.

Birthdays were a major event and Suzy came up trumps when she suggested a party with an American theme for Julia's.

Red white and blue was the compulsory dress code, and the whole cast helped turn the front of house bar into a star spangled jamboree. Linda and Ros were enthusiastic cheerleaders welcoming the birthday girl, who was dressed up as 'Dorothy' minus 'Toto' but clicking those red shoes for all she was worth. Ronald Reagan, the Statue of Liberty and even Superman made an appearance.

Suzy of course took it one stage further and rummaged through her garage for her precious roller skates, which she hadn't worn for thirty years. She collected the cake she'd had made, changed into her costume and put on her skates. After a few initial wobbles, she soon mastered her childhood skills and with the cake outstretched in her right hand she tentatively started along the pier, gaining confidence the nearer she got. Luckily for Suzy, it was a warm evening and the theatre doors were open to let in a welcome breeze. A small crowd of party goers standing at the entrance watched with amazement as Wonder Woman came hurtling at full speed towards them, and suddenly realising she wasn't going to slow down, jumped aside as Suzy flew past them into the foyer, where the rest of the party were drinking and dancing. Unfortunately in all the excitement Wonder Woman hadn't bothered testing her skills on manoeuvring through crowds or braking, and delivering the cake in one piece became a major problem. But catching sight of Julia who luckily was standing just inside the doors Suzy took the opportunity, practically throwing the now travel weary cake at her. The next problem was actually stopping. This proved more difficult as she careered straight through the back doors, into the auditorium, only coming to a crashing halt at the bottom of the small flight of steps leading to the stage.

Two days after Julia's party, Suzy collapsed on stage. She hadn't felt well for some time, with stomach cramps and overwhelming tiredness, which she put down to late nights and poor diet, trying to constantly please Richard who had started to complain of her weight gain again. She was devastated when she was told at the hospital that she was pregnant and the fall at the party had probably instigated her miscarriage.

Depression had never been a part of Suzy's life, with parents whose mood swings bordered on the unstable; she'd always been determined never to take life too seriously, which had proved to be a successful defence. So the black cloud that now engulfed her very being was beyond anything she recognised, therefore beyond understanding.

Richard had been in Birmingham when he got the phone call from the hospital, but as he explained, there was no way he could come home in the middle of a tour. He rang Suzy briefly at home on the second evening only to reiterate what he'd said all along, in that she had better make up her mind what she really wanted, because she couldn't have both.

'It's family or a career Suzy, not that you can call Cromer any sort of career!'

With Richard away Suzy had no choice but to mourn her loss alone. Back at home with Ben she took each day slowly, until a week later she insisted she felt well enough to go back to work and although her depression was short lived; her loss would stay with her forever.

Determined not to be bullied by Richard, she spent the following three summers on Cromer Pier, having the time of her life.

Her experience over the years in London brought her the chance to choreograph some of the more modern numbers and

Julia; always an enthusiastic dancer threw herself around the stage as if auditioning for Pans People. In the middle of frantic head rolls, she felt and heard a crunching sound in her head. Running offstage she flung herself on the dressing room floor hysterical, convinced she'd suffered a brain haemorrhage and was going to die. An ambulance was called and she was rushed off to hospital, only to return two hours later, looking disgustingly healthy, wearing a sheepish grin. She'd pulled a muscle in her neck!

Twenty years later that same neurotic drama queen was to become a very successful staff nurse and during their many reunions over the years the four middle age friends would enjoy reliving the dramas, which had brought them together.

THIRTY-ONE

Suzy's yearning for more children became an obsession and agreeing with Richard that of course it had to be her problem and not his, decided to seek help. Six months later, when an appointment came through the post for her to see the Oral Specialist, she thought at last help was on its way. On the day of the appointment, she skipped breakfast and nervously chain smoked all the way to the hospital, but confident she was sweet smelling in all the right places, having taken great care to shower, shave and smother the necessary area in Blue Grass talc. Arriving fifteen minutes early and tummy rumbling, she went to the canteen for a coffee and a bar of chocolate, then sneaked outside for one last ciggy.

When she was called into Dr Bartlett's room, she shook his hand and smiled, but couldn't take her eyes of the miners' lamp that he had strapped to his head. *"Blimey how far up is he going?"* she wondered and pulled a face at the nurse sat in the corner, who returned a stony stare.

'Good morning Mrs Parker, now before I examine you, I have a few questions. Are you pregnant?'

Suzy laughed, 'no, that's what I'm here for.' Dr Bartlett, relying on his nurse to take down the notes, ignored the remark. 'Now then, when are your periods due?'

"Ah, that's more like it" she thought as she looked in her diary. With her height measured, weight taken and all the formalities over, the doctor switched on his lamp.

'OK Mrs Parker, open wide please.'

Suzy couldn't believe her ears, '*you what?* She shrieked.

'Could you open wide please, so that I can examine you?' Suzy gave a quick quizzical look at the nurse and back to the doctor, but their blank impatient expressions, told her to stop making a fuss and get on with it.

'*I don't think much of your bedside manner, mate,*' she thought as she kicked off her shoes, unzipped her jeans and struggled to pull them over her hips.

'*Mrs Parker, what on earth are you doing?*' shouted the doctor, who seemed to be in shock. Suzy stared back, confused.

'You *said* you wanted to examine me.'

'I do, I want to examine your teeth.'

'*My teeth?*'

'Yes, your teeth, you're having problems with your wisdom teeth and I want to examine them, before we decide whether to take them out or not.'

'Oh my God, I thought you were the gynaecologist' she screamed. 'You see I'm trying for a baby' and suddenly feeling exposed, scrambled to haul her jeans up.

'Well I'm sorry, I can't help you there, I suggest you go home to your husband' he said tartly. But the nurse in the corner managed a wry smile.

'Do you know,' giggled Suzy, 'I thought it was a bit rude, when the card arrived.'

'What card?'

'The card for me to see the Oral Specialist.'

The nurse gasped and trying to hide her giggles, hid her face behind her notepad, while the doctor's eyes popped out of his head and not wanting to continue the conversation, tried to bring the situation to some sort of order.

'Yes, uh… right Mrs Parker, shall we take a look at your teeth?

'Oh no!' screamed Suzy in a panic, suddenly remembering her canteen visit.

'I'm sweet as a rose *down there,*' pointing to her crutch, 'but I must have dog breath, I'm *so sorry*' and ran her tongue around her teeth, as if it would instantly rid her mouth of her breakfast.

Three months later, Suzy sat in the hospital bed. She was finally having her wisdom teeth out.

'Mrs Parker?' asked a nurse, poking her head round the door. Suzy looked up from her magazine and nodded. The nurse smiled and disappeared. Within seconds another head popped round.

'Good morning Suzy, how are you today?'

'Bit nervous actually' smiled Suzy, flattered by all the attention.

As the second nurse fussed around the bed, Suzy was certain she could hear her sniggering.

'Oh don't worry; it'll all be over soon, I'll be back in a minute' and she practically ran from the room. Suzy went back to her magazine, but within seconds a third nurse breezed in the room, stopped at the foot of the bed, unhooked her chart and grinned as if they were long lost friends. 'So, shall we have your legs akimbo?' she asked, lifting the sheet up at the bottom of the bed.

Suzy stared. 'Wha...what? *No*, I'm having my wisdom teeth out' she said, opening her mouth and pointing.

Still holding the sheet midair the nurse beamed. 'Are you sure Mrs Parker, shall we turn the bed round?'

'OH NO!' screamed Suzy, her face turning pink as the penny dropped, 'how did you know?'

'It's all round the hospital. Sally Jacob couldn't wait to tell us. We've been dying for you to come in.'

'Sally Jacob, who's she?' asked Suzy, sweating from the rush of blood that swept up her body, turning her face from the delicate pink to a bright puce.

'Dr Bartlett's assistant. She was there, the day of your appointment, taking notes.' Suzy groaned and suddenly the room was full of uniforms, as at least five nurses, filed in to meet the woman who had managed to shock and apparently disgust stuffy old Dr Bartlett, who wasn't known for his sense of humour. She was a hero and her embarrassment turned to pride as she relayed the story once more.

But the whole episode wasn't over yet, for when the time came for Suzy to have a check up at her local dentist, some six weeks later, she wondered if she would ever live it down. As she lay back in the chair, mouth wide open once again, Simon Parks prodded and poked as he chatted away. 'Well they seem to be healing nicely, how do they feel?'

'Aah…arite…hanks.' Suzy struggled to reply, staring up his nose, but Simon seemed to understand and continued.

'I was at a seminar in Cambridge, last month and I heard a great story about a woman who thought an Oral Specialist was a gynaecologist. Isn't that a scream?'

'Aah…oh… ha…ha.' Suzy looked into his eyes for any suspicious knowing glint, but for now her secret was safe.

'I know and apparently she stripped off, expecting an internal. Are you all right? No wonder the poor woman can't get pregnant, she's putting it the wrong end…. can you keep still Suzy…oh sorry, you're choking, would you like to sit up…?'

'Arr…Yeh…Aaaah…'

Richard seemed to be the only one who didn't find the whole thing funny.

'You stupid cow, how could you embarrass me like that? When are you going to grow up?'

'*Never* I hope' she'd shouted, 'and don't worry Richard, the embarrassment was all mine.'

His constant criticizing and bullying was wearing her down, but was convinced that another baby would bring them closer again and everything would be back to normal. But even after a course of fertility treatment and she'd presented him with another healthy boy, Richard continued to find fault with everything she did and said, undermining her confidence more than ever. His present to her after the birth was a Raquel Welsh beauty book, to encourage her to get back in shape. Suzy had thanked him and promised she'd work hard, but deep down was gutted.

Over the years, she began to enjoy the times that Richard was away more and more, it meant she could relax and have fun with the boys without the constant threat of criticism, complaints and underlying tensions in the house, he treated it like a hotel anyway. And when the boys were in bed, she would relish her quiet time and reflect on her life. When did it all go so wrong? What happened to their perfect marriage? Surely it wasn't *all* her fault, was she so unattractive that Richard couldn't face making love to her anymore? She went over the same questions most nights, expecting the answers to jump out and smack her in the face. One day they would and when they did, she knew she would be prepared for the inevitable.

THIRTY-TWO

Mark Stephenson sat at his desk and watched as Suzy nervously perched herself on the edge of her chair opposite him.

'So Mrs Parker, let me take a few details. You have been separated for six months and now you want to go ahead with a divorce?' Suzy just nodded, aware that if she did attempt to speak, she might not be able to hold herself together.

'So could you tell me why you would like a two year separation, rather than go for adultery and abusive behaviour? Because we could have the whole thing wound up very quickly if you wanted to.'

Mark Stephenson was a kind man and had agreed to comply with his clients wishes of a 'friendly' divorce, even though he knew from the sketchy details he had of the case that she had enough evidence to take her husband to the cleaners.

Suzy had thought about nothing else for the past few months, and it was the only thing she was sure of. Finding her voice, if somewhat still shaky she replied.

'Because I still don't hate him enough to ruin him and I won't have the boys go through that. Besides it was probably my fault that he treated me so badly.'

Mark looked at his client with a puzzled look.

'Oh, and why is that?'

It was obvious to Suzy, 'because I *allowed* him to dominate me, I never stood up for myself, I'm weak, always have been, so you see I let him get away with it.'

'So why now, what's changed?' he asked gently, not convinced that she really wanted this divorce.

A lump came to her throat as she fought with the words. 'Be…because he's being unfaithful, probably always has been, but I only found out for certain six months ago. I've spent twenty years trying to please him, because I loved him, but I'm sick of being told what to do, who to see and where to go, I want my life back.'

'Do you have proof of his adultery?'

'Yeah, I hired a private detective, but I won't use it' she warned. 'I only hired him for my own peace of mind. You see I needed proof before I did anything about it.' Suzy suddenly felt her anger rise as she remembered the late night phone call confirming her suspicions and the strength she'd found to get her this far returned.

'I've had enough now, I want out. He can't tell me what to do anymore.'

'Ok Mrs Parker, I'll take few more details and then you can leave it with me, I'll be in touch' replied Mark, taken back by her sudden change of attitude.

Suzy stepped outside the solicitor's office and fumbling in her bag for a cigarette leant against the wall to steady herself. It had taken her six months to get this far and she knew she couldn't back out now.

Anxious to get home, she ran across the car park, but as she started the engine, she stared at the papers that she laid on the passenger seat. Papers that confirmed what she had refused to accept for far too long, that her marriage was over and it was up to her to bring an end to Richards bullying. Hot salty tears began trickling down her cheeks as she drove home. She had to talk to the boys, that was her first priority and as always she would protect them both as best she could.

Ben had been aware of the breakdown in his parents' relationship over the past year or so and wasn't surprised when his dad had moved out, but now Suzy had to tell him it would be on a permanent basis.

A gentle and compassionate eighteen year old, with his father's good looks and a smile that lit up a room, he was off to Bournemouth University in the autumn and Suzy was thrilled he was pursuing his dream of becoming a journalist. She was even more thrilled that he was moving away from Norfolk to fulfil that dream. Fred had been right, Norfolk was suffocating her and she didn't want the same for Ben.

It was Josh she was worried about and as she pulled into her drive she was grateful that she still had two hours before he came charging in from school.

Josh, who at eight years old hadn't even noticed his dad not being around for the past six months, he just thought his mum seemed quieter than usual, not so much fun and spent a lot of time sitting in the dark.

Suzy put the kettle on and lit another cigarette. She knew she shouldn't, the doctors had warned her to give up three months earlier as she lay in hospital with a collapsed lung, but right now she had more important things to worry about.

As she poured her tea she smiled as she thought of her little whirlwind, who reminded her of herself so many years ago, so full of mischief and unlike Ben, felt he was put on this earth to torment his mother. But after a miscarriage and years of probing doctors, Suzy was thankful for her miracle and loved the challenge.

But she worried, that not only was he losing his dad, who she had to admit had never had a lot of time for his younger son, but he would soon also be losing his beloved brother. How would he feel? Abandoned? Let down? Unloved? Was she doing the right thing? She was responsible for his well being and began to doubt her judgement, was she being selfish? Then she glanced across the table at the papers she'd been given by the solicitor and her doubts immediately vanished.

For twenty three years she had allowed the man she loved to dominate her, slowly chipping away at her confidence, reducing her to the shadow of the happy go lucky, ambitious, extrovert that he'd fallen in love with all those years ago, those same qualities that had irritated him so much in recent years. Or maybe she had always irritated him and she thought back to how he had always found fault with everything she did and particularly how she looked. The first mention of weight gain and she would diet until she was skin and bones, then when he laughed cruelly that he could play the piano on her ribs she would eat constantly to try and get her curves back, but it was never enough. In one row he told her he'd only married her because she made him laugh, but she didn't seem to make him laugh any more.

Suddenly she brought her thoughts back to the task at hand. There would be plenty of time to work out why things had gone wrong later, but for now she needed to be strong and concentrate on helping both the boys get through the next few months.

Josh took the news of his dad not coming home better than Suzy had ever hoped for. After the initial tears, it wasn't long before he seemed back to his normal self and happy to have his mum to himself. What she didn't realise was that Ben had taken it upon himself to reassure Josh things would be OK and promised his little brother that he could go and stay with him when he'd settled in at Bournemouth. This was good enough for Josh who immediately got back to the important issues of whether to have vanilla or chocolate ice cream after tea.

When Richard received the formal separation papers through the post, he was fuming. He stopped all payments, predicting Suzy would be begging him to come home when she'd run out of money. But he hadn't reckoned on her stubborn determination to cope on her own. Suzy's family history had left her well equipped to go without and Richards's financial blackmail only reassured her she'd made the right decision.

She found a new strength she never knew she had, and began to enjoy the power she had over her own life. She worked as a waitress in a hotel during the day and took aerobic and tap classes in the local leisure centre in the evenings, it was a struggle, but the spoilt rich bitch, a nickname friends had given her years earlier, was back where she started, with nothing.

Men were off the agenda, she hated them all, convinced they were all bastards and she vowed she would *never* be dominated by anyone again.

Suzy relished her freedom and as her confidence grew over next few months she craved for the company of old friends, that Richard had been so profoundly jealous of.

He had often accused her of living in the past and become intolerant of her constantly on the phone to her friends in London. Suzy had denied it of course, but admitted she still needed to feel a part of their world, delighting in all the gossip and deep down missed the excitement. Richard had flown into one of his regular rages, throwing her address book into the bin, insisting she grow up and concentrate on her family. Suzy had been equally enraged, having to defend her loyalties were beyond belief. Even in her darkest moments she never doubted her love for her family, with the boys coming top of the list every time, which is what she suspected was Richards's real problem, but never had the courage to suggest it.

She had retrieved the book from the bin later that day and hidden it, knowing that one day she would be glad she did.

That day had finally arrived and climbing onto a chair still didn't give her a full view of what lay on top of her wardrobe. Standing on tiptoe, her heart raced as she fumbled around blindly until she felt the hard cover, which she grabbed eagerly. Back in the kitchen, with glasses perched on the end of her nose, she flicked excitedly through the address book that she'd hidden from Richard over ten years ago.

Cigarettes and steaming tea at her side, she dialled the first of many numbers that night and for the following week went through the book, retracing old friends and trying to contact those who had moved on.

Fred was her first call, guessing he would have the most up to date news on everybody, but she got a shock when he burst into tears at the sound of her voice.

'Oh hen, I thought you were dead' he sobbed. Suzy laughed, he was such a drama queen.

'No Fred, not dead, just living in Norfolk, mind you I wouldn't call this living.' She waited for him to calm down and laugh with her, but he seemed inconsolable.

'Fred, whatever's wrong, tell me please.' It seemed an age before Suzy could get any sense out of him, but after he'd swigged back a much-needed scotch, Fred muttered, 'Is that really you hen?'

'Of course it's me. Who the bloody hell do you think it is, Ginger Rogers?'

'But I'd heard you'd died.' he whispered and poured himself another drink.

'Died! What the hell are you talking about?'

Fred, relieved to hear Suzy's voice, continued 'well I'd heard that you had....well you know ....'

'What? For Gods sake...what did I have? Apart from two kids and a bastard of a husband. Oh by the way, you'll be pleased to know he'll soon be an ex husband.'

Fred smiled but insisted on Suzy reassuring him that she was OK. And so Suzy spent the next twenty minutes explaining in detail what Fred had heard through gossip. How she'd survived cervical cancer some five years earlier and yes it was touch and go, but after a hysterectomy she was still here, alive and kicking! 'I'll show you my scar if you like?'

'Oh Suz, I'm so sorry'

'What, that I'm still here? Charming!'

'No no hen, but you were always going on about how you wanted loads of kids.'

Suzy smiled. Of course it was a shock at the time, but she had been dangerously ill and she was more than grateful just to be alive, besides she had her two boys who were the love of her life.

They chatted on for another hour, with Fred delighted to hear that hillbilly farmers hadn't kidnapped her and she reassured him she still didn't own a pair of dungarees.

She finally got to bed about 2am that night, after two more phone calls and yet more promises stay in touch. As she closed her eyes she wished she could make one more call, but still nobody knew of Beth's whereabouts, many assuming she was still out of the country, so for now she had to accept that Beth was still part of her past, with no chance of her being part of her present or future. She would never give up hope, but for now the girl who was always in her thoughts would have to stay just a fond memory.

Some months later Richard surprised Suzy with a decision that would force her to appraise her life once more. He decided to sell the house without consulting her, in fact the first she knew of it was when she came home to a 'For Sale' sign attached to the front gate. Her initial anger quickly turned to relief, realising she couldn't have struggled on much longer, coping with the high costs of running a big house, but had avoided thinking about her future, preferring the safer option of day to day survival. Now she was being forced to face a new challenge and in a way was grateful to Richard for making her move on.

The decision to move back to London was an easy one, with the help of Jackie, a close dancing friend who Suzy had stayed in touch with over the years and as she drove south towards the M25, she felt a sudden surge of excitement rush through her body as she felt for the first time in many years that she really was coming home.

All fear of what lay ahead and sadness of a life past that had plagued her for most of the journey vanished, as she glanced in the rear view mirror at Josh, who lay sprawled contentedly across the mountain of carrier bags and boxes on the back seat.

'Mum, how far away is Bournemouth from London? Can we go and see Ben? Can I really go to dancing classes? They won't laugh at me like they did at home will they?' She smiled at his impatience and had to fight back the tears as the small scruffy boy suddenly leaned forward and flung his arms round her neck.

'I'm so excited, what's the flat like? What colours my room?'

And for the umpteenth time Suzy described the two bedroom flat that Jackie had found and how he could have his bedroom sky blue pink if he wanted. He laughed out loud and for the rest of the journey they sang at the tops of their voices.

THIRTY-THREE

It was a bitterly cold December day, but Suzy didn't mind as she drove along the Newmarket bypass heading towards Norwich. The past five months had been hectic, settling Josh into his new school and finding work, which was surprisingly easier than she thought it would be. Teaching aerobics and dance at three leisure centres with ambitions to maybe have her own studio one day, she got a kick out of giving people a good time. But today she was giving herself a well-earned day off and looking forward to the yearly reunion with her pals from the Cromer Pier days.

Ros, Julia, Linda and Leslie, still living around Norwich had already arrived and as she approached the coffee bar Suzy could see the girls huddled round a table. It was so good to see them again.

'Here she is what kept you?' laughed Linda as they all hugged, keen to catch up on the latest news and reminisce about the good old days, when all they had to worry about was getting down the windswept pier in one piece.

They were eager to hear all of Suzy's news since moving back to London, with Ros commenting she'd never seen her look so relaxed.

'Well I haven't got anyone to boss me around like you lot, have I?'

The day was a complete success and as they said their goodbyes, promising to meet up same time next year, Suzy wandered round the city that had been such an important part of her life for so long. She decided to grab the local paper with one more coffee, before she faced the long journey home.

As she scoured the Norwich Mercury, the picture on page three made her stop in her tracks. The headline reading *"Choreographer Arrested on Tax Fraud"*

Suzy stared at the photo. It was Bobby, she was sure of it....yes, there it is....*"Bobby Brant, from Norwich"* in black and white. He certainly looked different, but those same cold staring eyes glared at her from the page. She had no idea he came from the area, but then it was all such a long time ago. Reading on, she found he'd returned to England after working abroad for many years and had been arrested at his flat after trying to claim social security.

"So, Michael was right" she thought, trying to remember all the details of his sudden disappearance, *"he was in trouble, the little shit."*

'Hang on' she blurted out loud, 'there's no mention of Beth' and raced through the rest of the article, looking for a clue. She read it over and over again, trying to make sense of it all. "So where is she? Did she come with him...is she in the country? She had to find out. Fumbling for her mobile in the bottom of her bag, she phoned Linda.

'Lindy Loo, hi, it's me. I need a favour.'

'Where are you?'

'Still in Norwich' replied Suzy, trying to keep the impatience out of her voice. 'Does your brother still work at the "Mercury"?'

'Yes why, what are you still doing there? I thought you'd be half way to London by now.'

Suzy tried her best to stay calm, but Linda sensed urgency in her voice. 'What's wrong Suz?'

'Nothing's wrong, I've just seen an old friend in the paper, I haven't seen for years, he lives in Norwich and I wondered if you could ring Matt and get an address for him, I'd love to surprise him.'

'Oh Suz, I'm not sure they're allowed to. Who is it?'

'A choreographer I used to work for, only it says he's in a bit of trouble, out on bail apparently and I thought I might be able to cheer him up' she lied, but knew letting Linda in on the truth of wanting to cut Bobby's balls off, wouldn't get her the information she desperately wanted.

'OK leave it with me, I'll see what he says and ring you back.'

Suzy ordered another coffee and frantically smoked another two cigarettes, willing her phone to ring. When it eventually did she nearly jumped out of her skin. Linda had worked her charm on Matt, making Suzy promise that she'd never say where she got the information.

'You're an angel Lindy Loo, I owe you one' she said scribbling down the address, 'see yer next year and thanks again.'

Finding her way out of the city was easy with the help of the local map she'd bought, and as she made her way into the area where Bobby was apparently living she suddenly felt unsafe. *'Maybe this wasn't such a good idea,'* she thought as she parked and surveyed the dismal overcrowded tower blocks that surrounded her. The estate was a casualty of tacky compulsive housing, with rubbish strewn all over the road and children playing among abandoned burned out cars.

Gripping her bag tightly under her arm, she made her way across the car park. Half a dozen grubby faces suddenly stopped climbing over a battered Escort and suspiciously followed her every move towards 'Canberra House', a block of flats at least fifteen stories high. Nervously she made her way up to number 12 on the second floor, preferring the stairs to the lift, which didn't look too safe and reeked of urine.

Her heart was racing as she took a deep breath and tapped lightly on the scruffy red door. She couldn't stop shaking as she saw a shadow shuffling towards her through the cracked glass.

'Who is it?' The gruff voice made her jump, but instinctively whispered 'a friend!'

She stood back as she heard the chain being taken off the door and open a few inches. Suzy peered at the beady eyes staring at her from the gloom of the hall.

'Yes, what do you want?' he shouted, without opening the door any further.

'Bobby it's me, Suzy' her voice was trembling uncontrollably.

'Suzy, Suzy who?' Bobby barked

'Beth's friend, Suzy….you remember me don't you?'

As Bobby opened the door a little further, Suzy heaved at the putrid stench of booze and body odour that wafted towards her. Instinctively she put her hand up to her face and faked a cough, while Bobby peered at her through sunken bloodshot eyes, searching his booze-fuelled brain for some sort of recognition. Suddenly his expression changed to a realisation and then anger.

'Shit, as if I haven't got enough problems with my past comes back to haunt me! So what do you want?' He demanded, as he turned his back on her and shuffled into the darkened flat. Suzy nervously followed the stooped wizened old man, and shocked by his appearance, did a quick calculation in her head. *"He can't be more than fifty,"* she thought.

'I'm looking for Beth'

'Oh piss off Suzy, she's not here, I don't know where the silly tart is and to be honest I don't bloody care.' They had reached his living room and Suzy suspected his bedroom as well, judging by the filthy blankets that lay crumpled in a scruffy armchair. By the window was a gate-legged table, full of rubbish and Suzy was sure she could see a syringe amongst the bottles and cans that overflowed onto the floor. The stench of sweat and alcohol was overwhelming and she took a deep breath, wanting to get this over with as soon as possible.

'So, how have you been Bobby?' she asked, sucking in the cold fresh air from a draft which whipped along the passage from the still open front door.

'How the hell do you think I've been, you stupid bitch, have you got a cigarette?' Suzy fumbled nervously in her bag and laid it on the table, avoiding any physical contact. He put it to his mouth and struck a match, unable to control his shaking hand. As he exhaled, he eyed her with a lecherous grin. 'So, life's been kind to you I see, I suppose you want hear about your precious friend do you?' He laughed in her face, revealing tobacco stained teeth. 'Stitched the pair of you up good and proper didn't I? Suppose you want to kiss and make up! Always knew you two were an item, she denied it of course…'

'Bobby where is she? I need to find her.' Suzy butted in impatiently, avoiding eye contact.

'Oh who cares? I bloody don't that's for sure' and he threw his head back and gave an evil cackle.

'I do you bastard; now tell me where she is.'

'All right all right, you always were a feisty one. If you must know I left her in that God forsaken hole. Thought she was going to be a supermodel, didn't she? Wanted the limelight that one, but of course she didn't make it. She needed me, but kicked me out she did….' and his words drifted away as memories of a lifetime ago lingered a while.

'So where is she?' demanded Suzy impatiently. 'Come on I haven't got all day, here have my cigarettes,' and threw the packet onto the table.

'Oh bribery is it. Well you must be desperate. How much is it worth?'

'How much do you want?' She needed to get out of there fast, before she hit him.

'Christ I've only ever seen this on the tele, how much have you got?'

She opened her purse. 'Here, there's forty quid it's all I've got, but it should keep you in whiskey for a day or two.'

'Don't get clever with me. If I remember you had a little problem yourself a few years ago' and he smirked as he recalled the incident which had caused Beth and Suzy such heartbreak.

'Got you into a bit of trouble didn't it….thanks to me…ha, you two were so stupid.'

Suzy was confused but didn't want to listen to any more of his ramblings. She held out the money and he snatched it from her.

'OK, I might as well tell you, it's quite funny really. I split you up and now I'm going to get you back together, ironic huh?'

Suzy had heard enough, 'OK, you got your money, now for God sake tell me where she is.'

Bobby took his time, enjoying this one last game.

'Toronto and she can stay there for all I care.' He mumbled, trying to push images of Beth out of his mind. 'Last time I saw her was in the paper, all eyes tits and teeth, modelling some fur coats. Looked quite good actually' and the lecherous grin returned.

'Which agency is she with Bobby?'

'Oh I can't remember the name, now piss off and leave me alone.' He stepped threateningly towards Suzy, but she was ahead of him, half running down the passage.

'Give her a big kiss for me; tell her I don't miss her.'

Suzy slammed the door behind her, sucking in the clean frosty air. She ran down the stairs and shook as she fumbled with her keys. Once inside the safety of her car she turned the engine on, raced out of the estate and continued driving until she found a lay-by, where she opened the window, ridding her lungs of the stench that engulfed her. She rang Jackie from her mobile and asked if she could hang onto Josh a bit longer as she was going to be a bit late. Turning the car onto the bypass she headed home, with her thoughts for the next three hours dominated by Beth, in Toronto. At last a positive clue!

THIRTY FOUR

The phone rang, 'Hi Beth it's me Penny, we're having a party on Saturday, please say you can come.'

Beth checked the calendar. 'Yes looks good Penny, what's the occasion?'

'My brother Andrew and his wife Sarah are over from England and Mike and I want them to meet some of our friends and show them some Canadian hospitality. You'll love Andrew he's a real sweetie, but Sarah's a bit of a snob, she's a big girl and a mouth to match.

'Er…. yes got the picture and thanks for the warning, we'll see you on Saturday.'

'Do we have to go tonight darling, I'd rather stay home and watch a movie' Beth whined as she did the finishing touches to her make up.

Beth still loved to dress up, with a tendency to overdress. Her friends often teased her, but she would just laugh, dramatically reminding them that she was a performer! But unlike the old days, after a couple of hours of socializing she became restless, usually bored and ready to go home, where as her husband, David enjoyed meeting new people and would talk for hours on his favourite topics, life, global concerns and spirituality, a subject he'd felt passionately about for ever since Beth had met him over twenty years ago.

'Actually you're right, I think I might enjoy tonight' she giggled suddenly remembering Penny's sister-in-law.

Arriving at Penny and Mikes they were instantly welcomed by a guest who'd obviously been there a while, by the state of his meandering bloodshot eyes. With a mouthful of food and a drink in his hand he ushered them into the kitchen where the bar was set up, and James the delegated barman for the night introduced himself.

'James at your service ma'am' he grinned as he poured two martini's, passing one to Beth and swigging the other down in one.

'Not Bond I presume!' she whispered to David who thanked James for his beer and watched as he poured one for himself.

'Perk of the job I guess' smiled David leading Beth away and into the crowded lounge.

'Hmm, he'll definitely need to be shaken and not stirred by the end of the night!'

Familiar faces greeted them both as they made their way across the room and before the usual boring chats of 'how's the job?' and 'Ooh, lovely dress!' got started, Beth was up for some fun and keen to meet the dreaded Sarah. She spied Penny in the corner chatting to a small crowd and grabbing David's hand made her way over, but before she had a chance to make eye contact was stopped in her tracks by a booming voice coming from the same vicinity.

'Bloody hell David, Pen's invited the Queen!'

'Well my dears I feel like royalty with all this fuss that's being made over us' Sarah was exclaiming to a bemused audience 'you are all so quaint.'

Beth inhaled on her cigarette, and David feeling her irritation, gently squeezed her hand in a failed attempt to stop her making herself known. Beth surged on through the crowd until she came face to face with Sarah. 'Well what you have to understand Sarah, is that although we are a civilized country, we're still not used to entertaining people of your status and are humbled by the presence of dignitaries such as yourself.'

Penny stifled her giggles, while Mike coughed politely and pushed David towards the bar, which ultimately left Beth smiling at Sarah, who was nervously fiddling with her pearls, unsure of how to take Beth's remark.

'Penny dear I need to go to the little girls room' Sarah whispered, keen to escape and as she squeezed passed Beth she mumbled 'It was so nice meeting you... err... I didn't catch your name!'

'Elizabeth, after *our* Queen as a matter of fact, but you can call me Beth.'

The two girls laughed as Sarah scurried down the hall.

'Oops, think I over stepped it, sorry Penny, but what a pain in the arse.'

'Don't worry about it; she needed putting in her place.' Penny had always admired Beth's wit, if maybe sometimes questioned her timing.

'Right then, I'm off to see 007 in the kitchen, it's time for another martini.'

'Eh? Oh, OK!' nodded Penny, not even attempting to understand.

Once the 'Welcome to Canada' cake was cut along with a chorus of "happy holidays" and the usual non humorous remarks about outstaying their welcome, everyone settled into the party pattern of drinking, flirting, drinking, laughing and yet more drinking which guaranteed James Bond in the kitchen passing out before the end of the evening.

Beth found a seat on the arm of a crowded couch and caught up on the gossip with Gaynor, a girlfriend she hadn't seen for ages. But the noise from behind them made it almost impossible to hear each other.

The two of them turned and watched for a moment smiling, as Sarah seemed to have captivated her audience with stories from "jolly old".

'Yes I've met a lot of show business people' Sarah was bragging 'and I can tell you they really are common as muck!'

'Beth what's the..?'

'Ssh' Beth put her hand up 'just a minute Gaynor' her attention caught by Sarah's loud voice.

'The way some of them carry on, you wouldn't believe it.'

'Have you met many famous stars then?' One man asked.

'Well, I was invited to a house warming a while back, and there were some theatre people there, mind you I was more impressed with the house it was beautiful and....'

'Snotty cow,' sniped Beth and turning back to her friend encouraged her to carry on with the sordid details of her latest catch.'

But within minutes Beth's attention was caught again.

'... *Well* my dears, I couldn't believe my eyes; there she was in the middle of the room doing a headstand with her legs wide open. I mean, I ask you, is that any way for a middle age lady and I use the word loosely to behave?' Sarah indignantly threw her fat flabby arms across her huge over exposed chest, causing it to wobble violently, searching the room for support in her disgust.

'*And then*' she continued 'after she'd made a *complete* fool of herself, she flung herself on Andrew's lap. Poor Andrew, he was so embarrassed, weren't you sweetheart?' She dared, glaring at her husband.

But Andrew's face told a different story.

Gaynor, fed up with the constant distractions went to get another drink, while Beth continued to listen more intently, aware of her heart beating faster. Then as if someone else was speaking she heard herself ask.

'Sarah, do you remember what this girl looked like?'

Annoyed with the interruption Sarah looked up and recalling her earlier encounter with Beth, replied with pursed lips 'Oh I remember all right, the little trollop.'

'Sarah, please tell me, what did she look like?' Beth pleaded, changing her attitude, trying to soften the tension.

'Why is it so important what she looked like?' Sarah barked. The other guests becoming acutely aware of raised voices, turned the music down, bringing the room to a hushed whisper, this was getting interesting!

'I can't explain, I just need to know, please try and remember.'

'Well let me think' Sarah said with exasperation, 'she had awful straw like blonde hair.'

'Long or short?' Beth cut in quickly.

'Umm…. I think it was long, Oh yes, I remember it was a real mess, all over the place, probably hadn't seen a comb for weeks.'

As Sarah gave thought to the bombardment of questions, she looked past Beth and round the room. Realizing that all eyes were on her she decided to put this irritating inquisitive colonial, probable half-breed in her place.

'Actually my dear she wasn't dissimilar to you, same height and skinny, but with a common cockney accent. Her voice was like gravel and on the whole quite coarse' Sarah finished with a look of utter triumph. Beth's head was reeling with questions, her stomach churning. "*Could it be? No it couldn't possibly…*" She took a deep breath, almost afraid to ask. 'Was she a dancer Sarah?' She held her breath.

'Oh it wouldn't surprise me in the least, probably one of those sleazy chorus girls' and turning to establish total understanding from the enthralled crowd. 'You know the type? Legs going in every direction possible, it was quite disgusting the more I think about it.' She shuddered, rolling her eyes until they almost disappeared into her head.

Penny, Mike and David began to worry that a full-scale war was about to declared, but the rest of the party were mesmerized; this was more fun than the usual shindig.

Judging by the blank expression on Beth's face, Sarah claimed an easy victory and was smugly making her way to the bar for a celebratory drink when Beth caught her arm. She had one more question to ask her.

'Sarah, I'm sorry but can you remember her name?'

Reluctant to continue the conversation Sarah turned and as if a nasty smell had suddenly wafted under her nose, brushed Beth's hand off her arm.

'Oh for goodness sake my dear why are you so interested? Don't tell me you know her!' But as she glanced at Beth's gold mesh mini dress and matching hoop earrings, she muttered under her breath 'Hmm, maybe you do!'

'I...I'm not sure, that's why I need to know her name. Please Sarah, it's important.'

Sarah looked thoughtful and took what felt like forever to Beth before she answered.

'I'm sorry I can't remember, but wait a minute Andrew might.' She looked around the room and seeing her husband, summoned him over. Andrew listened as Sarah recalled the house-warming story for him, and by the smile that crept onto his face it didn't take long for him to recollect the girl on his knee.

'Oh yes I remember now' He noticed the glare from his wife and toned down his enthusiasm. Taking the onus off himself he changed direction, 'in fact she nearly caused a divorce between Pippa and Ian didn't she Sarah?' He looked at his wife well aware of her feelings about the incident. Andrew turned to Beth and whispered 'apparently when they got home after the party Ian kept making lurid suggestions for Pippa to loosen up and get her legs behind her neck.' They both burst out laughing, much to Sarah's disgust, who was impatient to end the cosy chat.

'Andrew dear, do you remember the girls name or not?' she snapped.

'I don't I'm afraid, but I do remember us all laughing at the poor thing, she was very drunk and kept threatening she'd have an accident if someone didn't take her to the toilet.'

Beth fell back into the couch and stared at the ceiling, she couldn't believe her ears. In an instant everything came flooding back and there was Suzy, in her minds eye smiling back at her.

'Listen Andrew is there any way you can find out more about this girl, you see I...I think I might know who she is.' A lump came to her throat and tears were beginning to stream down her cheeks.

The couple looked at Beth surprised, 'you think you know her?' Andrew asked gently.

'What could you have in common with a cheap hussy like that I wonder' Sarah snarled. Andrew rolled his eyes and winked at Beth, who smiled gratefully.

'To be honest Beth we wouldn't have a clue who to ask, you see it was a couple of years ago, although it still seems to be the highlight of social stories for my wife' he added with a wry smile.

Sarah was becoming irritated by Andrew's interest in Beth and didn't like the way he seemed to enjoy the memories of that awful girl, so taking his arm in a vice grip, she suggested that maybe they should mingle with the other guests, who had long since gotten bored realizing that the anticipated cat fight was dwindling and no longer part of the entertainment.

The rest of the evening was a complete blur to Beth, unable to concentrate on what people were saying, as quick flashes of Suzy doing headstands, singing and dancing kept flickering through her mind like an old fashioned cine film. At last she found David at the bar with Mike, who had relieved his comatose barman, and after the usual twenty minutes of goodbyes and 'must stay in touches' she managed to drag him away. Once in the car she was impatient to talk about her exciting discovery.

'Don't you see David, it *must* be her, she was doing headstands,' he grinned at the thought. 'Suzy was always doing them at parties when she got drunk! The long blonde hair, the cockney accent, the weak bladder, it *has* to be her! Oh what if it is...? Oh darling I so want to find her. I miss her so much. Will you help me?'

David laughed at Beth's enthusiasm. 'Now calm down sweetheart, you'll hyperventilate if you're not careful, come on take deep breaths. Beth did as she was told, but it didn't last, she didn't want to calm down.

Suddenly she burst out laughing 'I can't believe it! Andrew said this party was only a couple of years ago didn't he?' but she didn't wait for an answer, 'and this girl and I'm sure it's Suzy was doing headstands and larking around like a teenager.'

'Yes...so?'

'Well don't you see? Suzy and I are the same age, so two years ago we were 46 years old! Which means she must *still* be in the business and *still* behaving like an idiot?'

'There can't possibly be another one like you?' David groaned,

'Oh David I've got to find her, I need to see her, you'd love her, she's so much fun.'

'OK, OK, we'll make enquiries, just calm down, I'm just grateful you've not got her bladder problem or we'd be swimming home.'

Beth flung her arms round David, causing him to swerve into the kerb.

'Ooh I love you so much' she said smothering him with kisses, 'you are the kindest, most gentle person in the world.'

David would do anything to make Beth happy, she had brought so much fun into his life and if finding a long lost friend that obviously meant so much to her, then he would do all he could to make it happen.

'I can't wait for you to meet her' she bubbled

'Hey, hang on we've got a long way to go, can we get home first?'

'Oh all right, but put your foot down.'

THIRTY-FIVE

The following few days were an emotional roller coaster for Suzy. Gathering all the information that she could on modelling agencies in Toronto, her initial excitement soon turned to frustration and despair with yet still no positive response from the names on the list, and anger at the limited information Bobby had given her, also confusion at his drunken ramblings of how he'd stitched them up. What did he mean by that? It was all such a long time ago and a terrible muddle in her mind. One day she would find her diaries and maybe then it would make sense. Despite all these mixed emotions she still clung onto the hope that Beth was out there somewhere, maybe sensing that she was trying to contact her.

Picking up a photo from her dresser, she smiled at the two of them posing for the camera, in their early teens, performing their usual party trick of Suzy supporting Beth in a comic 'Fishtail'. 'Come on Beth' she shouted 'use that bloody ESP you were always going on about and tell me where you are.' The phone rang, and still clutching the framed picture she ran to the hall.

'Hello'

'Hi, could I speak to Suzy Parker please?' The Canadian drawl made Suzy catch her breath

'Speaking,' she answered with a slightly shaky voice.

'Hi, my name is Belinda Cartwright from the Global Modelling Agency in Toronto; you left a message on my answer machine?'

Suzy's heart raced as she stuttered, 'Yeah... yeah, I did. I'm looking for a friend of mine Beth Carson, or Brant, that was her married name. She was a model in the Toronto area, do you know her? Please say yes,' she muttered under her breath, trying to stay calm.

'May I ask why you want to contact her, as it's not our policy to give out information on our models, we have to be so careful you understand?'

'So you *do* know her, bloody hell, that's *fantastic*. Oh, I'm sorry, yes of course I understand. Beth and I have been friends since we were kids, but we lost contact when she moved to Canada and I've been trying to find her for years.'

Belinda warmed to the cute cockney accent and wanted to help.

'Ma'am, may I ask, did you work with Beth in England?' Tears were now trickling down Suzy's cheeks as she nodded frantically.

'Yeah, we danced together, in fact we did everything together.' Belinda had one more question and she grinned as she asked. 'Ma'am, did you have a particular party trick that you were famous for?'

'Yeah, yeah I did, headstands, I did headstands....Oh please, it's her isn't it?'

'Well I may be able to help' continued Belinda, 'Beth did work for us, but moved to Calgary a few years ago' and sensing Suzy's disappointment, she was quick to continue, 'but I can give you the number of Carol Bennett, she was also a model with our agency and they were good friends. Carol moved back to Calgary to be near her family, and soon after, Beth split up from her husband, you did know she split?'

'Yeah I know, good job too.' Suzy blurted

'I agree Ma'am, anyway, Beth wanted a fresh start, so when Carol suggested she try her luck over there, Beth jumped at the chance. She's still modelling I think, mature ladies fashion now of course.' Suzy laughed, trying to imagine Beth as mature.

'Yes please, if you could give me Carol's number that would be great.'

Belinda gave Suzy the number and wished her luck with her search.

'Please give her my kind regards. I know she'll be thrilled to hear from you. She kept us entertained with stories of the antics you two got up to. Goodbye and good luck.'

Suzy put the phone down and stared at the scrap of paper with those magic numbers on.

'Nearly there Beth, just one more phone call!'

Carol was friendly and helpful, bringing her up to date with sketchy details of Beth's life. But at last she had what she wanted, Beth's phone number.

Suzy's hands shook as she carefully dialled the number.

Would she remember her? More to the point would she *want* to speak to her? The ring tone seemed to go on forever, when at last.

'Hello.' Suzy recognised her voice immediately, but was struck dumb.

'Hello?'

At last she whispered 'Is that you Beth?'

'Yes, who's speaking?'

Suzy held her breath and then stuttered 'It's me...Suzy'

Suzy was sure she heard a sharp intake of breath and then silence. 'Beth, are you OK?'

'Oh my God....Suzy is that really you?'

'Yeah, yeah, it's really me' and suddenly, twenty years of pent up feelings were released down the phone line as the two friends collapsed into floods of tears. After what seemed an age, Beth was the first to pull herself together. 'Suzy, my Suzy, I don't believe it, where are you?'

'In England'

'I don't believe this, Oh Suzy, you don't know how good it is to hear your voice, well it would be if you'd stop crying for a minute' and they both laughed through the tears. Suzy wiped her nose on her sleeve and giggled nervously.

'It's funny; I don't know what to say now'

'Well there's a first' and they fell about laughing again.

'Hang on what time is it there?'

'5pm'

Beth began to panic. Oh shit it's 10am here and I've got to go to work. Oh sod it, I'll phone in sick. By the way, how did you find me?'

'It's a long story, no don't cancel work, you lazy cow, I've got to go and pick up Josh anyway'

'Who's Josh?'

'My lad…the little bastard.'

'Oh my God, I don't believe it; I've got one of those.'

'What a little bastard?'

Beth laughed 'Yes and he's called Josh too, isn't that incredible? Oh Suz I've got to go, there's my ride at the door.'

'Sex so early in the morning…you tart'

Beth ran to the window and signalled to Jackie who was impatiently hooting the horn.

'What's your number? I'll ring you tonight, what about the time difference? You'll be asleep, won't you?'

'You must be joking' laughed Suzy.

'OK, Oh Suz, I can't wait'

'I know me too. You put the phone down first.'

'After three….1…2…3…Hello?' The giggling resumed, until Jackie reminded Beth with another loud hoot.

'Got to go, love you'

'Yeah, love you too.'

The next seven hours seemed interminable for both girls. Beth got through the day in a dreamlike state, while Suzy filled the evening with two classes, although on autopilot. By the time she got home she worked out she still had about three hours to kill before Beth would be ringing, so decided now was as good a time as any to find those diaries.

Bobby's words had haunted her ever since she'd got back from Norwich…. 'I really stitched you two up', what the hell did he mean? Maybe the answer was right here; maybe she'd written it all down and had the answers without realising. It was important for her to get things straight in her head before Beth rung. Now that she'd found her she didn't want any misunderstandings to come between them yet again.

Checking Josh was safely tucked up in bed, she flicked on the light switch in the garage and stared into the huge cavernous area, stacked to the rafters with books, furniture and boxes filled with a collection of treasures and unwanted ornaments of Christmases past and wished she'd sorted them all out before she left Norfolk, but of course at the time her state of mind was too fragile to face throwing her life into black bin liners.

As she searched and her eyes became accustomed to the dim light, she was immediately stopped in her tracks by four boxes piled three foot high, labelled "Suzy's Treasures KEEP OUT". She put her hand over her mouth to stop herself from crying out. Suzy Noden's life lay forlorn and forgotten in a dingy corner. Tentatively she knelt down and gently brushed away the cobwebs. She thought she was ready for this, but now with her heart pounding and tears threatening she wasn't sure.

It was a good ten minutes before she could bring herself to open the first box. With dusty wet smudges on her cheeks, she slowly lifted out her forgotten treasures. Every item brought back memories, good and bad. The first item she picked up caught her breath. It was the black leotard she'd worn to that first audition way back. She held it to her chest, closed her eyes and allowed her mind to wander back to that day when she'd rang Beth, telling her of the audition.

Suzy opened her eyes, reluctant to wallow in those lost years. She felt a renewed excitement that her life was about to change dramatically and brought her thoughts back to the job in hand. As she emptied the box, photos of dancers in underwear pulling faces at the camera, theatre programmes and posters of a life gone by surrounded her, and by the time she found the three leather bound diaries, she was completely engrossed in a world so remote from her present life, that it took her another hour before she could pull herself away. Having piled everything back, promising to have a clear out very soon, she returned to her kitchen and dusted off the years of neglect from the embossed blue covers, made a cup of tea and settled down to rekindle her past.

Although Suzy's schooling had been far from successful in gaining any qualifications due to her almost obsessive ambitions in the world of entertainment and total lack of interest in boring school subjects, her vivid imagination had produced a talent for free flowing writing that gained her unexpected respect from her peers and teachers alike. Embarrassed by the nerdy image of keeping a diary, she'd kept it a secret from everyone including Beth. Her scribblings weren't meant to be a day-to-day diary of events, but an occasional outlet of feelings and emotions, helping her get a perspective on a sometimes cruel, but more often than not happy time, creating an understanding of the people who were a part of her life.

Skipping quickly through the early writings of childhood, she wanted to find what she'd written at the time of Beth and Bobby's wedding and only then did she stop and digest the words on the pages.

Meanwhile, Beth rushed through the front door, throwing her bag across the floor. 'David' she yelled, 'where are you? You'll never guess. Suzy's rung me!'

She was fumbling in her bag for a cigarette as David ambled through from the lounge.

'Sweetheart, slow down, what did you say?'

'I said *Suzy's* rung, *this morning*,' she repeated excitedly, 'before I went to work. I can't believe it, after all these years. …Oh shit where are my ciggys?' David took the bag from her and calmly found her cigarettes.

'Beth that's wonderful, how did she find you?'

'I don't know I'm ringing her back now.' Suddenly she stopped. 'David, don't you think it weird, we were talking about finding her after Sarah's party, do you remember?'

'How could I forget, you haven't stopped talking about it all week' he smiled 'won't it be the middle of the night there though?'

'I know, but Suz said not to worry, she's too excited to sleep anyway, right where's the number?'

For the following few days Beth and Suzy spent every available minute on the phone, catching up with the lost years, until David decided to take things into his own hands. While Beth was at her art class one afternoon, he took the number from the fridge door and dialled.

'Hi Suzy this is David here. Hi… yes I'm fine thanks… yes it's great; I know…yes Beth's thrilled too. Listen Suzy I've got an idea that I think you two might like, before we all go bankrupt with the phone bills.'

Suzy liked the sound of this guy, he was funny and what he suggested made her scream with delight.

'You gotta promise me you won't say a word to Beth until I've got it sorted.'

'Yeah I promise. But David, won't she guess something's up when you drop her at the airport?'

'Yeah, well I'll tell her when it's all fixed, otherwise she'll be unbearable'

'Oh so she hasn't changed then!'

David laughed; this is just what Beth needs. 'Anyway madam will have to pack her own bag, I wouldn't dream of delving into her drawers.'

'No I don't blame you, dunno what you might find! Ooh David I can't wait, thank you so much. You're a diamond geezer!'

'A *what?*'

'It means a good bloke. Don't worry, you'll learn. Byee!'

THIRTY-SIX

A month later Suzy sat in her kitchen watching the clock, as Beth was boarding the plane in Calgary. 'Right it's 2am, she's on her way, safe journey Beth, and I'll see you soon' she whispered and turning the lights off, went into her bedroom, set the alarm and tried to get some sleep.

Beth now well on her way was doing the same thing. Earlier she'd chatted non stop to her neighbouring passenger, excitedly telling him the reason for her trip, but after two hours got the distinct impression he'd had enough, when without a word he moved to an empty seat four rows further back.

It was a fight for a parking spot at the airport, but Suzy was on a mission. Seconds before the Mercedes eyed the last spot she swerved her Rover in front of it, parked and half ran towards the arrivals terminal, ignoring the insults screamed at her. Today she loved everybody they could call her all the names under the sun, she didn't care, she was meeting her best friend.

She still had two hours before Beth's flight arrived, but ever since the initial phone call from David and the secret arrangements that compared to a military operation, she seemed to have been in a state of shock and excitement and wasn't taking any chances on being late. Laden with the biggest bunch of pink carnations she could find she staggered to the nearest coffee bar, oblivious to people sniggering at the 'Welcome Home' helium balloon tied to her jeans, swaying way above her head. Unable to concentrate on the newspaper she'd bought, she kept a keen eye on the arrivals information monitor.

The time ticked by slowly and every so often her tummy would flip as she realised that very soon Beth would be coming through those doors and they would be together again. She tried to imagine what Beth would look like and in a sudden panic, rushed to the loo. In all the excitement she had not even checked in the mirror that morning. 'Oh bugger, I look a mess' she mumbled, dragging a comb through her still untidy mass of hair, splashing her face with cold water and pinching her cheeks, trying to bring some sort of life to her tired face. She laughed at her reflection *'typical Beth, it's all your fault I look so rough, I've been too excited to sleep!'* and ran back to the arrivals gate.

As Beth gazed out into never ending blue sky that surrounded her, the announcement that they were approaching Heathrow, brought a shiver down her spine. Her first trip back to England in over twenty years and all her dreams were about to come true. She took out her mirror and refreshed her makeup, 'I wonder if she'll recognise me,' she babbled as she tidied her hair.

She hadn't slept for a week, ever since she'd come down for breakfast and saw the pink envelope resting against the marmite jar. 'What's this? It's not my birthday,' but without waiting for an answer she'd ripped it open.

'Oh just a little present, my sweet' David replied with a smile as the plane ticket fell onto the table.

'What's this?' She cried as she read the details. 'I don't believe it? Oh my God David, is this what I think it is?' And flung her arms around him. Suddenly she looked serious. 'What about work?'

'No problem, Jackie's covering for you.'

'Oh David, I don't believe this, but can we afford it?'

'Probably not, but it's still cheaper than the phone bill you and Suzy have run up in the last three weeks. So don't worry about it, this is too important to you. Just go and enjoy yourself, you've only got ten days.'

'Does Suzy know?'

'Of course she does she'll be at the airport to meet you.' And for the following week she could think of nothing else.

Glad to have her feet back on the ground, Beth could feel her heart pounding. It seemed to take forever to reach the baggage conveyer belt, but once she'd heaved the cases onto a trolley there was no stopping her. Weaving through the other passengers she manoeuvred the trolley like a hovercraft determined to be first in the queue to show her passport.

'Excuse me.' Beth whizzed past an older couple, struggling to control their wayward trolley, 'excuse me' she swerved and just missed flattening a small child!

Suzy had positioned herself in front of the waiting crowd and directly ahead of the arrival doors, she wasn't moving for anybody. Twenty minutes passed, it felt like forever and then the automatic doors opened and a sea of people flooded towards her.

It was like a film in slow motion, as Beth looked straight ahead, oblivious to everyone else, seeing the balloon first, jumping up and down and then Suzy attached to it, grinning that same huge grin. Abandoning her trolley she ran and they fell into each other's arms, crushing the flowers.

'Oh charming!' laughed Suzy through her tears as they eventually released their grip.

'Oh Suz, I'm sorry they're lovely,' giggled Beth as she accepted the bedraggled, squashed bouquet. 'I'm dying for a fag and a cuppa tea' she pleaded as she wiped the tears from her eyes.

'Me too, good to know some things haven't changed. Come on my treat.'

They didn't notice the traffic jam on the M25, they were too busy catching up to care about sitting in a jam for the next hour. But by the time they got back to the flat, Suzy had at least managed to explain how she'd played detective and bribed Bobby into helping her find Beth's whereabouts. Beth relished in Suzy's description of his downfall and probable future address behind bars.

'He kept rambling on about how he'd split us up though, I don't know what he was going on about do you?'

Beth thought for a minute, trying to recall memories she'd long put out of her mind. Gradually it all began to make sense as the two girls each told their tale of events that led up to their final fallout.

'The rotten bastard, I thought it was you that told 'em about my drinking and when I'd heard you got the part, I put two and two together and made nine. Oh Beth, I'm so sorry.'

Beth put her arms around her friend. 'Poor Suz your maths was never very good was it? And I thought you were too busy losing your virginity to care about me. I can't believe all those years we've wasted, because of that rotten lump of shite.'

Suzy's mind raced back to that day when she'd heard of Beth getting the show. 'Oh Beth, I can't believe it, I really hated you, Oh no, how could we have been so stupid?' Beth smiled. 'Come on you little hussy, it's all over now, he's got what he deserves, what goes around comes around. Now, I want to hear *all* your news.'

'What *all twenty years of it?* Blimey Beth, where do I start?'

Suzy's flat was filled with constant laughter for the following ten days, as the two friends swapped tales, slowly filling in the gap of the last two decades. Hours were spent round the kitchen table, looking at show programmes and photos, each one with a story to tell.

'What the hell are you doing here Suz?' asked Beth staring at a picture of Suzy, all in white, grinning at the camera, proudly holding up what looked like a ferret.'

Suzy snatched the photo, 'Oh, you'd have loved this Beth. That's my hair.'

'Your *hair*?' screeched Beth

'Yeah, it was an advert for Woodpeckers Cider, and they wanted girls with really long blonde hair, and of course I wanted to have the longest, so I wore a nylon hairpiece. We were filming at Battersea Funfair on the roller coaster, and just as we got to the top, there we all were waving at the camera and the bloody thing flew off and got tangled up in the track.' Beth waited as Suzy got the giggles.

'So, come on what happened?'

Controlling herself she managed to continue, 'well, someone had to climb up the track and get it down, and you can imagine the state it was in?' Beth nodded, 'but I had to put it back on, 'because mine was screwed up in a hairnet and looked a right bloody mess. Funny, I never got to work for that agency again. I wonder why?'

And so the stories continued, all day and often late into the night; there was so much to say and so little time. Beth loved listening to Suzy's adventures of the theatre that she missed so much and Suzy was fascinated by Canada, which seemed such a different world to hers. Beth told her about the mountains and open space, but after hearing about the long winters and −30 temperatures, Suzy decided that dirty, busy, crime-ridden London was a great place to live. She also couldn't believe the difference language.

'You live *where?*'

'What? Oh we live off the Shaganappi Trail, in the North of town.' Beth repeated.

'Shag a *what?*' Suzy asked and Beth laughed.

'Don't laugh, I had a long conversation with someone at a party about a Pawnshop or so I thought, turned out he was talking about a Porn Shop! He was telling me about studded collars and whips and I said I didn't think people pawned those kinds of things. He just stared at me and then the penny dropped, did I feel stupid!!'

'Beth, it's so good to have you back.'

THIRTY-SEVEN

The ten days flew by and before they knew it they were back at Heathrow for the tearful goodbyes, promising never to lose contact again and with the hope of maybe Suzy making the trip out to Canada. Realistically they both knew it would be years if ever, but the promises kept the dream alive.

The trip had been a great success, one of the highlights being the surprise party Suzy had organised. A lot of faces from the past, including June, Cloe and Lucy from the Tillers were there, and the two middle aged friends managed to demonstrate their famous party trick causing rounds of applause, as Suzy scooped Beth of the floor, proving they weren't too old for probably one last fishtail! Suzy performed the perfect headstand, which unfortunately wasn't caught on camera, as in her attempt to do the midair splits, her foot caught Junes hand sending the camera flying into the punch.

Suzy found it hard to settle back into normal life, reluctant to store away all the mementoes that she and Beth had spent hours reminiscing over. But when June rang asking her to join the original Tiller troupe again, Suzy initially fell about laughing.

'Are you sure people want to see a load of middle age women, throwing their cellulite around?'

'You'd be surprised Suz, we've done quite a few; mostly charity, but they love it. I would have contacted you before, but you were hiding in Norfolk and nobody knew where you were.'

'I wasn't hiding, I was being held prisoner,' she said and jumped at the chance to perform again.

She immediately rang Beth with her news. 'Christ who'd have thought, I spent all those years trying to get out and now I can't wait to get my legs in the air again.'

'For a good cause this time you tart, I wish I could be with you.'

'So do I.'

'When you're up there kicking, do one for me' asked Beth sadly.

'Promise' replied Suzy.

Her first show was in Brighton a month later, and as the curtain rose and the orchestra played that familiar opening signature tune, the audience got to their feet, with the cheers taking Suzy's breath away. She thought of Beth during the routine, as every kick and formation that had adorned TV's all over the country for so many years was welcomed with rapturous applause. It was the best feeling in the world and she was glad to be back.

She was happier than she had been for years, back in contact with Beth even though it seemed a million miles away; back performing again and she was free to make her own choices. Then along came Tony and changed everything.

She met him at a party and suspected Jackie had a lot to do with the contrived meeting and even though she denied it, the smirk said it all. He was the funniest man Suzy had ever known and a terrible flirt, actually he was very good at it. So when he invited her out for a drink, she found herself agreeing and then spent the following few days thinking up excuses not to go.

'But why?' asked Jackie one day over coffee, 'he's free and anyway it's about time you had some sex, cobweb crutch.'

'You *are* joking. I wouldn't know what to do, it's been so long, and anyway I wasn't any good at it apparently.'

'Who says?'

'Richard of course, that's why he played around.'

'Oh Suz give Tony a chance, not all men are bastards.'

'OK, OK, but if he tries anything funny, I'll…'

'Well he might, he *is* a comedian.'

Suzy found Tony's humour irresistible and they hit it off straight away. To Suzy he was Del Boy, Dudley Moore and a hint of Bob Hoskins all rolled into one and was just what she needed, a good friend who made her laugh, without the embarrassing groping at the end of the night. They became inseparable, with Tony helping Suzy realise her own worth and he in return finding a female who liked him for who he was, in his words, 'a short, out of work comic.'

Tony Peters was fifty-one and with two failed marriages behind him was happy to keep the relationship platonic and have some fun. He loved his work, having started in the business at seventeen as a jazz singer and over the years bringing his natural wit to into his act. But his personal life was a disaster, ever since his divorce from second wife Rachel five years earlier; his best friend had been a bottle of Jack Daniels and seemed to Suzy to be on a course of self-destruction. He was funny, flirtatious and totally outrageous and at five foot four, women thought him cute and wanted to mother him, but he had other ideas. 'I don't want a mother! Who the hell wants to fuck their mother?' Suzy knowing his passion for big boobs, was constantly trying to set him up with friends who measured up to requirements, but time after time he would either be knocking on her door, or on the phone with another disastrous but funny story to tell.

As the friendship grew over the next few months, Suzy found herself missing his company while he was away working.

'I wonder what he's like in bed' she asked Jackie, who knew him well, but insisted not that well.

'How the hell would I know, anyway, why haven't *you* found out yet?'

'Because he hasn't bloody asked me, that's why. Obviously my tits aren't big enough.'

Jackie shook her head, 'well you probably frighten the life out of him. Maybe if you stop telling everyone what bastard's men are! Believe me he's nothing like Richard, I've known him for years and he's a one-woman man. Bit of a flirt I must admit, but that's his charm.'

Suzy listened but wasn't convinced.

It was another six months before Tony plucked up the courage to say what he'd been rehearsing for weeks. He dialled Suzy's number and took a swig of scotch.

'Hi Tone, how did it go with Laura last night?'

'Total disaster Suz, I was in bed by ten.'

'Wow quick work mate.'

'Alone Suz, I was in bed alone.'

'What's wrong, you sound awful.'

'I've got something to tell you and I'm not sure how you're going to take it.'

And for the next twenty minutes Suzy listened as Tony explained. When he'd finished there was a deathly silence.

'Are you pissed?' was all Suzy could think of.

Tony sighed 'I knew you'd think it was the drink talking, but everything I've told you is true, I can't stop thinking about you.' For the first time in ages Suzy's heart began to beat faster, he was serious. Tony poured another drink, wondering if he'd made a complete Prat of himself and was about to lose his best friend.

'But I'm not you're type, you've told me enough times you like big buxom wenches and I'm not exactly Marilyn Munroe am I?'

'Oh Suz, looks aren't everything'

'Oh charming, you really know how to make a girl feel good'

'I didn't mean that you silly cow, just shut up and listen.'

An hour and a half later Suzy put the phone down and immediately phoned Jackie with her news. But Jackie already knew, having spent night after night on the phone with Tony, encouraging him to tell Suzy how he felt. She had watched the friendship develop and knew they were perfect for each other. She understood Suzy's reluctance to get involved again, for when Suzy had suspected Richard was playing away from home; she was one of the few people she'd confided in.

Suzy had been desperate for proof of Richards infidelity, so Rick, Jackie's husband who was in the police force had offered to help by asking John, a friend, who was stationed in Cardiff to watch for any funny goings on at the hotel where Richard was staying.

It was a cunning plan, if somewhat theatrical, verging on the farce.

Suzy was to travel to London and wait at Jackie and Rick's house for the phone call from John, which would confirm Richard had a girl in his room. The two girls would then drive to the scene of the crime, dressed in black of course, offer room service and deliver it by tipping out Richards's dirty underwear all over the bed.

The master plan would have worked, but for the two bottles of wine, which the girls needed to calm their nerves and so by 2am when the phone call came, neither was in a fit state to drive anywhere.

Suzy took her newfound love slowly; reluctantly agreeing that maybe Tony wasn't such a bastard after all. He brought fun into her life and socially they were a good team and great entertainment value at parties. Introducing him to friends she insisted that he was only "pencilled in" and Tony took this teasing in good spirit, not only was it a warning that he wasn't going to be allowed to rush things, but it also gave him the luxury of time to work out in the aftermath of previous disastrous relationships, whether he would ever, or indeed want to fall in love again. In the past he'd come to realize that the weaker one of a relationship makes an incredible effort to please their partner and the stronger normally makes no effort from day one and remains steadfast throughout. But in Suzy was someone who genuinely felt the same about friendship, and an honesty with regard to family commitments He encouraged her to be free and follow her dreams, loving her humour and natural ways and found that he not only had a soul mate, lover and friend, but most important of all she was a joy to be with. Her compulsive happy go lucky outlook matched his own, to such an extent that sometimes outside company was seen as dull and bland.

Suzy, seeing a kindness in him that she'd never known in any man before, was slowly falling in love. As the relationship grew, sensing in him an all too familiar insecurity, she reassured him that he was well on the way to being "inked in".

Their baggage was equally heavy, with two sons each, but Anthony at twenty-five and Tim two years younger, adored Suzy and on a boys night out with their father, threatened to "cut his balls off, if he screwed up this time". Ben was gentler with his advice, having watched Suzy's confidence grow over the two years, and with the knowledge that Josh loved Tony as much as his mum did, hugged her 'Stay happy mum, it suits you.'

Buying a house together was the obvious next stage and if either Tony or Suzy had any secret worries as to whether they were doing the right thing, Josh soon reassured them. 'We're "The Three Musketeers" now' he announced as he cuddled up between them on the sofa that first night. Suzy never happier smiled and with tears in her eyes, had to agree. The adventure was just beginning.

Tony encouraged her to take singing lessons, insisting it was only her lack of confidence that held her back and when he suggested she do a song with him on one of his shows, she nearly wet herself with excitement. Suzy's adrenalin reached new heights; she thought her heart would burst with pride as Tony introduced her as his 'Special Guest'. He was proud of her history in the biz and wanted her to pursue all her unfulfilled dreams.

'Why don't we go out as double act? You've got great comedy timing, can sing with me, but I'll leave the dancing to you' He was serious! Suzy couldn't believe it.

'But...but...!'

'No buts...you can do it, you've just got to believe in yourself'.

For too many years she had been told she was useless and now she was being told she could do anything she wanted. Oh how she'd dreamt of this, secretly knowing she still had something to give, but unsure of what it was, or how to prove it. But if she was to do it, she wanted to be the best she could. Tony had built up a good reputation over the years and she didn't want to ruin that. He would still work on his own, but whenever she could, Suzy would join him.

Over the next three months they rehearsed and within six months they'd developed the act so well, that regular bookings were coming in, agreeing that as long as the venues was near home for Josh, "Swingstreet" was on the road.

THIRTY-EIGHT

Then one cold November afternoon, on her way home from a tap class, her whole world was turned upside down. The rush hour traffic was building up and as she sat waiting to turn right, a bus came round the bend too fast and smashed into the back of her car, sending her across the road into the path of oncoming traffic. Tony rushed to the hospital as soon as he got the phone call and as he quietly drew back the curtain his heart lurched. Suzy, bruised and pale was smiling at him.

'Don't cry Tone, it's not as bad as it looks, but nooky's out for a while I'm afraid.'

A week later Tony and Josh helped Suzy down the hospital steps and into the car. Every step she took sent sharp piercing shock waves up her spine and although the injuries to her back and left shoulder were superficial, for next nine months she would have to endure daily gruelling painful physio.

Beth wanted to jump on a plane as soon as Tony rang her with the news.

'Don't worry Beth, it's far too expensive and anyway you know what she's like, hates lots of fuss and she doesn't want anyone to see her as she is.'

'Hmm, little miss independent,' Beth agreed, 'she'll be a terrible patient. Poor you! OK I'll phone her every day and nag her to get her ass out of that bed.'

'She'd love that, thanks Beth, but be gentle, because the doctors have told her she won't dance again.'

Tony couldn't bear the thought of Suzy hurting any more than she was already.

'Oh no! How's she taken it?'

'Worries me sick, she won't talk about it, just changes the subject.'

Beth understood his concern. 'Don't worry; she's always kept things close to her chest. I'll talk to her.'

Rather than collapse into floods of tears, the doctors' words had had the complete opposite effect on Suzy, who seemed to remain calm as she listened to his regrettable but inevitable diagnosis.

'I'm afraid Mrs Parker that although you're very fit for your age, your body will never recover enough for you to dance or exercise again. But with physiotherapy there is no reason why you shouldn't get some mobility back.'

'OK, thanks' was her only reaction, which caught him off guard; he was expecting a more emotional outburst. But he didn't know his patient that well, unaware that behind her seemingly accepting smile, he'd lit a fuse that ignited a steely determination, of rather than accepting the grim future he lay before her, saw it as one of her biggest challenges yet.

A week after being discharged from the hospital, Tony realised he had his hands full when he walked into the bedroom, to find Suzy laying on her back, legs dangling in the air, with a pair of knickers hanging from the end of a foot.

'What the hell are you doing?' He asked taking the pants, why didn't you call me? You know I'll help you get dressed.'

'Put 'em back' she snapped. 'Put the bloody pants back. I can do it myself.' He did as he was told and watched with admiration as she painfully bent her knees to her chest, put on her pants and rocked herself slowly up to a standing position.

'There see? I can do it.' And he was treated to a repeat performance as she fell stiffly back on the bed and struggled to put on her jeans.

This was just the beginning of her campaign to beat the odds. Six weeks later she asked Tony to take her swimming. The car journey was excruciating, but once Tony had helped her down the steps, she felt the pain ease as the warm water took the weight of her body. Using her fitness experience she spent the next hour gently exercising her damaged muscles and stiff joints. Swimming became her saviour and she spent every available minute there. As she slowly got stronger, she followed it up with exercises at home, until one day, she called Tony and Josh into the lounge.

'Close your eyes' she told them excitedly, 'I've got a surprise for you.' They rolled their eyes, without daring to question and obeyed.

'OK, you can open them now.'

'*MUM* what are you *doing*?' and they both rushed to her side.

'I'm touching my toes, what does it look like?' she giggled, proudly poking her head between her legs. 'Mind you I'm not sure I can get up.' And for once she was grateful for their help.

Tony took her in his arms.

'I'm so proud of you' he whispered.

'Thanks' she said warmly and turned to Josh. 'See my man, six months ago the doctors told me I was finished, never dance again' and putting her hands gently on his shoulders, she looked into his beaming face. 'Believe in yourself Joshy Boy and you can do anything you want and *don't* let anyone tell you otherwise.'

Tony couldn't believe what he was hearing. Was this the same woman who had spent her whole life being dominated by other people?

'Oh my God, I've created a monster.' He laughed.

Josh grinned his cheekiest grin. 'So I can go to Guys party on Saturday then?'

'*NO!*'

It was now nine months since the accident and financially they were struggling. Tony had to take on building jobs during the day, before driving off to do a show, getting home in the early hours. He was becoming tired and irritable and Suzy although still in pain, was determined to help.

'Did you know I was quite good at painting?' She was sitting on the edge of the bath, as Tony relaxed before facing another two hours in the car. The show in Bournemouth was a late one, 10 o'clock and he really should make a move.

'Hmm, I remember your flat, you did a good job, why?' he asked sleepily.

'Oh nothing, come on your tea's ready' and she pulled out the bath plug.

The next morning, instead of waking him as usual, she strapped on her back support, took the keys from his trouser pockets, took the phone off the hook and crept out of the house. The flat he was working on was the other side of town. She had been there a couple of times, with a packed lunch or to help him clear up at the end of the day, and as she lay out the dust sheets and stirred the paint, she felt a thrill at imagining Tony's face when he saw what she'd done.

At two o'clock her mobile rang. It was Tony and he was furious.

'Suzy, where are you? Why didn't you wake me? And where are the flat keys?'

'Did you have a good sleep sweetheart? Now just calm down, I'm at the flat and I could murder a sandwich.'

Tony, still bleary from such a rare deep sleep was confused. 'You're...where?'

'At the flat, I'll put the kettle on if you bring me a peanut butter sandwich. See you in a while.' She was grateful for the break, but was determined not to mention the pain that was shooting up her spine.

'Suz it looks fantastic, are you OK though? How's your back, you haven't done yourself more damage have you?' He eyed her suspiciously as she slid slowly down the wall, landing gently on the floor.

'No it's fine, the exercise is doing it good' she lied. 'We could work together when you haven't got a show and when you've got a gig, you stay at home and I'll come on my own.' He knew her well enough to know there was no point in arguing, and so the new double act was formed. "Bodgit & Scarper" were in business.

They worked well together, even though there was an unspoken knowledge that each were suffering in their own way. Tony's dizzy spells were becoming more frequent, tiredness was taking its toll, but with the bank on their back with late mortgage payments, he refused to take time off.

One Friday morning, after only four hours sleep, he wearily climbed the ladder. It was the last room to be finished and he needed to fix the centre light. As he reached the top he missed his footing and crashed to the floor. Suzy drove him home, tucked him up in bed and returned to the flat where she did the final coat on the bedroom door, cleared up and rang the client, explaining what had happened and that he'd have to get an electrician in.

It was the last straw and Suzy made up her mind there and then that things had to change. She raced home and crept into the bedroom. Tony was sitting up, nursing his bruised shoulder.

'We're selling the house.' It wasn't up for discussion. 'You're too talented to be up a bleeding' ladder.'

'But you love this house.'

'I don't care where we live as long as I'm with you. You're no good to me flat on your back.'

Tony laughed, 'well I could be if you stop behaving like the Gestapo and give me a cuddle.'

'Don't start all that dirty business, I've got things to do, besides I can't go on much longer, my backs agony.' And she swept out of the room.

The house was sold within weeks and after paying off the bank loan and clearing all their credit cards; they moved into a rented two bedroom flat in Bromley, keeping what little there was left for emergencies.

'Now you can concentrate on what you're *really* good at.'

With the pressure off, Tony used the time to ring agents and Suzy concentrated on her obsessive fitness regime. She would get up two hours before Josh and Tony to work out in the lounge. She was on a secret mission and nothing was going to stop her, not even the latest x-rays showing damaged vertebrae. The only person she told of her plans was Beth.

'I really want to do the show Beth and I've still got six weeks to get fit. What d'yer reckon?'

'But Suz, the kicking routines are killers, they'll cripple you.' Beth wanted to cry. 'Please don't Suz, I couldn't bear it if anything happened to you.'

'But it's the Palladium Beth, I've *got to* do it.'

'But why?'

'I just have to, that's all.' Suzy knew she sounded childish, but she didn't care.

When June had rung to find out if she was well enough to do a show with them, she didn't have to think about it. 'Yeah, I'm fine, what's the show?'

'It's for Bruce Forsyth's Seventieth birthday, we're opening the show, are you sure you're Ok now?'

'Yeah, of course, I'll be there and thanks for thinking of me.'

Beth knew only too well that whatever she said would make no difference to Suzy's decision and in a way she understood. Since the accident she'd noticed Suzy's growing impatience. Every time they'd spoken on the phone she'd moan how she felt useless and frustrated at not being able to do the only thing she felt she was any good at. She had lost her confidence again. Beth had tried to reassure her that she'd find something else, but she would just laugh and say 'Crap, who the hell wants to employ a cripple, middle age dancer. I'm not exactly brain of Britain?'

'Ok, then just promise me one thing.'

'What?'

'Promise me you'll talk it over with Tony first, because you're not really being very fair to him.'

'OK, I promise. And Beth thanks. Luv ya.'

Suzy kept her promise, but as expected Tony was devastated when she told him.

'Oh Suz, please don't...'

'Look Tone, I'm not stupid, I wouldn't do anything to jeopardise what we've got, I love you too much for that, but I need this like breath. Don't you see I've got something to aim for; I never thought I'd be performing back at the Palladium...not at *my* age. Just this once I promise, please doesn't be cross with me' and she nuzzled into his chest, squeezing him hard, smiled a sickly sweet smile and fluttered her eyes at him.

'Oh, here we go... "Pretty Pleeese" he'd seen that face before.

Suzy managed to get through the show, but only just. Tony knew there was a problem, when at the after show party, instead of the usual enthusiastic rush to the bar, Suzy sat quietly in the corner with a glass of water, seemingly happy to watch the others enjoy the electric atmosphere.

'I'm sorry Tone, you were right, I shouldn't have done it.' There were tears in her eyes. He pulled up a chair and gently put his arm round her.

'Go on, say I told you so' she added bitterly.

'Ooh no, I like living too much' he grinned, but could see the obvious pain written all over her wretched face.

'Do you want to go home?'

'Yeah, but I might need a bit of help getting out of this chair,' she groaned. Tony slid his hand round her waist taking her full weight, as she struggled to her feet. They slipped out unnoticed and as they stepped out into Argyle St, Suzy turned and with tears streaming down her face, this time of sadness and not pain, gazed back at the theatre of dreams and said goodbye to her past.

'It was worth it you know, I know I shouldn't have, but I'm glad I did, just one last time.'

THIRTY-NINE

'It was all Tone's idea' admitted Suzy.

Beth thought the idea outrageous '*A book? Us* write a book, are you mad?'

'No honest, I've already started scribbling notes down, and don't forget I've got my diaries. Remember you laughed at me when I told you about them, come on Beth I can't do it without you.'

'But we don't know the first thing about writing a book.'

'I know but we could find out stuff as we go along. Please Beth I need this.'

'What the hell Suz, lets do it'

'*Yes!*' Shouted Suzy into the receiver, 'now you've just got to get a computer'

'Oh is that all' laughed Beth.

A month later a computer was sitting in Beth's spare room and with Josh's help she managed to manoeuvre the mouse, email, and with Suzy write the first page. That was the easy part. For the following six weeks, chapter one was emailed back and forth between London and Calgary until the girls were happy with it.

Suzy spent hours going through her photos; show programmes and diaries, collating events and dates, while Beth compiled as many stories as she could remember.

After six months a successful formula was worked out. Suzy would decide the order of events and write the basic outline, admitting she was too impatient to fill in the boring details.

'It'll be a bloody short book, if you have your way.' Beth teased one day on the phone. 'Once upon a time…they lived happily ever after…THE END!'

'Yeah and they'd need a lorry to get yours home from the bookshop. Five chapters describing the colour of the vicar's grandmother's moustache.'

Beth who, as Suzy put it 'flowered it up' would fill in the details send it back, leaving Suzy to have the final say.

E-mail: September 24th 2001

Allo my Sweet, it's me Beth, so we did it the first chapter, can't believe it. We're on our way, love ya Beth

E-mail: September 25th 2001

At this rate we should have it finished by the time we're eighty! Forgot to tell you, Josh had his audition for Italia Conti today. Love you back

As they had with every adventure throughout their lives, the budding authors threw themselves into their latest with unsurpassed enthusiasm. Christmas came and went in both countries with the usual festivities, Beth and Suzy both making excuses to their respective families, so they could sneak away on Boxing Day and finish chapter two. It seemed like a good idea at the time, but Beth had eaten too much and Suzy was pissed, so chapter two was in need of a rewrite two days later!

Excitement rose during the next three months, the book was taking shape and then Beth got an email from Suzy.

Email: March 2nd 2002

Shit! Poo! And Big Hairy Bums! Computer crashed and lost last two chapters; can you send them to me? I'm such a dick, didn't know you had to save it to a disk. Hope you've got a 'Floppy One?' So upset I went for a drive and sat in a lay-by for an hour, gave myself a right bollocking. By the way Josh got his scholarship into college, he's so excited, Love lots.

Email: March 3rd 2002

Allo sweetness, give Josh a big kiss from me... XXX ...and say well done. Here's stuff you lost. Don't be too hard on yourself and yes I have my "Floppy" in all the time! I've got 'Potty' to talk to and me fags as well. 'Potty' never did take up smoking, tried once and it made her sick! Love you

Although for Beth and Suzy the book was top priority, their duties as wives and mums all too often shifted their venture to bottom of the list. Frustrated, the girls managed to cope with husbands, children's problems, ailing Mothers and Beth moving house. Proving to be experts at multi tasking, the prized project came flying back to number one on the 'sod off everyone, this is my time' chart.

Email: October 18th 2002

Allo my sweet, well winters here again and we're knee deep in snow. Can't get the car out of the driveway but that's good I can keep writing. Thx for attachment you sent, only made minor changes, have a look-see wot you fink. Love ya Beth.

Email: October 19th 2002

Got your email but where's the att' you silly cow! Think your memories going. How did Josh's exam go?

Oops! Forgot to send it, here it is sorry, ha ha!! Love Beth. P.S. Nothing wrong with my memory, its menopause...or is it 'memo-pause!' Damn I'm funny! Josh passed, he's now qualified, and so now I can be a total hypochondriac, I'll have my own personal paramedic....

Beth was in full swing with winter almost over and settled in the new house. All she could think about was the book and every spare minute was spent writing. Many a night she'd wake at two in the morning, unable to sleep and armed with ciggys and tea, creep downstairs, working on the book, sometimes creeping back to bed just in time to hear the alarm go off, for David to go to work.

Suzy was doing exactly the same thing, although there'd been a slight hitch one afternoon, when dashing back from London full of ideas, she locked herself out of the flat. 'Oh Sod' she mumbled as she rifled through her bag a third time, hoping the key would magically appear. Undeterred she sat on her patio for the next two hours, until Josh got home from college, scribbling notes down on any bits of paper she could find, the back of her hand and a used tissue!

'Bleeding 'ell I'm sure Geoffrey Archer doesn't carry on like this, 'have to tell Beth about this one' she muttered.

Email: April 27th 2003

Glad you got all the ideas down, but used tissue- snot nice! Love Beth.

One of the few people who hadn't laughed cynically at Suzy's venture was Ben, who was proud of his mum, and with his writing skills helped her find her own style. He'd bought a flat in Sutton with Kellie, a bubbly attractive girl who was full of fun he'd met at university. Suzy and Tony adored her and were thrilled he'd at last found the love he deserved.

236

Hi Beth, this is Ben here. Have come over to take mum out for lunch, but I can't get her off this computer. Please tell her to take a break...I'm starving!!! Watch this space! Love Ben

Email April 29th 2003

Wotcha mate. Needed that lunch yesterday...burp!!! Too excited to eat lately. Think it's time to get in touch with publishers, hurry up & send me your ideas on the last chapter...luv me

Suzy managed to get hold of the 'Writers & Artists Yearbook' and spent hours searching through, sending the synopsis and the first two chapters to publishers listed as dealing with their style of book. A few showed some interest, but not enough, with most of them, as Suzy so delicately described in an email to Beth, 'having as much personality as a worm!'

However, the regular nighttime chanting, around the dream catcher hovering over her bed worked its magic powers, when she got a phone call from Nigel Breton. He ran 'Quirky Publishing' even the company name appealed to her. Nigel had been really helpful and set up a meeting. From then on it was like a whirlwind. All Suzy could think of on the way home from their meeting was the last sentence Nigel spoke before he shook her hand.

'Suzy you've got three months to get the book finished, then I want to meet with you and your friend to talk seriously about publishing! She raced home, barging in the door at 7pm, praying she hadn't gone through any red lights, or driven over someone leaving them blood splattered, screaming for help. Once inside she made a beeline for the phone and dialled the code for Canada. It seemed ages before she heard a bleary voice at the other end.

'Hallo'

'Allo, guess what?'

'What?'

'We've done it!'

'Done what?' Beth yawned, fumbling in the dark for a cigarette.

'What d'you think you silly cow? We're gonna be published.' Suzy could hardly contain herself, 'what time is it there?'

'Oh my God what did you say?'

'I said what time is it there?'

'It's 2am, but what did you say first'

'Ooh sorry I was so exited, forgot the time change.'

'*SUZ!* What did you say' Beth was alert now.

Suzy smiled, enjoying winding Beth up. 'Oh, you mean the bit about the publisher?'

'YES!'

'Oh that!'...She paused... *'We've done it.* His name's Nigel and he wants to publish, *but* we've got to have it finished by the end of September.'

'Oh God Suz I don't believe it, let me light another fag, so, are you a precious angel or what?'

'Yes I am and don't bloody forget it!'

The summer of 2003 was the hottest England had ever known, but Suzy, the sun worshipper hardly set foot out of the door, while Beth put her insomnia to good use. By the end of September the book was completed and presented to Nigel.

The wheels were set in motion and the book *Not Just for Kicks* hit the stores on March 20th 2004, a date the girls would never forget. Another memorable date on the calendar was April 10th and Beth had flown in especially. Two days later, David had flown in as a surprise for Beth; he wasn't going to miss out on this.

They sat in the green room of the BBC Studios waiting nervously in anticipation for their appearance on the 'Steve Calvert Show'. Beth was applying lip-gloss for the fourth time while Suzy pulled faces in the mirror.

'If you put any more of that gloss on mate your lips will slip right off your bloody face!'

'It's all right for you, I've got to look stunning, it's my first T.V show in thirty years and never mind me, if you keep pulling those faces your eyeballs will be on the floor with my lips!'

The scene was all too familiar for the two middle age teenagers, laughing uncontrollably. Suddenly a knock at the door brought them to their senses.

'Everything all right in there?' a mans voice asked, 'we want you down on the floor now please'

'We *are* on the floor' Suzy blurted as Beth gave her a shove.

'Thank you, we're on our way down' Beth called out, rolling her eyes at Suzy. Just like the old days the girls fell into 'quick change' mode and with make up redone and clothes adjusted, they made their way to the studio floor.

The excited pair were surprisingly composed during the interview, except for when they unintentionally crossed their legs at the same time, looked at each other and slowly crossed them back again. Steve laughed, showing great generosity in his compliments and interest in their amazing "overnight success". Raising one eyebrow, he dryly quoted the title of the book

'So now that *'Not Just for Kicks'* is a huge success, what are your plans for the future?'

'Well, we're going on holiday first and from there, who knows, right Beth?'

Beth put her hands up and shrugged her shoulders, 'This is all just for kicks'!

Champagne flowed at the party Tony threw for the girls and for those who'd dare to miss the show, the video was set up, but of course even those who had, were summoned to watch it again. Plenty of obscene remarks flew around the room, with peanuts and crisps thrown at the screen during their close-ups and by the time everyone left at 4am the foursome were exhausted, but still on cloud nine. Sat amongst the debris of the night, they sipped their coffees and reminisced over the past amazing two and a half years.

The day before Beth and David left, arrangements were made and tickets booked for holidays. Tony and David were off to Vegas to check out the shows, then on to meet Suzy and Beth for the last week at their destination. A place Beth and Suzy had talked about for years and only dreamed of until now. The final date to remember was their departure on April 15th for Jamaica!

The private beach was quiet and deserted except for two slightly wrinkled but tanned bodies lazing on the white sand, sipping drinks that had more props than a Las Vegas production.

'What's in this drink anyway?' Suzy asked, eyeing her glass suspiciously.

'Haven't got a clue, can't get my nose past the umbrella and fruit.'

'Well I'm not surprised with the size of your nose, here watch this.' Suzy grabbed the tiny umbrella, jumped up and went into a chorus of "Singing in the Rain," dancing across the sand to the vivid aqua warm water, that lapped gently along the shore, kicking and splashing for all she was worth.

'You've got the job!' Beth screamed, 'now sit down and behave yourself, before you do your back in again, or you'll go back to your room.'

'Yes mother.'

Looking down at her body Beth started to laugh 'you know, all things considered the bod's not too bad'

'That's what you think. What's that purple thing, running through your leg?' 'It's a vein and it's because I've got thin delicate skin, not like your crocodile hide!'

'Well at least I'm tight "Flabby Florrie".' Suzy turned and sucked in her bum.

'Tight?' Beth laughed 'we are talking bollocks "Miss Euro Tunnel", if the tide comes in, you'd better keep your legs together' and as always the laughter started, but this time stopped by Suzy's mobile ringing.

'Where is it?'

'Here under my shoe' Beth quickly handed the phone to Suzy.

Suzy's face lit up and she gestured to Beth to listen in on the conversation. With both ears stuck to the mobile they listened with open mouths. Turning it off Suzy turned to Beth and after a moment's stunned silence they both screamed,

'SCREENPLAY!'

Printed in the United Kingdom
by Lightning Source UK Ltd.
119076UK00002B/61-198